DON'T LET THE SUN GO BROWN

First Published in Great Britain 2018 by Mirador Publishing

First edition: 2018

Any reference to real names and places are purely fictional and are constructs of the author. Any offence the references produce is unintentional and in no way reflects the reality of any locations or people involved.

A copy of this work is available through the British Library.

ISBN: 978-1-912192-91-5

Mirador Publishing
10 Greenbrook Terrace
Taunton
Somerset
TA1 1UT

Don't Let The Sun Go Brown

Bryan James

~ CONTENTS ~

~ PREAMBLE ~

When we look up at the night sky from our tiny planet, and wonder at the vastness of the universe that fills our view in every direction, with colourful and awe-inspiring stars, it is so easy to dismiss our local domain as being less than impressive, and not even significant. After all, our sun is not even close to the centre of the Milky Way. We live in a quiet backwater, a sleepy neighbourhood within a small galactic arm we call the Orion spur. When this is compared to the major arms that wrap themselves around a spectacular black hole at the centre of our galaxy, each containing billions of multicoloured stars, we get some perspective of scale.

Should we study our own solar system, we can see just how remarkable it is, that it is not something to be ignored, or dismissed carelessly, for it has a beauty, and a presence all of its own. Each planet has its own characteristics, marking them as different; even so, we often choose to notice those that have specific attributes.

The Goldilocks zone, within which humans can survive, thanks to the fact that it is not too hot and not too cold, not too close to the sun nor too far away, contains our Earth, and Mars. Both Venus and Mercury are too close to the sun for our comfort, with Venus's surface resembling a lava flow, and Mercury having a similar appearance to our moon.

The physical construction of a planet can vary, but there are some common attributes. They all have a core, which can be a solid metal or liquid, normally quite hot. The inner planets also have a mantle and a crust.

The mantle is the second layer of a planet, after the core, and on Earth it is made up of silicates of iron and magnesium, sulphides, and oxides of silicon and magnesium. Heat and materials are convected within this region, while the consistency of the material can be described as a paste, about 1800 miles thick. The crust is put at 3 miles deep, while Venus, sometimes called a twin of Earth, has a similar sized mantle and a thicker crust of about 31 miles deep.

Mercury's mantle is 310 to 435 miles thick, covered by a silicate crust, probably less than 25 miles deep. Mars has a crust of around 30 miles, and a mantle of about 1000 miles deep. Out of all the inner planets, Mars would offer the best migration opportunity for Earth people when our tiny world gets too full. However, life support would be a major hurdle, and a lot of investment would have to go into making the planet habitable.

Out beyond Mars is the asteroid belt, a 113 mile wide barrier of rocks, most of which are capable of inflicting severe damage to Earth, should they ever move in our direction. A dwarf planet, called Ceres, resides in this region.

Jupiter, the largest gas giant, has its own asteroid belt, preceding it, and following in its wake. The gas giants like Saturn, have rings, but none are as impressive as the sixth planet, while large rocks, usually called satellites, orbit the outer planets in great quantity. Uranus, then Neptune, more correctly called ice planets, mark the end of the planetary region. Although Pluto is even further out from the sun, it has been downgraded to the status of a dwarf.

Jupiter could be called a sun that didn't ignite. It had the same mixture of elements as the sun, (hydrogen and helium), but was not massive enough to have high internal pressures and temperature to cause hydrogen to fuse into helium. In many ways, this gas giant is similar to a brown star, except that a brown star would have commenced the process of making helium out of hydrogen, although it would have failed to come alive as a real star due to it having a mass below the necessary level for thermonuclear fusion of deuterium.

Space is cold, but that's not to say that incredible levels of heat cannot be found within our system of rocks, moons, and planets. Inner planetary cores have temperatures between 1230 and 5400 Celsius, while the cores of the outer planets can reach 24,000 Celsius, hotter even than the surface of the sun, but not quite matching the sun's core of 15,000,000 Celsius.

The next major component of the solar system, known as the Kuiper Belt, resides just beyond Neptune and contains Pluto, when its elliptical orbit takes it that far out, as well as hundreds of thousands of icy bodies and trillions of comets. After that there is a huge amount of space until we come to the Oort Cloud, another region that holds even more icy comets.

This Oort Shell, or Oort Cloud, which marks the physical limit of our system, surrounds the entire solar system. It occupies an enormous space starting between 2,000-5,000 astronomical units (AU) from the sun and stretches out to as far as 50,000 AU, around 4.6 trillion miles, or about a quarter of the distance to the nearest star, Proxima Centauri. It is believed that the Oort Cloud formed as trillions of comets where thrown out of the inner solar system by Jupiter and Saturn, as the solar system was reaching the end of its formation. Residents of the Oort Cloud can be ejected by the passage of a star, nebula, or by actions in the disk of the Milky Way. These movements can knock cometary nuclei out of their orbits and send them on a headlong rush towards the sun, to temporarily brighten up the night sky.

The whole of the solar system is contained within a magnetic bubble called the heliosphere. It is shaped like a long windsock as it moves with the sun through interstellar space. The heliosheath is the outer region of the *heliosphere*, just beyond the point where the solar wind slows abruptly.

The ability of the universe to surprise us, time and time again, will become more evident as we continue to explore our own amazing domain. Needless to say, there is plenty of scope for man to understand more or to know it better, as he explores this fabulous adventure playground.

~ CHAPTER 1 ~

~ FIREWORKS ~

It came out of nowhere, and gave the people of Earth their first suspicion that, perhaps they might not be immortal as a species, after all.

"Julie, how come NASA missed that comet till it was right on top of us?" Gary exclaimed. "Somebody should give them hell, as we are getting beaten up about it."

"They will be getting plenty of stick about that don't worry, but my main concern is trying to work out how close it will come to Earth," replied Julie. "Without knowing where it came from, estimating a future trajectory is nigh on impossible."

The unknown comet crept forward, with most of the telescopes of the world watching its progress, as it lit up the night sky. Astronomers continued their vigil, even as the potentially destructive ball of rock and ice approached level with the Earth's orbit.

"That was a close one, but not dangerously so," said Julie, when it was clear that the comet was a whole day early. "Just as well that this a Thursday rather than a Friday, otherwise we would have been right in this thing's path."

Astronomers in Peru were the first to announce the fact that a lot more comets were heading for the sun from the deep reaches of the solar system.

"My God," exclaimed Julie, after getting the images of what Peru had seen, "just look at that, a whole bunch of comets, now spread out between Pluto and Uranus. For sure they must have been ejected from the Oort Cloud, and every one is brand new as far as returning comets are concerned."

"According to ESA," said Gary, "these are all travelling even faster than ordinary comets normally do, approaching 240,000 miles per hour."

"Hmm, sugar!" said Julie. "That is quite a speed, and all of this means we will be bombarded for at least a week, starting in about 10 days' time. Our top priority is to work with NASA and ESA to plot the course of each of those bad boys."

"Hey, that's not fair," said Mike, having caught up with the images and fresh data, "I reckon most comets are female by their nature, so I would call them bad girls."

"We can disagree on that," said Julie smiling, "as long as we can get accurate trajectories."

The vigil continued with the team pulling in fresh data constantly and doing the analysis, concentrating on the bigger lumps of rock coming their way, or the ones that were in the lead.

"With luck," said Mike, "Jupiter and Saturn will either take them in, or seriously affect their paths due to the heavy gravity of both planets."

"Hope so," said Julie.

The team worked long hours to get accuracy on if, or how, the comets would fall to Earth. There was no point in issuing warnings if Earth was going to be somewhere else when the comets zoomed in.

Fortunately, many of the comets were pulled in by the gravity of Saturn and Jupiter, to end their days in the depths of a gas giant.

"Thank goodness for our gas giants," said a happy Mike, "they really are good to us, but there are still too many more rocks working their way towards the inner planets, even if most of them will end up falling into the sun as burnt ash, with luck."

The media got wind of the fleet of comets on its way, and started to run with the story of Earth potentially being bombarded by large icy comets, and being wiped out in the same manner as the dinosaurs were. Television broadcasters recycled their old worn out disaster movies, especially those that involved people dying with anything connected to outer space.

Numerous television panel programs spent many hours discussing why we were seeing so many active comets, and how this could change the future. Some new-Earth activists even spoke of a new beginning for planet Earth, after man had been killed off, and speculated what a marvellous place it would be. While many Liberal Democrat supporters liked this view, even more of those that didn't want to die just yet, took to social networking websites to protest at such juvenile anti-humanity hogwash.

The *Panorama* program on the BBC went into great detail on exactly how we were all going to expire, painfully, one way or another, with so many comets moving towards the Earth. They made it seem that it was a matter of fact that life on Earth was due for a mauling by nature, for all of our crimes against her.

According to the BBC there was a one in ten chance that at least five large comets would land on Earth, each one having enough destructive power to completely obliterate whole nations. They would trigger earthquakes and tsunamis, after which there would be the dust to contend with, which would cloud the sun from the skies, polluting the air, and causing untold deaths.

Amongst thousands of others, Jenny of Ipswich wrote into the BBC to complain, "I strongly protest about the *Panorama* program you broadcast, telling us we were all going to die, in many horrible ways. You should be ashamed of yourselves. This is nothing but scaremongering, and was backed up by very little evidence, but well done, you've managed to scare the kids, and the grandparents, almost to death."

The BBC switchboards were jammed also, but in its normal apathetic manner, the BBC responded with the usual worn out unsympathetic line that they felt the program had been well balanced.

Typically, human nature took over this news item to make it profitable to some. Astronomy books and equipment sold very well of course, and physics became a sought after class at most schools. The scientifically unproven theory on dinosaurs being destroyed by asteroids resurfaced, again and again, prompting toy manufacturers to go to town on large cuddly prehistoric creatures, and disaster games featuring these long since dead animals.

"Oh look," said Steve, son of Jenny, "cuddly dinosaurs are back in fashion," as they passed by *The Entertainer* toy shop. "Guess what I don't want for Christmas."

"You've still got your old ones in the cupboard. You used to love them, never stopped playing with them," said Mum.

"I was only three then," proclaimed Steve.

"Anyway," said Jenny, "I bet your new girlfriend would love one of those cuddly monsters to keep her warm at night."

"Thanks, Mum, but I have other ideas for keeping my girlfriend warm."

A certain amount of media time went into showing how the large outer planets were actually saving us from great swarms of rocks that would be heading our way were it not for the gravity of these planets taking a hand.

Jupiter especially came in for a good deal of approval, with more people getting interested in the solar system and our place in it. It wasn't a perfect method for us to avoid trouble, of course, and it was only a matter of time, given the large quantity of comets moving towards the sun, before some would come too close to Earth.

Politicians started to question astronomers for an explanation for the excessive number of comets now active, and there was no real answer, except for the usual one of funding. "Give us more resources, and we can do more." Subsequently, someone pointed out just what they *were* getting from government funds and asked if we were getting value for money. That put the scientific community under scrutiny. This was another subject that ran and ran in the media. "Is astronomy helping mankind in the way it is set up? Should astronomy be under military control? Why were astronomers studying distant galaxies when they knew so little about what was happening in their own backyard?" And so it went on.

Two weeks after the comet near miss, Julie and Mark were on a trip to Copenhagen in Denmark, thoroughly enjoying their first real vacation in years, away from the would-be grandparents who were becoming ever more persistent that it was time for them to start a family. But even more so, it was a break away from work, and the late nights they both often worked. They'd already seen some of the sights, and had spent much of the previous day at the Tivoli gardens and amusement park, getting plenty of thrills on the rides, while they loved the very special flora.

From their hotel that towered up high, they could see out over the Stadsgraven, a beautiful series of lakes surrounded by greenery and paths. Mark couldn't resist going for a walk around it when they first arrived, giving Julie time to relax. He took a walk across a small bridge, over some well-worn paths to eventually find himself in a busy commercial street, with shops and an enticing cafe. It was on his way back though that he regretted his trip, having gotten himself severely lost and unable to find the correct path across the lakes. He walked for miles, looking out for the final little bridge across the big lake that would take him back to the hotel, but it was in vain. There was no option but to walk on, and on, still half trusting his sense of direction, which wasn't so far out, as he'd simply joined the lake paths at the wrong point. After walking past some very strange little houses built very close to the lake, and enduring some very strange smells, "and it wasn't tobacco," he had told himself, he finally made it onto a real tarmac road. Turning left instead of right he found he was heading towards the sea, and only finally getting the correct direction when he asked someone, something he always avoided doing as it made him look so silly. "Excuse me, do you speak English?" Most Danes do. "Is this the way to town?"

After getting back, with legs aching, to be confronted by an angry Julie who had been waiting to eat dinner, he felt a huge relief, and decided he wouldn't take any more such walks without a proper guide.

When she'd calmed down, and while Mark got changed, Julie said, "I can see why you were so long, it is a big lake to walk around, and it is so very attractive, from up here at least."

"Yes," sniffed Mark.

Next day, they were drifting gently along the city canal system in a glass topped boat snuggled up together against the cold, for although it was now May the weather hadn't really warmed up greatly.

Mark was looking up at the sky. "Fantastic fireworks they're putting on. I didn't know that they had any celebrations here today."

Julie looked up lazily to take in the spectacle, which almost filled the portion of the sky they could see from where they sat. She could only stare for some moments, but with some alarm said, "Mark, those are not fireworks." She stood up to see more sky.

"What?" was all Mark could manage.

"That," insisted Julie, "is a meteor shower, and a damned large one at that. Now that one really crept up on us. We were not expecting a display until October and nothing like that. From their direction of travel, it looks as though they didn't come directly at us from beyond Uranus, which is very odd."

Before Mark could think of anything intelligible to say, Julie had whipped out her phone, taken a number of pictures, and was very soon talking to her colleagues back at the British Astronomical Society, in Cambridge.

Fortunately for Mark, there were no more meteor showers, meaning Julie had no excuse to rush back to work and spoil their holiday. The subject did, however, occupy their conversations a lot as they explored the sights of the fascinating city.

They did avoid the hotel casino as Julie insisted that no gambling was allowed, even on holiday, instead they visited some of the castles, like Rosenborg, and even better Amalienborg, the home of the Danish royal family, which was most spectacular.

ॐ ♈ ॐ   ॐ ♈ ॐ   ॐ ♈ ॐ

A large number of rocks were now hitting the atmosphere in what initially looked like random periods. One EU weather satellite had been knocked out, the one that had been in a geostationary orbit above Russia. Fortunately that had no effect on the weather predictions made.

No other damage from meteorites was reported, indeed, those that dared approach Earth were burned up well before they got to terra firma. Newspapers were still headlining the showers as they happened, and even provided a daily schedule, provided by the British Astronomical Society, of what to expect to see in the heavens as far as melting rock spectacles was concerned.

Astronomers had gotten a whole lot better at informing everyone when a shower was due, yet still were unable to say why it was happening so frequently.

While the world was concentrating on the unusual number of impacts in the atmosphere, another event was almost ignored, save for those that had a very special interest in large stars coming to the end of their lives. For a good number of years, astronomers have been watching a giant pulsating red star very closely, by the name of Betelgeuse. It was the second-brightest object in the constellation of Orion, and around 642 light years from Earth. Astronomers frequently informed us that although this super giant was at the end of its life, it could take more than 100,000 years before it would explode in a spectacular light show. On the other hand, it could already have gone nova and the evidence would still be on its way, given that light doesn't travel that fast on a universal scale.

Earth astronomers had over the years observed, or seen, data collected from a good number of stars going nova, however, as they kept saying, "every one was a little different," and while they knew generally what to expect, they also emphasised that each event was unique and there were always some surprises. With a gigantic star, such as Betelgeuse, the surprises were likely to be bigger and very different from past events. In terms of size, Betelgeuse is over 500 times bigger than our sun and emits 16,000 times more visible light.

It is not the biggest star in our skies, for it is dwarfed by stars like UY Scuti, which has a radius more than 1,700 times greater than the sun, and is 1.925 times the size of Betelgeuse. The media that bothered to report on the changes in Betelgeuse did so quietly, saying, "Alpha Orionis, or Betelgeuse to non-astronomers, is getting larger, astronomers have told our science reporters." Relegated to page seven of various broadsheets, it was given less attention than it might have been given, due to the comet situation. It was also reported that the pulse rate had changed, as though the huge sun was spinning faster.

The British Astronomical Society stated that, "Measuring the new pulse rate would take time; nevertheless, initial observations put it at weeks now rather than months."

There then followed some high level discussions on what might be going on with Betelgeuse. Even so, what really took over the front pages on news channels the world over was the confident report from NASA that man-made climate change was the most significant news story that was happening and was beyond any doubt. They had statistics to prove that the Earth was going to warm by 3 degrees centigrade in the coming year. The head of NASA pleaded for more government money to get better predictions on how many people were likely to be killed by the severe change in climate.

The US President, who was a non-believer, announced that he was cancelling all programs related to climate change, which was not happening, to concentrate all resources on the straying comets, which was happening. The head of NASA was sacked, unceremoniously.

ॐ ♈ ॐ   ॐ ♈ ॐ   ॐ ♈ ॐ

Julie was giving her team a hard time because everyone else was giving her one. From the association director down to her direct boss, they wanted answers to questions before they even knew what the questions were. "Daniel, when will you have those start locations verified? I need them yesterday."

A frustrated Danny went a little red at being picked on. Like the rest of the team he'd been working long hours sifting through the data on comet movements, and nothing was clear. It was still impossible to trace exactly where the comets that were closing in on Earth, originated from apart from suspecting the Oort Cloud, generally. Small comets they might be, but with every spectacular firework show the pressure grew for them to know everything about the relocating comets. "It will be a little while," he replied, "the problem is in tracing any given comet back to where it was behaving normally, and the data has big holes in it. We simply do not have the capacity to monitor every single potential comet out there."

"I know that," said an equally frustrated team leader, "if we'd been tracking these things earlier we wouldn't be in this mess, yet we don't decide what our priorities are. Take a best guess at a couple, and see if they could be from a specific part of the Oort Cloud.

"Gary, how are you doing with the comet's speed analysis? How fast are they travelling and does that vary?"

"Yup, getting there," said Gary, "give me another 15 minutes."

"Mike, how close are you to giving an accurate total quantity of comets out there in the cloud?"

"Two secs," pleaded Mike, "nearly done, ah yes, OK. I have a best estimate based on a study George did last year, and cross referencing that with a report on the subject from Venezuela. There are literally billions of comets in total; it's actually close to 2 trillion. Most of these comets have a nucleus of around 6 miles, nonetheless, what makes up a comet is mostly dust and ice, so trying to estimate how many pose a threat to Earth, given that we do not have any data on the core density of more than a dozen medium sized comets, means we are into a guestimate or fingers in the air job. That said, we do know most comets we have studied have a core of less than 15 miles in width. Now if they were all solid pieces of rock, Earth would really be in trouble if they start coming our way, however, we do not know how many comets are solid rock. For our purpose we are calling everything from the Oort Cloud a comet, as it's easier for the media to deal with single terms."

"Thank you, Mike, that is pretty insubstantial but our bosses love numbers. Give me that analysis as a soft copy, please."

"Already sent to your email box," chirped Mike.

"Cool," said Julie with a half-smile on her lips. "Now I have to go and get my daily rollicking for being unproductive. At least I will have something to say and some numbers to throw at them."

ॐ ♈ ॐ   ॐ ♈ ॐ   ॐ ♈ ॐ

Jupiter and Saturn continued to pull in large numbers of comets, although a good number bypassed the gas giants and headed towards the central part of the solar system. One 5 mile long monster hit the moon on the dark side, so any damage was not immediately visible, but with it making the news for several days running, it became a general concern. The moon kept to its normal path, so no immediate concerns arose about the moon being pushed out of orbit, but the Americans decided they had to know. A probe was launched to assess any harm done to the moon, and some 2 weeks later, happily they found only one new significant crater. The comet itself lay splattered all around the depression it had made. Other than that no effect was visible, after all what is one more impact crater to a body that has been hit countless times in its long history?

The comets appeared to be moving in waves, from well past the orbit of Neptune, towards the inner planets, and the centre of the solar system. The stream of comets was triggered by some unknown effect, after which there was a pause while everyone caught their breath. Subsequently that unknown factor drove another batch of comets in the general direction of Earth.

Initial thinking focused on gravitational forces of some undiscovered large body or bodies, as certainly that could account for the way the comets moved. However, due to the way in which this seemed to happen at regular time slots, observers had tended to rule out causes from outside the solar system.

The JWST-2 space telescope already had a full program of research that needed to be done on an urgent basis. In fact the schedule was solid for the next 3 years comprised of requests from many different organisations that each saw their project as being absolutely vital. The American President fixed the predicament in one brief conversation with the new head of NASA, "Cancel all outstanding requests to use JWST-2, unless it is comet related. Focus only on the comet issue, and if necessary, specifically train the JWST-2 on the Oort Cloud and find out what is going. Priority one."

The world of astronomy thereafter started to receive pictures of clarity that only a state-of-the-art optical lens could provide. However, it still worked hand in hand with radio telescopes to get a complete picture of what was being viewed.

Most Earth telescopes now focused on the different areas of the very distant Oort Cloud to locate anything that could possibly be disturbing the icy rocks. Some television commentators suggested it was a way for us to be softened up for an alien attack, despite no evidence of an invasion fleet being found. It was noted however that the areas where the potential comets had been were now showing high radiation levels. These areas were notable simply because of the large gaps where comets should have been. The broadsheet media of course continued to splash front page illusions of aliens being the root cause of the comets misbehaving, as it sold more copies than it would have done without having something dramatic to say.

Sometimes they went a bit over the top. One misty drizzly day, the *Daily Chronicle's* lead article was entitled 'ALIEN SPACESHIPS HIDE IN THE SHADOWS'. They showed a very grainy picture of what could be seen of the Milky Way in the centre, and some dark shapes to one side. The article claimed these shadows had moved, getting a little larger to indicate they were coming towards Earth. The author suggested that the picture proved aliens were waiting just outside our solar system, to attack us when a few well-placed comets had taken down our defences. The story would have had more credibility if only the picture had come from a reliable source, but the paper initially refused to say how they obtained the picture or provide the photographer's name. It eventually came out, following pressure from other media, that the image was manufactured by a 17 year old named Timothy O'Leary, a trainee decorator from Cheetham Hill in Manchester. He had used enhancing software on some images NASA had released, to make the picture more bold and in the process made the shadows more distinct.

"The only problem is," said an expert from the British Astronomical Society by the name of Julie Banks, "that the alleged shadows in this picture could be from anywhere between Mars and Alpha Centauri, if they were indeed real. We do know a lot of metallic debris is flooding into our view of the Milky Way and the stars all around us, meaning optical telescopes are liable to show inaccuracies that have to be filtered professionally with data from radio telescopes. Using a cheap piece of software to enhance something which started off as a very poor image, with unknown debris in the way, is about as unscientific as it gets. It is about as useful as waving your arms at a comet to see if you can create a big enough wind to blow it away."

Even the people on the streets had come to the conclusion that each wave of comets was due at a fairly regular period of 5 weeks. Nevertheless, it took an official announcement from NASA, to show that the experts were on top of this, and were leading with the developments as they happened. It was a short message, put out from the NASA news website that told the waiting world, hungry for exact data on the comet situation that the cycle was exactly 36 days and 20 minutes.

A great deal of hot air was generated by politicians on what was to be done, yet very little actually got decided, except that the Russians and Americans started to collaborate on a wild scheme, using recalibrated satellites, to shoot down any large comets that got too close. It was rather reminiscent of the Strategic Defence Initiative from 1983, a plan proposed by Ronald Reagan, when he was president, to protect the USA from Russian missiles, except that this new approach would be much less sophisticated. Enough satellites were already in place to detect any encroachment into the Earth's atmosphere, however to save the Earth the comet had to be destroyed well before it got close to the top of the atmosphere, and this needed different technology.

ॐ ♈ ॐ   ॐ ♈ ॐ   ॐ ♈ ॐ

Geoff was sitting in his easy chair, memorising and picking out unusual patterns in the wallpaper, neither happy nor unhappy, but certainly not full of the joys of spring. His limbs were too old for that. A light breeze blew in as a form of alert, although he didn't stir. Thereupon his peace was truly shattered.

"I don't think I've ever met such a useless piece of meat in all my days," said a very shrill voice.

Geoff put his hearing-aid back in so that he could enjoy the full pleasure of his wife returned from her morning sweet shop job.

"You daft ha'penny, you didn't hear the postman again, and I've got to walk all over to the blooming post office to pick up my parcel."

He knew it wouldn't do any good, even though he always did try to console her. Who knows, one day it might work. "I'm sorry, my love, but you know they don't stay too long these delivery people. By the time I'd gotten to the door they were nowhere in sight. I reckon they have those little collection cards already printed before they even ring the door bell."

"Yes, yes, any old excuse will do," shouted one irate woman from the kitchen area.

Geoff tried again with his well-rehearsed lines, "I don't know why you stick with that job of yours if the little blighters get you so worked up by the time you get home. I reckon life would be more peaceful if you gave that job up. We don't need the money anymore."

"What?" she spluttered, knowing her lines all too well. "I have to get out of here to have a proper conversation with someone. I'd die of boredom otherwise."

The drama over for now, Geoff removed his ear piece and picked up the book he'd borrowed from the library. A rather interesting analysis of life in the British Isles, starting at 1600 and coming up to present time, pretty well. The first chapters had been mainly about kings and queens, which was interesting to a point. Now he'd moved on to where globalisation started to take hold and that was more relevant to how things had played out since. Although the two world wars had ended with nations broken financially, they went on to greater prosperity and trade. After this, several things came in to destroy the peace, namely corruption, socialism, greed, poor government and drugs, but mainly stupidity and corruption summed it up.

"Got your nose in a book again?" The shrill voice was back, although Geoff managed to ignore her, for the moment. He was reading now about the EU, a misbegotten entity that put the interests of people behind bureaucracy. It should have been strangled at birth, instead it went on to cause many years of suffering and misery for millions.

Thank ye gods for BREXIT, thought Geoff.

A slightly less shrill voice tried again. "What is that you keep chuckling at all the time; is it so funny?"

Geoff responded to that by putting in his aid and having her repeat what she said; although almost stone deaf, he could still recognize a reduced shrill when it reached him.

"It's amazing," he said, showing her the book, "ever since the doctors have been treating ear loss, they have not been able to grow back the little hairs in the ear that cause us to hear. Science has not advanced that far in 600 years if you ask me."

"Hmmm," she managed, "that's not enough to keep you laughing all the time. There must be more to that history book than that."

"It's about," he said, "history repeating itself until the idiots that would repeat the same old mistakes are locked up somewhere and can't do anyone any harm. A darn shame they haven't recognized socialism as a sickness yet, the world would be a much better place without it."

She nodded in agreement. He continued. "From the 20th century onwards, the book says, socialism had gotten an increasing hold over life in the Western world and the future was looking very grim."

Geoff made space for Thelma to sit next to him on the couch, and he went on, "What gets me most though, is that in spite of all the progress that has been made, they still have no technology capable of spotting an irrational person before he gets into power. The near-insane are allowed to do whatever they want with no checks made. The book mentions psychiatry, says it is a failed science. Most of the practitioners it seems are ready for a straitjacket themselves, so no wonder we have so many deluded and half crazy people around. It's not as though the drugs cure anybody, unless them acting out their nightmares is seen as a cure."

Thelma leaned closer, pleasing to Geoff, and they read the same page together. Soon both were smiling at the nonsense that was still being pursued in the name of political correctness.

"Geoff, do you ever regret retiring from your job? I mean you are only 68. You always seemed so cheerful when you were working. Now you rarely seem to be happy except when you are reading books like this."

"I did have an interesting job," he said, "but I'm afraid I'd outlived my usefulness, they simply didn't need me anymore. I was responsible for storing the data, managing it and making sure it was cycled properly. It seems that they discovered a way to create sulphur-ionised-wafers or some such fancy thing, that they said can hold so much information that the data cycle happens naturally. They didn't need me, nor want me anymore. Before I left I was asked to make sure the housekeeping batch would run daily, to scratch the old data and to make the virtual tapes ready for re-use. I did such a good job they got rid of me early."

"Had you thought of retraining?"

"No, I wouldn't be any good at anything else. I'm a poor learner. Took me years to pick up the knowledge I had, and that was mainly by rote."

"You're too young to vegetate at home," managed Thelma. "What about the radio system you built? You made a great job of that, and you used to talk with friends all over the place."

"Hmm, yes," said Geoff, "I haven't been in contact with any of the Hams for a few months. Maybe I will call them up again, really used to enjoy chatting to those two Russians."

Yet it was true, Geoff thought, he had been much happier working. It gave him a purpose. Even though he didn't fully understand any more what they were doing at Counter Sensory Containment (CSC). One rumour had been that they'd been able to isolate the human spirit, however, Geoff and others had no idea how mankind might benefit from that, or even if there was any profit in it. All sorts of rumours had started up with each new production building that was erected. Space travel, faster than light transmissions, and water generation were just some of the possible secret MOD projects being worked on. CSC did a lot of work for the government, and ever since BREXIT, innovation in many areas had boomed, creating some amazing scientific breakthroughs. It seemed, however, following the way the EU treated the UK, that the British government was less willing to share its new ideas, preferring to go it alone, and subsequently doing very well.

He decided that he'd read enough for now, put the book down, and told Thelma to come closer as he wanted a good snuggle, and wrapped his arm around her. She protested of course, as she always did. "We had a good snuggle only last Friday, and I'm not sure I'm ready for another one; besides, we haven't had lunch."

"Never mind that, my love," said Geoff, "maybe I can make you forget all about food, for a while."

ॐ♈ॐ   ॐ♈ॐ   ॐ♈ॐ

Normal space, if there is such a thing, has a low density of gasses and dust, and this was typical of the Oort Cloud under normal circumstances. This had changed dramatically, for the space where the comets were now missing from, not only contained high density radiation particles, but these particles, being composed of mainly metallic, iron, or cobalt, were moving towards the sun.

The JWST-2 telescope confirmed the general lack of rocks and ice, in specific areas of the Cloud, while the increasing light from Betelgeuse illustrated all too well just how dense the gaseous material now occupying space from within the Oort Cloud right up to the region in front of the sun was. Pictures from JWST-2 went around the world, and got people very excited. They showed just the very brightest of stars glowing through the dense darkness. The gaseous dusty material flowed towards the sun, spreading in all directions. As it did so clarity of observations from Earth became more limited. The moon took on a halo effect, making it seem as though winter was excessively cold. Optical telescopes were blurred, as were any pictures taken. The sun was starting to form a halo as well.

Efforts to see what was happening switched primarily to infrared and radio equipment. At least these technologies were used to looking through dust, although even they struggled to give an accurate and clear picture.

Extensive searches were conducted by several different astronomy groups around the world for any large body at the edge of the solar system, an unknown dwarf planet, or some other space object that could be responsible for the comets moving. Different theories on gravity being the culprit came up, yet with no sign of any large enough mass, there was no evidence to support those views, although, of course they persisted.

They started to study, and restudy the sun to see if any unusual activity there could have contributed to the situation. For example, they investigated if the sun could actually be attracting the comets. Perhaps, even, there could be a combination of reasons for the comets now becoming hyperactive. What it came down to was a thorough re-evaluation of everything, in context, that was known about the solar system. Facts were examined and rechecked, and all assumptions up to that point were shown to be 90 per cent consistent, with some very small differences, none significant.

More by good luck than anything else, several radio and infrared telescopes, as well as the JWST-2, were viewing the next area of evacuation within the Oort Cloud when it happened. What was observed still amazed the people watching. It was as though an invisible hand, or could that be a reversed, high power, solar wind, was pushing the comets in front of it out of the way. All that was left in place of the frozen rocks was the radioactive metallic dust and gas.

The invisible hand sent most comets within one part of the cloud towards the sun; some went sideways and stayed in the Oort Cloud, taking a different trajectory. To either side of the part of the cloud now containing the dense gases, comets were changing course slightly, as though the hand that was pushing the comets was also creating turbulence all around. This meant that the Cloud was now in a more chaotic state than ever before with more disturbed ice-cold rocks likely to shift away from their home space to travel towards Earth. One thing that this all promised for the future was that there would be no shortage of comets lighting up the sky with their long tails and reminding us all that the solar system was bigger than our own tiny planet. Without Earth the solar system would carry on as normal. Without the solar system, Earth would die a thousand potential deaths.

ॐ ♈ ॐ   ॐ ♈ ॐ   ॐ ♈ ॐ

A shrill voice was disturbing Geoff while he was signing off after talking to his HAM friend Ingor. "...and your dinner is getting cold as well." He took himself into the kitchen before the rest of the complaint could be uttered, almost silencing his wife, but not quite. "So you did hear me!"

"Yes," said Geoff patiently, whose ears were still sore after wearing the headphones with the volume turned up to extreme.

They ate in silence for some time, until the food started to make Geoff feel a little better. "Hmm," he said, "these mangled potatoes are really nice tonight. Are these the ones from the farm shop?"

His wife agreed that they were.

"Oh," she said, I've brought home some travel brochures. Time we had a holiday somewhere different. I really fancy a trip of a lifetime, something so different it will knock your socks off and give us great memories for years to come. It will be fantastic. I don't mean anything like Sophie has planned, we're a bit too old to go without a good deal of comfort."

Geoff agreed, "Be nice to get away somewhere warm, exotic maybe, where I can get a nice shiatsu massage."

They continued feeding, after which Geoff started on the washing up. He soaped a plate, scrubbed it, and finally held it under the hot tap to rinse it. All of a sudden his body jerked, almost as though he was having a heart attack, although he remained standing, with his hand still under the hot tap.

"Damn, that was hot," Geoff said in a very gruff voice he'd never used before. He turned off the tap and looked around. "Where the hell am I, and what the heck went wrong?"

Thelma didn't know what to say, which was not something that happened often, she just realised that her Geoff was no longer with her that was all she knew.

The man looked at Thelma, realising she must be in some sort of shock and was surely wondering what was going on. He started to explain, a little, "I'm not your husband as you have probably realised. His spiritual self is far away. Basically, we have swapped bodies. God only knows how it went wrong, I was supposed to be moved in to a different body altogether."

Thelma managed a look of total bewilderment, eyes staring at this man who was not who he was 2 minutes ago, and gave a strangled, "Oh," before collapsing to the floor.

~ CHAPTER 2 ~

~ SPIRITED AWAY ~

NASA comet trackers became alarmed at the trajectory of three large frozen rocks that had escaped the clutches of the gas giants, telling the world that their paths would take them very close to Earth. Following this on the TV or newspapers was like watching it frame by frame in a movie, inch by inch as the comets moved closer. The questions were always the same, "Had they changed in any way? Had their bulk dissipated at all? Just how solid were they inside?"

One of these big boys would certainly have hit the moon as it skimmed past Earth, a mere 250,000 miles away; happily the moon was on the other side of our planet at the time. The second one gave us a wider berth of almost one million miles, really lightening up the night sky as it passed by. For a time the people of Iceland imagined that summer had arrived very early. That left one major worry still in the deep darkness of space.

Probably the biggest of the three comets, A/5009 Crick trailed the other two by a whole day. It was soon noticeable by anyone that cared to train their telescopes in the right direction, despite the amount of dusty gas in the vicinity. It became a big blob in front of the moon and this was when the Russians had their first attempt at destroying a stray comet. The moon now looked like it had a big scab, not a pretty sight, and one everyone was keen to cut out and wash away.

No harm was done to the comet from the first rocket, which missed by a lunar mile, after which the rocket went on past the moon to explode some 50,000 miles away. By that time it was fortunately behind the moon, allowing the brightness of the explosion to create a perfect, if brief, silhouette of our nearest permanent neighbour.

The Russians sent up another missile. There was still plenty of time before the rock hit the atmosphere. Yet again it was a superb miss, exploding in a dazzling flash some distance away. The last Russian missile was a total flop, initially heading up nicely towards the target, only to loop away to one side, after which it fell back sideways into the atmosphere. The warhead didn't explode this time; the rocket nose dipped in shame, headed for, and fell into the Caspian Sea.

The EU with great fanfare had promised a fleet of comet killing missiles. However, in the end they had to admit that the plans were still on the drawing board, but, they also admitted, as Britain had left the EU there were no funds available for extravagant gestures. The Americans did little better than the Russians with their attempt at handling the threat from the huge comet. Their rocket was fully on course, actually hitting the side of the comet, and slicing a small piece from it. However, the warhead failed to blow up at that point, seemingly waiting for an additional few moments after which it did explode, and gently pushed the comet further towards the eastern sky.

North Korea was the next player to announce that they would destroy the intruding rock. Having built up a good nuclear arsenal with which to frighten the West, they felt certain that they could get the job done. Their missile went up 9 miles, after which it crashed back to Earth with a small nuclear explosion, wiping out the town of Huanren in the northeastern province of Liaoning, in China. Not only was the town, and 300,000 people destroyed, the whole area became contaminated with nuclear fallout. Additionally, just outside Huanren was a spectacular water reservoir that looked like two dragons fighting, from the air. The waters and all around were also polluted, fish killed and the whole area was declared unfit for human habitation.

The Chinese people were extremely angry at the North Koreans, while the Chinese President was apoplectic, almost unable to speak coherently. He sent a delegation to North Korea, 'inviting' the whole North Korean government and President to Beijing to explain what went wrong. Upon arrival they were promptly executed. China subsequently imposed a governor on North Korea, whose army was moved, on foot, to the Chinese border with Mongolia, and forced to patrol that area, while many faithful Chinese troops arrived in North Korea, to keep the peace, we were told.

There was nowhere for the comet to go except down, and it hit the atmosphere with a crackle that could be heard across the Himalayas. Nine mountaineers were halfway up Mount Everest when the avalanche of snow and ice came down on them. One climber who had not tied himself completely to the rocky surface in time had his safety line ripped, and he ended up in a snow filled gully, still breathing, some 200 feet below. The others got covered in snow, which they had to burrow through, and shake off, before moving back down to their injured colleague.

The comet was being filmed from the International Space Station, with pictures beamed directly, via global satellites, to terrestrial broadcasting stations. NASA had predicted it would hit somewhere in Eastern Europe, possibly towards the Middle East, however the path taken would depend on several things including the physical shape and internal structure of the whole comet. If it started to roll that would also affect its final destination.

The whole world was able to watch the drama unfold, with many breaths held, as the burning mass came in low over Ukraine and Georgia, missing the Black Sea completely, as though it were headed for central Iran. After that it fizzled brighter and curved to one side, finally hitting the east of Turkey, and obliterating the border close to Iran and Iraq, just south of the towns of Hakkari and Yuksekova. Both towns were wiped out and the devastation carried on for over 100 miles across the borders. Thousands of people were killed; most of these had been ISIS fighters, gathering for an attack against Turkey.

Every 5 weeks, as if synchronised by a big clock in the murky sky, the new wave of comets would drive through the solar system. Occasionally some small ones would hit the Earth, burning up in the atmosphere; however, the general panic that had started to swell on the subject subsided down to interest of the great views of fireworks in the sky on a fairly regular basis. The threat seemed to have lessened, and people were more relaxed about it all.

Scientists reported that the solar wind was failing to push away the dust and gasses coming into the solar system, saying that more of this 'debris' was accumulating closer to the sun, which would affect the degree of light received by us on Earth. Astronomers were complaining that they could see very little through the dust, making it harder to predict the paths of comets. One scientist, by the name of Dr. Martin Banishton, stated that the Earth would not be getting so much heat from the sun, and this alone would throw out the predictions on climate change. Most people put his comments under the 'any excuse will do' pile, as most predictions on man-made climate change were already proven to be inaccurate at best.

So it was that the Earth started to cool. The dust increased close to the sun, inhibiting the heat of its rays, while the solar wind was barely noticeable. Climate change 'experts' suggested that whatever we were doing previously to warm the planet, by using carbon fuels, that we should increase it. Some believers started to chop down trees and make great bonfires, but of course it made no difference to the temperature. Several Saudi oil wells were deliberately set on fire, sending huge amounts of carbon into the atmosphere. None of this changed the way the planet was cooling, and after 2 months of this burning of natural resources the American President, in a speech to the world, begged everyone to stop as it was only making things worse. Certainly the air was more polluted, with fog now becoming widespread, and air traffic was being badly affected. The president requested that all those scientists who had been predicting chaos from alleged man-made climate change should be purged from their positions within the UN-IPCC.

With temperatures now down by an average of one degree Celsius, over a year, winter seemed to last longer. The air was perceptibly cooler, even in summer, and that following winter saw the ice around both poles extend further than ever before. Strangely there had been no change in the polar bear population, which seemed to carry on living as though nothing had changed.

ॐ ♈ ॐ　　　　　ॐ ♈ ॐ　　　　　ॐ ♈ ॐ

Bang. One moment he was washing dishes, the next he was sat strapped into a chair tightly with a silver metal cap on his head. None of the images in front of him made any sense and he seriously wondered if he had just died. He couldn't move his jaw to speak. He sat there feeling desperate, yet angry.

A bright light to his right came on, next there were hands working on the straps that held him. He was aware of figures around him, but his vision wasn't clear due to the bright light in his eyes. "Won't be long," said a friendly voice.

Someone helped him to stand up and he looked around himself in total confusion at what seemed to be a small, dentist's room. "Where the hell am I?" he almost shouted, ready to hit out and hurt someone.

"You are in the middle of an asteroid called 1017 Kientsch," a confused voice responded, "but you should know that."

"I don't know anything except that 2 minutes ago I was standing in my kitchen at home, and now I'm here," snarled Geoff.

"Oh my God, something has gone seriously wrong. You'd better come in here, have a seat and we will explain, as best we can," said a voice.

They went through an archway that had a sealing hatch attached to it, Geoff and three men. One of them went to make a strong coffee while the others sat down around a small table carved out of the floor. Geoff looked at the other two men, trying to know them, trying to work out what or who they were.

"I'm Henry Jones, lead scientist here," said one man, offering Geoff his hand. "This is Richard Baker, and the guy making the coffee is William Bonnerfield. What should we call you?"

"Geoff or Geoffrey," managed Geoff.

Henry, Geoff noted was of medium height with dark brown hair with a few grey streaks, and his most noticeable feature was the overgrown brown goatee beard. Richard was taller and slimmer with hair starting to thin, and he had pain wrinkles around the eyes, this was combined with an easy smile. William was the youngest, not as tall as Richard, with a full head of dark brown hair, no wrinkles and a deep sadness in the eyes. Geoff noticed that like them, his hair was very long. It made him feel like a hippy.

"I don't expect you to know any of us, however, we have to start somewhere with telling you what is going on."

Geoff noticed his own fingers were different when he shook hands, bigger and rougher than usual. He barely recognized his own voice. Something very odd had happened to him. He took the hot coffee, warming his hands, for he had suddenly gone very cold inside, anticipating with a degree of fear what was to come, except that he was not able, nor willing, to imagine what it might be.

"Sorry we do not have any fresh milk," apologised William, "that's one luxury we have learned to do without."

Henry continued, "We are part of a special science project, a British one I should say, and we are sitting inside a huge rock that has been partially hollowed out. There are all sorts of sensory equipment on the outside because we are studying the solar system."

Geoff felt like he was losing his mind, his reality had been turned upside down and scrambled, and he was having great trouble accepting anything being said, what was that about stuff outside?

"OK," managed Geoff stiffly, "but what happened to me, what am I doing here?"

ॐ ♈ ॐ   ॐ ♈ ॐ   ॐ ♈ ॐ

Another medium sized comet struck the Earth, this time it hit the northern part of Qaasuitsup Municipality, Greenland, well inland from the nearest coastal village of Qeqertat. Nobody was killed, even though the transit, which was observed from as far south as Royal Tunbridge Wells in southern England, did illuminate the night sky considerably more than was usual for a passing comet.

ॐ ♈ ॐ   ॐ ♈ ॐ   ॐ ♈ ॐ

After 12 months, families of the North Korean soldiers were allowed to join them, and they were permitted to build themselves little houses with materials provided by the Chinese state, on the condition that they became Chinese citizens, and swore to work for China's good health. Any dissidents saw their families removed back to North Korea.

South Korea welcomed the change in their neighbour and very soon both Koreas were starting to trade. The North Korean Governor stipulated the extent of the new-found friendship, saying that North Korea would always remain as a buffer zone for China against the imperialist Americans.

Natives of North Korea were told they were now Chinese citizens, almost. First they had to show they were good workers. After that they could apply for full citizenship.

Chinese soldiers that had taken the place of Korean ones were given special instructions to stay on professional terms with the soldiers of the South. The fence and extreme security barrier between both countries would remain. Strangely, in a very short time, the happier people of North Korea soon forgot that they had ever been ruled for so long by a half crazy neurotic despot.

ॐ ♈ ॐ   ॐ ♈ ॐ   ॐ ♈ ॐ

Many international gatherings of experts and politicians took place, and for once they all agreed on something. "Due to external conditions the planet is cooling down."

Such a short statement, but high in significance. Normally any comments issued after international conferences were long winded and wordy, to hide the fact that very little was actually agreed on and common ground was scarce. This surely was a giant step for humankind.

There was little mention of climate change at any political conferences, although some die-hards at the world conference for nature suggested that man-made climate change as a subject was far from dead. Other than that those that had been predicting one upcoming man-made disaster after another, including those from the IPCC, were keeping their heads low, as all disasters to date were clearly instigated by a bigger force than humans.

Nobody had any idea if the situation would recover, or how long it might continue for. There were many promises from politicians that the public could be assured that everything possible was being investigated and done to improve things.

At the G20 in sunny Mexico, exact location unnamed, the politicians came together to thrash out some global policies while they were able to relax in unrestrained luxury. The finance minister from Argentina was working hard beside his own personal swimming pool, giving directions to his assistant. "Make sure my foot massage and pedicure doesn't clash with my head massage. I need some more detective novels, so go and buy me ten books that look interesting, so that I will have plenty to read during the conference. Before that rub my shoulders with more sun screen and pour me another tequila."

Likewise, two commissioners from the European Union were deep in discussion over how they should handle the crop failures in northern Germany. "I just don't know why these people are complaining so loudly," said the French commissioner for financial integration. "What do they expect of us? It's not as though we can actually do anything, but they should know this by now."

"Agreed," said the Swedish commissioner for energy integration. "It is the same thing with keeping the lights on. Don't they know that unless we put all of the energy producing options in one bundle we won't be able to monitor what each household uses, which means we will not be effective in being able to limit supplies when energy becomes scarce, as it will do. They have to take responsibility themselves. We are far too busy with important matters to have to worry about them having light or full bellies."

"We are misunderstood and unappreciated," said the first. "Are you ready to go on that little horse ride into the mountains now?"

"Yes, almost," said the second, "I just have to make sure that at least some of my eight assistants have some work to do while I am away for 2 days. It doesn't look so good back home if it seems we only come here to make fun and get drunk."

After well over a week of hard pleasure the G20 conference closed, with the prime minister of Mexico issuing the headline announcement about working together and cooperating to improve our understanding of how nature was changing.

The USA called for a UN conference on how the world should prepare for a colder future. Very few fruitful ideas came out although there were several speeches on what should be done about the dust cloud hiding the sun. Most of these proposed some means of sending up a gigantic bomb to put things right.

Mr. Takahashi the Japanese PM asked, "Would an atomic bomb close to the sun help to clear away these particles? Would it help in any way?"

Mr. Abdullah Al-Buloushi the Kuwaiti PM said, "I'm not sure we can rely on the two superpowers to actually explode a bomb from a rocket in the proper place, especially given recent history, besides introducing this factor could complicate it and make it worse."

Ms. Smith the Canadian PM wanted to know, "Has NASA or any other agency completed any real studies that would help us in moving forward with removing this debris?"

Mr. Drunker the EU commission president stated, "If it was a huge force that brought this debris to us in the first place, surely a powerful push is what we need to get rid of it. The EU is looking to send up a nuclear bomb to test this theory."

Mr. Bannerman the American President told the audience that, "NASA has been working around the clock, investigating the problems, and trying to come up with a solution. I am told that exploding a very big bomb will only have a local effect, if that, so before we get into the realms of science fiction, we need more in-depth analysis of what we are dealing with so that we can come up with a viable solution."

Ms. Dinkleman the Australian PM said, "Our scientists have suggested that exploding a 500 megaton bomb in the centre of Mercury will turn the planet into another asteroid belt and that has the potential to sweep away the debris in front of the sun."

Mr. Agawal the Indian PM asked, "If the Americans or Russians have the ability to send up a rocket with a bomb, do they not also have the ability to send up an ionised vacuum cleaner type rocket to attract this debris to it and send the mess into the sun, out of the way?"

Mr. Obarmie the Nigerian PM wanted to know, "How are first world western countries going to help undeveloped countries like Nigeria to survive this coming ice age, and what resources in terms of money will they commit to making available?"

Nothing was agreed on at that conference except that they all agreed to have another one when more data was available.

In the meantime individual nations, and unions, were pressing ahead with their own ideas. The American ambassador to the EU was invited in for a special briefing by the EU technology integration commissioner, who declared that they were seriously planning to detonate a huge atomic bomb in front of the sun to see if this would help. The commissioner said, "There is no scientific evidence that exploding an atomic device will change anything, but we have to be seen to be doing something. People are getting restless about what has been going on with the spreading coldness and we fear that the EU will collapse if these fears are allowed to continue. Most importantly, we in the EU will be using quantitative easing to fund this project while insisting that our citizens contribute more in the way of taxes to sustain the economy." The ambassador grunted something in acknowledgement.

The commissioner continued, "Oh by the way, you will be invited to a prestigious brick laying ceremony for the commencement of a brand new project to relocate the commission and parliament to a sunnier location in Spain. I'm afraid that our last 5 year plan had no contingency in it for such an expensive project, around 3 trillion euros at the last count and a lot of the working class already complain at the alleged luxury we provide for ourselves, but they don't understand the importance of having a government that can function under all circumstances. There has to be someone in authority making decisions even if half the population has died of cold or starvation. No doubt there will be more riots when we reduce the quantity of food available to the markets, but we have to sell more than our surplus abroad to pay for the air-conditioned transport between Brussels and Murcia in Spain."

The ambassador nodded ruefully, wishing he didn't have to deal with such people.

It was suggested, by more and more people on the street and on TV, that at last this was the much talked about, delayed ice age, beginning to hit us. Up until now, there have been periods where the planet had been covered with ice for thousands of years, and the last one was about 10,000 years ago. This seemed very plausible, now that they could see a likely reason for periodic ages where the planet was frozen. Perhaps this type of event was the trigger, and maybe it had happened before. Some clever astronomers started to re-evaluate the undiscovered effects, and dates, of dying stars.

Most governments were generally in apathy about what could be done, although they still focused their attention on the planning and construction of large shelters, to house people and support food production for when it became impossible to live on the surface. They dug into hillsides and some mountains even, seeking some potential warmth from inside the planet. Where feasible, shelters would be linked by tunnels and in some cases, high speed transit cars. The ambition was that enough survival shelters should be built before the ice took over completely, if indeed it went that far, for it was still possible that the cooling would taper off so that an ice age was not inevitable. In any case, the physical landscape of currently unpopulated areas was being changed dramatically.

A huge bubble of plastic glass was proposed to be put up to cover London's Westminster area and the City of London. Other communities around the world were all working to put up some similar protection over their main cities. Some schemes were more practical than others, and always there was the question of how many people would be allowed inside, how many should be left to freeze to death, and how would they fare for food and water once inside. The bubble technology was innovative, coming from some research the UK had been doing on colonising Mars. Details of how to construct such bubbles was made freely available to grateful world leaders.

The rate of planetary cooling was variable with worst estimates allowing only 5 years before ice covered much of the planet at the perceived rate of cooling. In previous ice ages, only that land close to the equator had escaped the worst of the cold. All of a sudden, Mexico became very popular and many thousands of Americans became illegal immigrants. Southern Spain and Italy, and northern Australia started to see a huge influx of people, with these governments warning that feeding so many would become an impossible task the longer the freeze went on.

Economic, benefit seeking, immigrants that had previously plagued Western Europe suddenly decided that their survival came first, and what good was a free house if it was under several feet of ice? Many of those that had come to the UK seeking a subsidised better life started to flood back home. At least it wouldn't get as cold as England promised to become, they hoped. Northern and middle Africa became a target for migration as well, especially from China which had invested so heavily into this continent.

Britain concentrated a good portion of its newly gained innovation in attempting to master the weather above its skies, in addition to the shelters. The intention being to channel warm air over the entire kingdom to keep the ice at bay. This little project was worked on by a very select few people and no details were passed to anyone in the media. Only a handful of government ministers knew about it, yet with so many other projects on the go to ensure the protection of the country, and survival of as many people as possible, it was just impossible to know about everything.

ॐ ♈ ॐ ॐ ♈ ॐ ॐ ♈ ॐ

While Geoff waited patiently for a succinct reply, he realised that he didn't have his hearing aid in, and yet he could hear perfectly well. This came as another shock. One of the men got up and left the room.

"A few years ago, a company called CSC devised a means to isolate the human soul, or the spiritual being himself, if you get me. By isolate I mean they could locate it and even move it to a different body," Henry said boldly.

Geoff blinked; here was something real from his own past. His mind relaxed a little, willing to accept some small part of what was being relayed to him.

Henry looked Geoff over, trying to find words to explain what had gone wrong without causing more upset. "I can only imagine," he said, "that at the crucial moment when the beam was activated from Cambridge, that the guy who was supposed to come here twitched or moved very slightly. That would have caused the beam to interact with the next person in line, no matter how far away, which just happened to be you."

Geoff produced a frown that told Henry he hadn't been successful in calming the situation, and quickly changed tack. "Have you ever heard of CSC, Geoff? They do a lot of work for the British government."

The frown lessened a little with Geoff's thoughts coming back to more solid ground. "I used to work for CSC, and there were often rumours about how they had found the spirit within a person."

"Quite so, and good to hear you know about CSC."

"Yes I'm very familiar with CSC. I used to work on the mainframe until they told me I was surplus to requirement."

"Well, that is interesting," said Henry pursuing anything that could increase Geoff's reality. "We actually have a mainframe here that is in need of some maintenance. We were supposed to be getting a software expert to help with that, and then you arrived."

"I just hope I didn't drop that plate I was washing," smiled Geoff, "the wife would kill me."

"Don't worry," said Henry, "I'll make sure CSC buy you a whole new dinner set when we get back." That seemed to please Geoff somewhat, and the haunted look in his eyes eased a little.

Henry continued, "I guess by now you have realised that you as a spirit have been transferred to another body?"

Silence all round as Geoff took this concept in. They pointed him at a mirror, and for the first time he saw the body he was occupying. He looked about 50 with an almost handsome face, a reasonable physique, but no noticeable pains in the joints. This last point definitely helped to sway Geoff's feelings. In fact, Geoff wasn't too unhappy, still doing his best to come to terms with his new situation.

"Quite a good exchange there, my body was getting a bit worn out." Smiles all round and a sigh of relief from Henry that they had gotten so well past the difficult part.

"William has gone off to inform Cambridge base that they have badly screwed up," Henry informed Geoff. "In the meantime, if we describe our mainframe problem, perhaps there is the chance we can rescue something worthwhile out of what must seem like an incredible situation to you."

"Incredible, yes," said Geoff. "Tell me all about it," he urged, anxious to concentrate his mind on things he knew about, that were real to him.

"Well, it's not something I fully understand," said Richard, jumping in. "We had the error codes analysed back at base, although all it said was to add in more scratch tapes. Now we've looked everywhere. There are no spare magnetic tapes, and even if there were there is no way to get any physical tapes into the EMC virtual tape library."

Geoff could really relate to all of that in terms of his own experience, it was something he grabbed hold of to stop his mind wandering away at the otherwise impossible position he was in. He pushed the more crazy thoughts away, concentrating on what had been said about tapes. Now that was his universe. He could handle that in his mind. It was something very tangible to focus on, something he knew about, his entry point to this seemingly crazy world of Henry, William, and Richard.

Geoff laughed, laughed, and laughed some more. Partially this was the tenseness he had been feeling being relieved, but mainly it was at what Richard had said.

"Ye gods," muttered Geoff, "that was my job back in CSC, until they told me I wasn't needed as they were now using sulphur-ionised-wafers, or some such fancy name, in the cache, and scratch tapes were no longer an issue." He laughed some more. "They could have asked me before bringing me here, though. I would have told you how to sort it all out."

Henry and Richard both looked confused. "So what are scratch tapes, if that is not a daft question?" asked Henry.

Putting on a posh voice, Geoff stated, "In the beginning... when mainframes first came out, they used magnetic tape, on round spools, to write transient data, and data backups to. In fact they used tapes to store the operating system on and everything else, until magnetic disks were developed. They came up with that term for making the tapes reusable. They would retain the data on tape only so long as that data was valid. In the case of backups, a tape would be retained for 4 weeks so that there were always at least three copies of the backed up data if they wanted to restore it or get something back from an earlier version. At the end of the life of the data, they would run a process to scratch that tape, so that it could be written to again. That's all there is to it really. With a virtual tape library you cannot physically provide extra scratch tapes, you do it logically. I suspect though that it is just a case of managing the cycling of tape files correctly."

"Amazing," muttered Henry. "By a freak accident we get just the right person from all the people in the solar system to fix our problem. You just couldn't make it up even if you were writing a novel."

They all had a good laugh at this. For Henry and Richard a certain amount of their own frustration blew away with some degree of relief that their problem might have a solution. Having been stuck inside the comet with an insurmountable difficulty that threatened to wreck the whole project, and having Geoff turn up was enough to make anyone smile.

"Geoff, if you are feeling up to the task, I can show you the TSO terminal and provide a LOGON and password," said Richard.

Geoff was keen to be physically involved, and to get his hands on a mainframe after so long away from work, so he agreed to start right away. "Oh, and I'll need the website and sign on details for the virtual tape GUI, as well."

"That will be one of these," said Richard, handing Geoff a short list of mainframe details.

Jokingly, Geoff asked, "I should probably ask what my pay will be for all of this consultancy work, and I'm expecting a bonus."

"Agreed," said Henry, "and with travel expenses that should work out at about £500 per hour."

"That will come in handy," smiled Geoff. "This method of call-out takes some getting used to, even if it has some potential. Just remembering all of those times I would get a phone call from Operations at CSC in the middle of the night to fix a problem, slowly waking up while the PC was booting up, and Thelma never happy about being disturbed like that. I just hope she is not getting too upset about all of this," he said, with sadness creeping into his voice again.

ॐ ♈ ॐ   ॐ ♈ ॐ   ॐ ♈ ॐ

The Russian winter had been a hard one, persisting well into the spring, and even though they knew what to expect from a very cold spell, this coldness was a little different. Despite this, they refused to accept the propaganda coming from the West that a new ice age was starting, and said so. The president announced that his people were hardy, and what was a bit of a chill to them?

The Russians did, however, start to make some plans, just in case. They became very friendly with several African nations, proposing to bring some badly needed skills to improve townships and roads. In reality, Russia migrated a lot of her people south and built them large compounds to live in. It was said that Moscow was going to get its own air bubble, and all of a sudden the city became very crowded. They were also advancing plans to build survival stations on the moon to hold many thousands. It wasn't known how they expected to obtain water or oxygen, that was what the initial explorers would be tasked with finding out, if they survived long enough.

The US government, amongst other things, decided to move to southern Florida, taking over a large part of Hendry County to build a slightly smaller set of requisite government buildings including a mini White House and a mini Congress. Large parts of Clewiston were earmarked for expansion, with new highways planned for easy access to international airports at Miami and Tampa. Local airports were also due for expansion. Roads to the local airports had major upgrades planned for them, and a lot of building went on to house the extra people that would potentially be moving south to allow full functioning of government activities. Clewiston was about to be changed from a backwater into a real metropolis.

ॐ ৺ ॐ   ॐ ৺ ॐ   ॐ ৺ ॐ

The rich of course had their own way of dealing with a potential disaster. They sunk money into buying up remote islands and property close to the equator and paid locals to work farms that they established. Large boats, some as big as small towns, were designed and financed, with only the very rich being able to afford a berth for a decent length of time. With the assumption that the promised ice age would last for a very long time, people were willing to pay huge fees to be able to live in some degree of comfort on the boats for the rest of their lives. Very few planned for a future that didn't include the planet being almost engulfed in ice.

~ CHAPTER 3 ~

~ BACK TO WORK ~

"Hang on a sec," Geoff said, after following Richard and Henry into what they described as the computer room. The room itself was formed from solid stone walls, not always straight, with rough bits projecting out a bit, and the lighting wasn't that great. They could just about stand up straight, although with three people it was a bit of a squeeze. The CPU was tucked under a high arch with just enough clearance to open the access panels. The virtual tape library was in a rack, edge on to the wall, as it needed full access, front and back. A disk subsystem was squeezed in under another arch, while the system console and TSO console were against one wall that was reasonably straight. There were other boxes and racks around the room, with cables going this way and that. A clear sign that it had all been put together and cabled up by someone who had never touched a mainframe previously.

"Hang on a minute," Geoff repeated. "I'm still in confusion about all of this. For example, where are we? You said inside a rock, but where is that rock?"

"You," replied Richard, "me, Henry, William, and this computer equipment are sitting inside a huge rock, an ex-asteroid, about eight times the size of your house. The rock itself, actually we prefer to call it the 'Comet', has had rooms carved out for different purposes. We stole it from a group beyond Mars and converted it, as we are now in the land of comets we gave it that name."

"OK, I get that," said Geoff, "what I don't get is *where* this 'Comet' is physically located?"

Henry took Geoff's arm and indicated that he wanted to show him something. They went just outside the room to a small alcove in which a small window had been installed. "What do you see out there?"

Geoff looked, his eyes blinking with the brightness. "I see stars, far brighter and more colourful than I've ever seen them before."

"That is because you are not looking at them through an atmosphere, and we are not seeing distortions. Neither are we looking at them through the gasses and dust that normally exist within the solar system," said Richard.

Geoff paused, half guessing the full answer to his question; still, he needed to hear it from the men telling the story.

"Our 'Comet', Geoff, is very, very, far away from Earth, and the sun. If you looked towards the sun, it would be just a tiny dot of light. We are at the absolute edge of the solar system, looking out towards the Milky Way."

Geoff blinked, beginning to think mind exploding thoughts, again.

"Does that clarify that question for you, is that real?" asked Henry.

"Yes and no," managed Geoff after a moment, head beginning to spin a little. "Now more and more questions come into my mind. If we are in outer space how come we have gravity? How come we can walk around like this? Where does the oxygen come from? What about water and food? Why is this happening?"

Henry said, "I can understand how you are feeling. This is all very strange to us and we've had over a year to get used to it. Let's take it easy, we can talk about all of this calmly without raising any blood pressure."

"To be honest," said Geoff, "I feel like I'm in something very unreal, and I need something solid to hold my mind together. Perhaps we should go one point at a time. Tell me why I'm able to stand up straight inside a rock on the edge of our solar system, in space, and Earth being less than a dot. Why are we not floating around here and banging our heads against the protruding rocky bits?"

Henry and Richard smiled a big satisfied smile, having wanted to boast a little of a major achievement. "I promise to show you more, and we can talk about all the other questions you have while you are with us," said Henry. "On the subject of gravity, I have to say that it is something we are really proud of. On our way out here we had extensive time to devise a way to monitor and measure gravity waves, with a lot of help from the big planets. By the time we got to this area we knew more about the subject than any living man, having seen it up close, in regular use in different ways. So, using that knowledge we created an artificial gravity."

"Just let us explain a little about what we found out about the subject. It will hopefully give you something real to hook your thoughts around. Anyway, it comes in waves, rather like the sea, unlike light or sound waves that bounce around," said Richard.

Henry continued, "The waves consist of very, very, tiny particles that exert a pull against objects as they meet, also these particles are absorbed into physical objects as the wave passes through, affecting the way the object moves, slowing it down a little and slightly altering its course. A planet like the Earth would have many different waves affecting it, main ones being the sun and large outer planets. You can bet there is also a strong pull, although not as strong as the sun, coming from the black hole in the Milky Way. The moon also exerts a force, just as the Earth exerts a pull on the moon. We discovered how these particles were created, and that was key; once you know how to create the particles you can manage them. At first we could only make a few randomly, but as we said, we had a lot of time on our hands during the journey down here. By trial and error, we perfected the process, and what amazed us was that the energy required to do so was minimal. The gravity particles themselves are part of the same family as neutrinos, both being fundamental particles, both having a very tiny mass."

Richard interjected with, "Of course, it helped that we could deploy our most sensitive instruments while in the vicinity of Jupiter, and then Saturn. As we passed these great planets we could actually watch gravity particles forming, with our revised instrumentation. That was so amazing. It seems that gravity particles cling to solids and generate a pull action towards their source. The next thing was to work out why they formed, what was the trigger mechanism that started them. That was more difficult to identify, even though we had noticed that these waves started to grow when a slight disturbance in the mass of a planet took place. For example, the red spot on Jupiter slightly changing position or growing. Or on Saturn when something hit the rings. The disturbance seemed to generate a push effect on the planet that was met with the formation of the gravity particles themselves. It was a little like the nervous system in the body reacting to some impact or pain. We were able to see that formation happening time and time again. Even when there seemed to be nothing to trigger the disturbance, it was as though the mass at the centre of the planet was creating its own disturbance to balance internal pressures."

"Yes," agreed Henry, "it was as though it were all laid out for us to discover. It would not have been possible of course without all of the research that preceded us, nor without the extreme sensitivity of the devices we had to work with. At the end of the day we were the right people in the right place, with the right equipment. This discovery alone will pay for the whole cost of the mission, and believe me that wasn't cheap. It has many practical applications, for example, when you take a sleep, you will find the bed is the most comfortable you have ever known. To put it simply, we have turned down the gravity in our beds."

"Super," said Geoff, "in that case I will be staying for breakfast. Sorry to say that explanation nearly put me to sleep. You have to imagine I came from the slums of Birmingham and my ability to take in raw data is very limited, unless I hear the same information at least four times, I just don't absorb it."

Henry continued, "Understood, although I feel you are much brighter than that. I will explain it all over again if we have you stay long enough. However, just to finish off the subject, I should add that by the time we reached here, we had already rigged up the necessary gravity generators, so it was easy just to turn it all on. Only one initial bug, we'd made the ceiling the floor, although that was soon corrected."

"Wow," said Geoff, you are clever people, "despite the fact that I didn't get all of that, this is still pretty amazing." They both agreed.

"Yet not so clever as to be able to fix the scratch tape problem," mumbled Richard.

They smiled and Geoff took this as a hint, moving back towards the computer room. At this point William rejoined them with a very humble apology to Geoff from Cambridge, who were still running diagnostics on the whole transfer process. They were over the moon that he knew about scratch tapes though, and begged him to stay and fix the problem. They would get him out of there as soon as he was ready to go home. Geoff liked the sound of that, even though he was reluctant to leave, just yet. He was just getting very interested in this amazing project.

"I'll look into that," agreed Geoff, but I've been promised a great night's sleep and breakfast, so maybe I will stay at least for that."

"That's a deal," said Henry, and we aren't going to rush you away, we need to give you plenty of time to find those scratch tapes and shove them in to the tape library."

Laughter filled the room and corridor.

ॐ ♈ ॐ   ॐ ♈ ॐ   ॐ ♈ ॐ

Julie and team now spent most of their time examining data produced by a variety of radio and optical telescopes of the Oort Cloud. The only thing they could say for sure was that whereas before there was total randominity in the way comets moved around, this had changed to a whole bunch of them moving towards the sun, while others, at the edge of this great broom effect, that had swept through a portion of the cloud, had literally been brushed aside into an even more inconsistent orbit within the cloud. Collisions happened, yet made little difference to the overall picture of general chaos within the cloud.

"Julie, will we get a bonus if we find this big broom?" Gary wanted to know.

"No, instead you'll get a broom up your bums if you don't come up with something," Julie sarcastically replied.

They were no closer to understanding the issue than they had been 5 weeks ago, and that applied to many teams around the globe, who were trying to digest data that was infected with the misinformation caused by so much dust and debris. Still, they all kept searching, hoping their team would spot something vital.

"OK," announced Julie, I'm as sick as everyone else is of poring over this crap data. Time for a mini conference to work out what we have and what we can do to take this to a better state of play." The team gathered around the big table with their notes, trying to be positive. "Let's start off with what we know. Mike, please summarise."

"This will be quick," said Mike, "what do we know; nothing."

"Alright, now let's be serious, Mike."

"If you insist."

"I do," replied Julie, and that is not an agreement to consummate any imagined nuptials." That made them all smile and relieved some of the group's tension that had started to show.

Mike started writing on a large flip chart. "Right, what we know is this:

For some unknown reason comets are leaving a portion, or portions, of the Oort Cloud.

The section of the Oort Cloud affected is getting wider, in that the broom affects a different segment each time, but close to the previous one.

The comets are travelling at high speeds, approaching 300,000 MPH.

Most are heading towards the sun, some diverted within the cloud.

It happens periodically, regularly, at approximately 5 week intervals.

The movement is accompanied by large amounts of radioactive metallic dust.

The dust is starting to impact on the sun's rays.

The dust makes normal astronomy extremely difficult.

Solar wind is being held at bay."

"Number ten," said Gary, "there is no sign of the brush that is doing the sweeping. Eleven, astronomers are getting a very bad name and blamed unfairly for all of this chaos."

"Hmm, OK, leave off that last one, Mike, it's one of those things we can take for granted. Let's see what we have. The other items really define our problem nicely. Let's discuss."

They talked at length on each item, after the last item they started again, going through many times, often repeating what was already said. They kept throwing in ideas until no more came. Before they all left for the day, Julie reminded them, "Our objectives are to find out where the push is coming from, and what controls that big broom, as well as finding a way to predict if any comets might be coming our way, potentially to harm Earth. If we can find the source the rest of the things should fall into place and maybe we can do something about it all."

Julie had been keeping notes, which she typed up after the others had left for the day. After that she assigned a group of tasks from the notes to each team member. *That will stretch everyone*, she thought, telling herself it was a good way forward.

ॐ ♈ ॐ   ॐ ♈ ॐ   ॐ ♈ ॐ

The weather became gradually more grey and dull, and not just in Britain where they were used to it. More rain fell around the world than was usual. El Nino, although overdue, appeared to have hibernated, with water temperature in the Pacific Ocean cooler than many would have liked. The Gulf Stream moved well to the south of Great Britain, and stayed there even through the summer months, making the weather wet, windy, and cold. Norway cooled dramatically as the warm winds from the Rocky Mountains failed to warm the area.

The sun, when visible, took on an orange tinge, which became stronger as the months passed. Some wondered if the sun itself was changing, or if it was simply the way the sun looked through all the debris in between itself and the Earth. Scientists were not a great help on this question, some saying it was very feasible that the colour spectrum of the sun could conceivably become more like that of an orange star. Others said that was nonsense, and the sun would remain the same type as it always had been, we were just seeing it through a screen that was mainly dark orange.

As the days passed, the rays of the sun continued to take on a deeper orange hue, and some die-hard alarmists in the IPCC, who were still trying to find ways to blame the comet situation on mankind, suggested that the sun could turn into a brown star due to pollution, and it would no longer be able to support life on Earth. The media picked up on this although every reputable scientist, including Julie Banks was saying that, "It is impossible for the sun to become brown as that is fundamentally a different type of star. Brown stars are normally much smaller than our sun and create far less heat. They still glow, well, in a very limited way, but have nothing like the intensity of yellow stars. The magnitude of output produced by our sun would not change, but it is harder now for that energy to reach out into the solar system."

Following the discussion in various media about the deepening colour of the sun, a DJ on Radio Two, by the name of Ned Grimcrack, started to play an old song he'd dug up from his personal archive. It was called '*Don't let the sun go down on me*', by Elton John, a popular classic from 1974. The sun being a topical subject, Nick played the original regularly, until one day he was talking over the introduction, as DJ's often do, and managed to change the main line of the song so that it sounded like, 'don't let the sun go brown on me'. His engineer gave him the thumbs up to show he liked the rephrasing, which prompted Nick to regularly distort the opening words of this song and it became a regular feature of his show, as well as his ad-libs on the subject, and talking in a comical fashion about brown this, or brown that.

Subsequently, whenever he played this song he would always dub in the word 'brown' in place of 'down'. The music buying public enjoyed the humour, and the recording again found itself in the pop charts.

The recording company liked this idea from the DJ so much so that they remastered the recording in this fashion. Very shortly, this became an iconic song of the times. It got so much airplay due to the subject being so vivid to everyone that it got into the psyche of the nation, such that nobody could complete a sentence with "don't let..," without someone singing out, "the sun go brown." In the streets, some sensitive people would look up at the orange grey sky and start singing, "don't let the sun go brown... don't let the sun go brown..." and the record company made another fortune.

ॐ ♈ ॐ   ॐ ♈ ॐ   ॐ ♈ ॐ

Geoff signed onto the TSO terminal which allowed him access to manipulate the settings that managed tape processing. The first thing that he found, as he investigated, was that tapes hadn't been set up as generational files, so they wouldn't automatically cycle out. He fixed that by a slight name change to the files created, with a generation number at the end. Henry said they would like to keep at least 100 versions, so they settled on 250 to be sure.

The virtual tape library had exhausted all of the logical scratch tapes that had been configured to it, so after checking in the tape management system that enough tapes had been assigned there, he added in 10,000 extra tapes from the appropriate range into the library. He had to do that before he could run a job to scratch old tapes, because that job required a scratch tape, which was really an unfortunate design feature.

As soon as the job had completed, everything burst into life, with jobs that had been waiting for quite some time, writing their valuable data to virtual tape.

Henry slapped Geoff on the shoulder to congratulate him on fixing the problem so quickly.

"That should get things moving for now, but you'd best explain what all these batch jobs are doing. I will need to do a more thorough check to make sure there are no other issues sitting there," said Geoff.

"OK," said Henry, and went on to explain how it all worked. "Basically, we have the sensors picking up the data and digitising it before sending it to its own cache. When the cache fills up no more observations are taken, and that's the position we've been in for over 2 months. Normally the raw data goes from cache to CPU, picked up as a feed, but if the CPU is not running jobs, then no data can be processed. It's a wrap around cache so processing will take all data available and free up that bit of the cache for re-use. The jobs are scheduled to run daily, one for each sensor or telescope, of which there are 48. The jobs do an initial tidy up of the data, some basic logic checking, and then they compress the data on to tape. Finally, the tape is re-read and the data streamed back to Cambridge using our super-fast laser link."

"Nice summary," agreed Richard.

"Cool, I get it," said Geoff. "I only changed one procedure so I will need to check if there are different ones, but for now it should all run happily."

"Sounds good to me," said Henry.

"So what are these sensors you talk about? Are they like big telescopes?"

"Yes and no," replied Richard. "We interchange names between sensor and telescopes, but they really are the same thing, except that ours are at least three times as penetrating as the most powerful telescope that Earth has."

"Have you heard of the JWST," Henry wanted to know, "with its large infrared telescope using an 8.5-meter primary mirror array?"

"Oh yes," said Geoff. "The James Webb space telescope number two, there were some great pictures produced by it and its predecessor, of distant galaxies."

"We don't use an array of mirrors for our telescopes," said Henry. "In fact the devices are quite small by comparison, following a rather amazing breakthrough by our lab people. I can't explain the theory behind it all too well; however, it is based on computer generated imagery to expand on what has been viewed. Another project that we have been testing to destruction. If I hadn't seen for myself how accurate it was on something I could verify, I would still be having doubts about it, but it is brilliant."

"Super," said Geoff, "so does that mean you've been able to get images beyond the edge of the universe? Have you found the big bang?"

"I should have guessed that one would be coming," smiled Henry. "Quick answer is no. It seems that no matter how far we look back into the depths of the universe there is always something more to see, there is always more time to go back in."

"Should you ever get to look at 'Comet' from the outside," said Richard, "you will also come to think of it as a spiky potato, which is what it looks like with so many sensors jutting out."

The only way to really appreciate that view, though," said William, "is to take a spacewalk. How would that take your fancy?"

"That sounds like quite a sight, although it must be rather scary," said Geoff. "I've always fancied doing that, you know, walking around in space, in a spacesuit, and moving about without gravity. At the same time I find it quite terrifying."

"It's a great feeling if you can control it," said William, "and that isn't easy. We'd have to make sure you were tied very securely to anchor points on the outside."

"You're almost getting me wanting to do it," said Geoff.

Henry thrust a small booklet at Geoff. "Read that before you even think about going outside. It demonstrates the principles of being weightless, and we all found it very useful, however, we did also get weeks of training to operate without gravity."

Geoff read the booklet and rather than putting him off the idea, it only increased his desire to go for a walk outside.

"It's not a bad idea," suggested Richard, "if Geoff is going to be with us for a short time, he should know the emergency procedures, and getting into a spacesuit is definitely a part of that."

"You're probably right," agreed Henry reluctantly. "Will you and William escort Geoff?"

"We can do that," said Richard, "if we get a clear yes from Geoff."

Geoff nodded his head up and down vigorously.

"This way," said Richard leading the way to the suit room. It took them a full 20 minutes to get Geoff into the lower part of the suit, after that he had to have a short rest, so while he did that, Richard and William showed him how to do it without help, and in another 15 minutes it was all done except the helmet.

Once fully suited they made their way into the airlock, where the air pressure was gradually released, allowing the outer door to be opened. Geoff found it a bit of a waddle using the big heavy boots, and he decided he certainly wouldn't be walking far. Before moving outside, lines were attached to each person and secured at a big metal ring just outside the door. Additionally, William and Richard had a cable each that was attached to Geoff as well.

Richard stepped out into the void first and floated some 3 feet away from the entrance. Geoff took a little jump in the same direction, colliding gently with Richard and making him turn around. Richard quickly corrected his motion, while grabbing Geoff to steady him. Pulling on the main rope, Geoff pulled himself back towards Comet, drifting up until he could plant his feet on the top side of the outside wall of the huge rock. For the first time he saw just how big it was. He walked up and down a bit, gingerly exercising his limbs in a slow manner and getting familiar with what he needed to do to stay in control. Looking at the full length of 'Comet', which seemed to stretch on a long way, he couldn't help but agree with the spiky potato description, little protruding prongs were everywhere.

Even looking through the thick glass of the helmet, that blurred his vision at the edges, he couldn't help but notice the emptiness of the space and the bright lights of distant stars all around. The stars burned into his soul, energising him, making him so aware of the amazing vista around him. It enthralled him, almost hypnotically. He couldn't help thinking that only a few days ago he was living his normal humdrum, but comfortable life. If anybody had told him then that within a very short time he would be taking his first spacewalk, he would have laughed his head off. He looked in his make-believe diary, and oh yes, there was an entry, looks like a Thursday at three PM, for a walk in space, strange how he hadn't spotted that before. *Oh boy*, he thought to himself, *this is quite a leap for a couch potato.*

Geoff looked around at where he might tread with his heavy feet, without tripping over a spike, and found a little path that took him almost to the centre of the top of 'Comet', and gingerly he moved his bulk towards it. Slowly he gained confidence in walking and moving about without gravity to keep his feet below himself, and managed to reach the centre point on the topside of 'Comet'. With arms outstretched he simply stood there, like a king, absorbed in the moment, luxuriating in the feeling of freedom, appreciating and yet in awe of all around him, the brilliance of the stars and such a glorious feeling of being weightless, with no Earthly pains to disturb his thoughts. "Brilliant, absolutely brilliant, this is truly fantastic," he told the local universe.

Inside 'Comet' Henry had been following the progress of the spacewalk. Using a sensor at one end of the rock, just above the comm's area he viewed and recorded the image of this inspirational guy, enjoying the moment and seemingly so pleased with himself. Henry captured a still image of the newest spacewalker, which he printed off in black ink, while saving a colour version to his own mainframe storage area, for posterity.

Still with arms out wide, Geoff started to turn in a circle, taking in the vastness of empty space and the tranquillity of it all. It wasn't just darkness, for the stars illuminated everything so well. It was unreal and yet so inspiring at the same time, unlike anything he'd ever experienced before. Still turning slowly around, marvelling at the colourful universe before him, the cable resting against 'Comet' hooked itself around a nearby spike. Richard noticed this and started to warn Geoff, "Geoff, don't move." It was too late; the motion of one body moving in one direction against the sudden tautness of a restraining cable could only result in one thing. Geoff lost his balance, with his feet sliding away from him and his body taking up a horizontal position to the surface of 'Comet'.

Through the gap in between his feet Geoff could just make out the distinct smudge of the Andromeda Galaxy, yet despite his precarious position, and before the idea that he might be in trouble reached his overactive mind, he just wondered at the beauty of it, and how that majestic image had been coming towards him, for his eyes to take in at this very moment in time, for two and a half million years.

The thump against the surface of 'Comet' was enough to jar his thoughts and wake him up to his present time problem, for now he was sliding outwards, away from the spiky surface towards emptiness. His first thought was to plant his feet more firmly, which had the reverse effect when he tried it, causing him to tumble, until the second cable tightened and jerked him back. Now he was heading back towards the airlock, with both William and Richard positioned ready to catch him, which they did nicely and pushed him in the direction of the open airlock. Geoff felt a little like a ping-pong ball as he could do very little to control his own motion, grasping at small rails only to lose his grip as his body shifted yet again. Now Richard and William each caught hold of their cable attached to Geoff's suit, and like a wild stallion he was pulled in towards them both, his progress to and fro eventually becoming calm, until he could see the empty airlock before him, and reached out for it. He scrambled, and got pushed, until he was well inside, allowing William to get the external hatch closed. Geoff was still feeling the effect of no gravity, moving up and around slowly within the chamber, and his heart was beating faster and harder than he was comfortable with. Finally the oxygen returned to the exit chamber, along with gravity, allowing the inner hatch to open. Several pairs of hands were helping Geoff release the straps and zips of his cumbersome suit, but which had kept him safe. The helmet came off and he breathed a great sigh of relief when he was finally helped out of the suit. Still in his underwear, he sat very quietly on the bench, trying to relax the tenseness in his body and calming the overworked heart.

"You were doing OK there for a while, Geoff," said Henry, "until you did that little twirl."

"I suppose I got a little carried away," suggested Geoff, "it was such a fabulous feeling to be out there unencumbered by anything, just floating. Thanks for letting me try that, it was magical."

Richard was a little breathless, though smiling. "Glad you liked it, but next time, no more dancing, eh?"

"Agreed," said Geoff, smiling his thanks.

"Here's something for your scrapbook," said Henry, handing him the picture he'd taken before Geoff started to have difficulties.

"Wait till I show that to Thelma," said Geoff in an excited grateful response, "and this is me, my love on a spacewalk, standing on top of our ship, just before I made a total idiot of myself and had to be rescued. Thanks, Henry!"

Geoff soon became familiar with his new temporary habitat. It was bigger inside than he'd originally expected, with a whole assortment of different rooms for unknown purposes.

"Those are our individual bedrooms," said Henry, indicating some solid wooden doors, numbered one to five. You should take over Dave's room as you will need to use his clothes. That will be room number three."

Geoff entered his room to find it comfortable, if sparse. A single bed was against one fairly straight wall, while cupboards were built into another wall where the clothes and other items belonging to Dave were stowed. An easy chair was in the corner with a light just behind it.

"There's the shower unit," said Henry, "and a supply of towels in that cupboard next to it. We are each responsible for our own laundry, and I'll show you where that happens."

They went along the corridor a little way to a room with no door. It had a great metal contraption within. "We posted the instructions on the wall for using that beast, but you'll soon get used to working it," said Henry. "Washing powder is kept in that cupboard."

"Very nice," said Geoff, "and I've noticed how clean and tidy you all keep everything. Just tell me what I have to do to help with that."

"We will," said Henry. "Take a look in your room, you will find there is a little booklet in one of your cupboards to explain how things work. Richard put it together on the way down here so that we would be productive and not tiresome to each other by being untidy."

Henry went back to the comm's area while Geoff explored his temporary accommodation. He imagined that as soon as they were happy that there would be no more mainframe issues, he would get swapped back into his own body. Still, in the meantime it would be interesting to explore 'Comet'.

After he'd digested the 'How to keep things tidy' notes, and he'd checked all the cupboards and crevices in his little suite, he decided he should explore some more as there was clearly many other rooms off the corridor he hadn't investigated, nor indeed had he looked into the big cupboards along the walls of the corridor.

Most of the rooms had no door, which made access easier, although a lot of rooms hadn't been converted into any particular use. He found a gym room with treadmills, exercise bikes, and a weights machine, which he promised Dave mentally that he would use. At the end of the corridor that went across the width of 'Comet' he found another observation area with seats and some screens. A really ideal place to get away from the main activity. On his way back he looked in a few cupboards, not finding much of interest to him personally. He did find the scientists' office, close to the computer room, also there was a room he almost missed just opposite because it had initially seemed to be empty. Taking a closer look, he discovered a full kitchen, with cupboards half full of canned food, and a freezer with ready meals, and a great deal of sliced bread. There was a large carved table to one side, with four chairs, so clearly that was the dining room as well. One nice little surprise he stumbled on behind the freezer room made him smile. At first glance it looked like a display of fresh green vegetables like you used to see in specialist greengrocer stores, but moving in closer he found a real garden, a boxed growing produce kind of a garden. Nonetheless, it had the capacity to grow many varieties of fresh foods.

One other large room back towards the little observational area, which initially confused him, was worth another visit he decided. It had what looked like a very large cage inside. Certainly the room had the smell one associates with animals, not overpowering yet more than a hint. He couldn't work out how or why live animals would be kept there, besides it would have been more suited to monkeys than cows.

In the very centre of the main corridor, there was a big room that held a trio of big glass tanks, full of water, and above them there seemed to be a big sponge. "That," said William who had seen Geoff wandering about looking puzzled, "is where we get most of our fresh water from. That is the supply we use to drink, eat and cook with."

"From a sponge?" asked Geoff.

"Not exactly," smiled William. "On the other side of the sponge, which is actually a big filter unit, is a big mushy mess of what was once an ice comet. Above that there is a very large trap door for the comets to enter."

"What happens when you run out of fresh water?"

"That's when we go hunting for another supply. We find another comet that is mainly frozen water, after which we drag it in here."

Geoff felt a little better after considering this, but wanted to know if they got oxygen the same way.

"That's a lot more complicated," said William, "we had to bring a great deal of that with us, although one of our tasks here is to find out how we can make our own, or get a supply from something or somewhere. We have been attempting to extract oxygen from our water supply, so far with only limited success. The whole process needs streamlining before it could be even considered partially effective."

"Considering how colourful the stars are, the walls, floor and ceilings here are very dull, with that washed out grey colour everywhere," said Geoff, "has anybody considered decorating, or at least painting some murals?"

"Not sure what we would use for paint," answered William who had just been joined by Henry.

"What do you want paint for?" asked Henry. "These grey sombre surrounds match our collective mood perfectly."

"Exactly," said William, "Geoff thought we should brighten up both."

"Well," said Henry, "we have plenty of oil spare. Geoff if you want to experiment you could try collecting some coloured fruits from our garden and mixing them all up with a little oil. We have a machine in the lab that can shake it all up very well. If you do have a go, please start the painting somewhere that is not too prominent, in case it all goes wrong. I couldn't be sure how, or if this rock will absorb any colouring."

"Alright," said Geoff, "I could start in the room with that big cage in, just tell me where I can get some oil and empty bottles, and I'll give it a go."

The garden was full of so many different types of fruit and vegetables that Geoff had little problem in finding red or purple colouring. Lighter shades were harder to find. He plucked a pound or so of broccoli for green. Carrots would either come out yellow or orange, while peas would provide a different shade of green or could be mixed in with other ingredients.

"Okey-dokey," said Geoff to Henry, "I'm ready with six samples, each bottle has a spoonful of cooking oil and all the veg and fruit that I could mash up and squash in. Now they need an extremely good shake."

"Right," said Henry, "no guarantee that this will produce anything like real paint or that it will even stick to the wall."

Geoff found a little tray to pour the mixture into from the first test bottle, and he used a bit of cloth to soak up the colour and apply it to the wall next to the big cage. Then he tried the other colours in turn, considering this his first abstract art submission. The colours mainly stayed on the wall, some streaky, some covering well, although he wasn't sure Darren Fitzgerald, famous abstract painter, would be impressed by his conceptual randominity, but it certainly brightened up a 3 square feet patch of wall.

"This will cause some nightmares for whoever sleeps in there," he said to himself, "if they ever get any wild animals to put in there, or wild men."

He gave it all a while to dry off before asking for the critics to appraise his work.

"Hmm, interesting," suggested Richard, "you could certainly use the deep red purple colour as a band around the windows to show them off."

"That green could be used to mark a centre point in the corridor walls," suggested William, with occasional squares or oblongs above with a deep colour border."

"Not bad ideas," agreed Henry, and I'd like to see a nice pale yellow and bit of red on my bedroom wall."

Soon they were all doing their bit to make 'Comet' a little less grey, in the first bout of redecoration. The colours were often weak, although even these relieved the greyness. As for Geoff, he painted a big Union Jack in his room and copied it at various locations. "Now I know," he said to the others, "how cavemen felt about living in a dreary cave, and that urge they must have had to brighten it up just a little with a handmade drawing of animals and people."

"Absolutely," agreed Henry.

~ CHAPTER 4 ~

~ ABDUCTED BY ALIENS ~

The main control area that housed a host of screens and several different sets of mechanisms, was towards one side of the corridor where it was fattened out somewhat. Within this comm's room, as it was called, a very large observational window was the main focus. It covered all of one wall and stretched way over the ceiling in a wide arc to show a great deal of what was outside. It was pointing head on, out towards the Milky Way, and the rest of our neighbours in outer space. The amount and variety of the spectacles on view through the observation window, not to mention the colours of the stars and galaxies,

was totally staggering, enough to leave anyone in awe and frequently mesmerised by the view. It was all so bright that the darkness in between the specks of light was almost negligible.

Making himself comfortable in one of the chairs in the comm's room, Geoff was feeling very cheery, and he could judge that his mood helped the others who had been having a hard time of it lately, having been locked up for quite a while in this stone ship of limited pleasures, amazing as it was. He started to jabber away, as he often did when the conversation anywhere started to die, throwing in some of his lighter questions. "So, Richard, what did you do to get locked up here? Something very bad, eh?"

Richard smiled. "We all volunteered for this, believe it or not. The chance of a lifetime to be able to work in raw space, with so much data to view, and just looking out of the window almost makes it all worthwhile."

"I noticed," said Geoff, "that you have a problem with your back. Hope that's not too painful."

"It hurts like hell at times," admitted Richard. "I damaged my spine in a silly accident when I was young, and that slowly affected other parts of my body. The spine itself is rather weak, which subsequently puts pressure on my neck and lower back. It's the gradual erosion of a disk in my lower back that is worse and causes me most pain, especially whenever I try to bend or stoop. It's only thanks to the anti-gravity bed that I can get a good sleep and not wake up in pain, so there have been some benefits from the trip for me personally. That will be something to take home with me when we get back."

"Sorry to hear about the back," said Geoff, "I know how painful these things can be."

"I get by," said Richard. "It's only the young and fit amongst us that don't suffer physically on this trip," he added looking towards William. "Still not sure how you, William, qualified for this trip, not technically, you are very well qualified, but they were looking for disposable scientists. It was a risk doing all of this and so many things could go wrong. Henry and myself qualified due to age mainly, and we had no dependants."

"Neither did I," said William. "My wife had died in childbirth a year before this project started and I lost them both, so I was happy to get away from sad memories."

Oops, thought Geoff, *so much for a light subject.*

"This certainly gives one a different perspective being out here," said Geoff, "so much to see and learn about, although I just realised, I am not qualified on any level. I can barely spell science, I'm married, happily, and I'm still a youngster." This prompted some smiles from the three of them, and relieved a little of the gloom that had descended.

"Nice excuse," said Richard, "actually you qualify for this project because you know more about the mainframe than Cambridge and all of us here put together."

"That's odd," said William. "Just to change the subject. Our laser transmissions are getting to base OK, but it looks like Cambridge is unable to find us. Oh hang on, this might be something."

A short burst of words came through the laser comm. "... trouble sending to you... Have you moved or have you had a..." After that it just went quiet.

Geoff knew exactly what that all meant. When he worked for the European Space Agency in Germany, occasionally the technicians would fail to send a command to a satellite because it wasn't in exactly the same place as it should have been by their calculations. It was usually a hit and miss affair to re-establish the link and command the satellite afresh. Geoff guessed that this was happening here. Cambridge was a fixed point and any re-fixes would be calculated automatically by the on board computer when sending. Earth was in a known orbit and predictable in terms of location, the rock wasn't.

The three scientists got to work, attempting to verify if they had moved and by how much. They conferred using their different observations to come to an agreement. Henry announced that they were no longer following the trajectory laid down. "It's like a great gust of wind has blown us sideways," said Richard.

Geoff watched as the other men worked through the observations and technical data from the sensors, not disturbing them, just mildly fascinated until it became repetitive, after that he took himself off to his own suite, some way up the corridor, and had a most refreshing sleep in his bed. The lessened gravity made him feel almost as though he was floating. His back and neck sunk lightly into the mattress and pillow in a truly comfortable way. They really had just got it absolutely right, at least for Geoff. He had no aches or pains when he did awake and lay there daydreaming and wondering what an incredible invention this gravity control feature was. He immediately decided he wanted a bed like that at home, no matter what it cost. It meant he would have to save up all his pennies to get one, though.

Normally the air was kept clean of odours; however, there was one in the air right now. Slight as it might be, that smell grabbed him and got him into the shower and dressed pretty quickly. "Hmm, bacon," he said as he walked into the kitchen, "smells like the real thing anyway."

William was in the kitchen and smiled a good morning at Geoff. "It sure is the real thing. No substitutes when it comes to breakfast. Grab yourself a coffee, or there is orange juice in the metal jug. Breakfast is ready." Right on cue the other two men arrived and they all tucked into the bacon served with tinned tomatoes and bread that had been frozen so long it took 30 minutes to toast, but it was indeed the most enjoyable meal Geoff had had for so many miles.

Geoff realised how hungry he was after the first bite, and it was two more mouthfuls before he got his first question of the new day out. "How's it going with the analyses?" He swallowed another bite as he waited for a reply.

"Well," mumbled Richard, through the bacon, "we know how much we have moved, in which direction and how fast. So far we have no sign of what did it to us and all the comets that we were close to before. For now we will close that cycle and get back to our normal routine. We will take it in turns to get some sleep. One of us three will be awake at all times so you won't get too lonely."

Henry interjected, "Geoff, it's going to be your job to keep one of us awake, if you would please, but nothing too loud."

"I can be as quiet as a mouse and still keep people awake," smiled Geoff.

ॐ ♈ ॐ   ॐ ♈ ॐ   ॐ ♈ ॐ

One not so cold morning in England, although wrapped up in their winter woollies, people were surprised to see that a fountain in the centre of Oxford, that had been frozen over for months, was now mostly a pool of very cold water, with pieces of ice floating within. It seemed it had thawed out, and nobody could say why. They suspected someone was playing a trick to get them excited, yet even if it was due to warmer air, the chances were it was only a short respite from the coldness they were becoming used to.

The following afternoon there was no ice in the fountain, and happy faces welcomed the news that similar things had occurred in several other places.

Astronomers came up with the reason for the thaw, and scientists confirmed temperature everywhere had improved. It seemed the wind associated with the comets had been blowing very warm radioactive gasses instead of metallic debris. Thanks to this new effect the Earth had actually warmed a little. Everyone of course wished this would continue, which it did for several weeks.

People were still chanting to encourage our star to emerge from behind the orange barrier, "Don't let the sun go brown... don't let the sun go brown..."

The media speculated that the big freeze might be over, even if there was still a general concern that the sun was still only visible as a dark reddish orange colour.

The chill effect came back, just as astronomers announced that the warming effect from the warm wind blowing past the Earth towards the sun had stopped. Gloom once more spread around the world. The only hope was that the sun would somehow recover its strength and blow away the metallic debris from all around the inner planets. Astronomers had no good news on this, and the Earth gradually cooled again.

Comets were of course still a big worry, and the solar system was regularly searched for anything that might be coming Earthwards.

A lot of people turned to religion, continually asking why God was punishing them so much, with one big problem after another.

"Ah, that makes sense," said a blurry Richard, "we are heading in a wider curve, well within what we understand to be the boundary of the cloud."

After breakfast the scientists had continued their deliberations and having been able to plot their course with some accuracy, they sent the details back to Cambridge, who were able to link up with 'Comet' once more. Several hours later a reply came through on the radio confirming the data had been received and implemented.

"We know that," said Henry, "now all we have to do is work out what caused us to drift."

William interjected, "Has anyone noticed how bright Betelgeuse has become?"

"Yes," said Henry, "it's a fascinating sight. We will take a closer look at that once we solve our little question."

Geoff wandered off to an observation area to view the stars for a while; afterwards he did some more work on the TSO terminal.

"It's all very odd," muttered Richard, as they took a much needed break from their work. "There doesn't seem to be anything in the opposite direction to our new course that could have caused the change, no gravitational waves, no hidden planet. I don't really understand why the comets that were sitting to one side of us have all started to move sun wards."

"Could the push or whatever it is be coming from some distant source?" asked William.

"Unlikely," replied Henry, "we just aren't seeing a consistent cause point. If this was an insurance matter I'd say it was the hand of God, but damn it, we are scientists and need a real answer. It seems to be something that turns on only for a short time."

"I wonder if we could be looking at a pull rather than a push," said Richard. "Has anything happened to the sun that might cause this?"

"Not sure about that," said Henry, "it is as though we are feeling the effects of a galactic wind, similar to the solar wind, but stronger. Could it be coming from the black hole at the centre of our galaxy?"

"Too many possibilities," suggested William.

"Well," said Henry, "Cambridge has all the data we have been studying, and there are more brains there. Perhaps they can solve it."

As if on cue a laser message came in from Cambridge to ask that all sensors and telescopes be directed towards Betelgeuse. "We confirm the data provided has allowed us to lock onto your position and predicted course. Let's hope that doesn't change again because it's an absolute bugger to code it all in," said Cambridge.

It took over 8 hours to realign all the telescopes and sensors. Each one had its own control console. Geoff found out how to adjust the direction and focus of the sensors and helped with setting some up to the new orientation.

The newly collected data was run through a special mainframe process, with software traps in place to select key types of digital information. This was left running for a week with nothing significant having been isolated by the end of that time. This continued on for another 4 weeks without anything useful coming up. Cambridge had not requested any change so the focus point stayed as it was. Sometimes the traps were amended, however there was still no data to suggest that Betelgeuse could be the reason for comets shifting position. The term 'Galactic Wind' came into play more frequently and time was spent on proving its existence without a great deal of success or evidence. Yet another theory that was likely to find itself on the agenda of most astronomy classes in future.

Geoff found things to do even if it was only serving coffee or making a sandwich for them all, or just asking questions. Whenever talk came up about sending him home he would find something he had to fix on the TSO terminal. Mostly, Geoff was still in awe at being inside a huge rock, and the amazing things that were being done. He loved the stars most of all. He had gotten used to being inside another person's body, and was still admiring the fact that everything worked properly. He often reached for his hearing aid to turn it down when some noise got too high, and even now, was still surprised to find it not in his ear.

"Geoff," yelled Henry. Geoff took himself into the control room where the yell came from. "Not sure if you can help with this alert that has just come up on the mainframe. It is saying something about paths unavailable. Not sure what that means, although there is a message number and a string of error codes."

"Nasty," said Geoff, "I don't suppose you have a cable map?"

"Errrmmm no," mumbled Henry, not knowing a cable map from a telephone directory.

"That looks like either a port failure on the CPU or a storage device, or a cable problem." He went into the computer room and logged on to TSO to see if he could identify where the problem lay. Displaying the channels, he was able to spot the connection not working. It was one of the eight FICON connections between the CPU and the disk unit. Geoff made the channel offline which pleased Henry as the alerts stopped on his console.

"The fault," Geoff muttered to himself, "could be the port at either end or the cable itself." He took the easier option and went searching for the spare cables. A large box of used ones was all he could locate. He extracted the longest, which was shorter than the one he wanted to replace. It only just fitted, with the disk end needing a bit of a stretch to make it click onto the port in the disk unit. The channel was made online and it was a full 30 seconds before Henry's yell reached him to say that the alerts were coming again. The channel was made offline again.

"Henry," yelled Geoff, "I can't find any new FICON cables. Any idea where they might be?"

"William will come and help you," Henry yelled back.

Together they looked in all the storage areas, some of which Geoff hadn't previously been aware of, still not finding any new cables. "That's a bugger," said Geoff annoyed.

With William's help he edged the heavy disk unit rack a fraction closer to the CPU. It meant the replacement cable had a little slack in it, so might make a better connection. The alerts came up again as soon as Geoff attempted to online the channel.

"Drat," insisted Geoff, "that suggests a port problem. I wonder if I can reroute to another port on the disk unit. All depends if there is a port there physically, and it's been genned by a systems programmer, however that's way outside my comfort zone."

He entered a different command on the TSO terminal to look at all ports genned, and yes, there were three that showed as 'NOT CONNECTED'. He relocated the new cable at the disk unit into a spare port, made that channel online, and waited for Henry to yell. Silence.

Geoff checked the system log and no errors were showing. He was a bit rusty on the format of some commands. All the ones he could recall displayed the appropriate details, showing all disk channels working properly. He breathed a deep sigh and gave William the thumbs up. They were back in business with full throughput between disks and CPU.

"Geoff has done it again," William yelled to Henry.

At the end of the sixth week, after the direction of the sensors had been recalibrated, they got everything they were seeking. The sensors picked up the radioactive blast that clearly came from Betelgeuse, identifying within the blast huge quantities of metallic dust and particles.

Then there was something else that was verified by the telescopes. Their position had changed dramatically again. Comet 1017 Kientsch was moving towards the sun at a very fast pace, along with dozens of real comets. Again, almost immediately, they lost laser communications from Cambridge, and despite trying were unable to plot the slightly wobbly path they were heading in, so they had no other feedback on what had been observed from Earth, or what was happening there. Indeed, was the world even aware of the large number of comets being affected by whatever it was? A radio message eventually came through with much crackle, to the effect that Cambridge would prefer if they could keep 'Comet' from moving about too much, and could they send positional and directional data again?

"Why can't I get any accurate data anymore?" cried Julie. "All we get is distorted telescopic images and even the radio telescopes are failing to provide a totally clear picture. We know things are moving up from the Oort Cloud, though the details are too sketchy, and I still have those idiots upstairs on my case." Julie was not happy.

"Tell them we are under resourced and lack proper equipment," suggested Gary.

"That would not go down well," cried Julie, "they'd just want to know exactly how we are spending our time in minute detail. I've seen it before. It wouldn't be long before they brought in the time and motion people to kick us into working to a very specific set of criteria and trust me that can be painful."

ॐ ♈ ॐ   ॐ ♈ ॐ   ॐ ♈ ॐ

"It was fortunate," everyone agreed, "that the sun had not changed from orange to brown." It was no doubt helped by all the chanting, but now everyone was waiting hopefully for the orange to fade into a natural yellow to signal that some aspects of life could get back to normal, now that the flow of comets appeared to have stopped. They did finally get their wish as yellow streaks of sunshine started to warm the planet once again, but still, it was 3 months before temperatures returned to close to what they should have been. Now all they needed to worry about was that one last enormous comet, recently reported to be on a collision course with Earth. The world began to return to something like normality, the northern and southern icy sea lanes reverted to ordinary salty water, and people began to speculate on their future again.

The people who had banked all their money on living on a floating island, or similar, were most unhappy to hear that refunds were not available, even though building work had stopped on the huge arc ships. This forced a good number of people who had previously had a large bank account and several houses to consolidate what wealth they had left and to downsize their properties, while they looked at how they could recover their previous status. This was a bonus for many British people as a great many homes now came onto the market, pushing prices down, and allowing first time buyers to get a foot on the housing ladder.

Most government projects to create people shelters were mothballed, although some consideration subsequently went into working out how they could be utilised for some other purposes.

ॐ♈ॐ   ॐ♈ॐ   ॐ♈ॐ

The four of them were sat in the comm's room, talking about how Cambridge still couldn't get in contact with them when they heard a rather loud bang. William checked externally with the cameras to see if something had bumped into them. All he saw was blackness, not even one star, and the cameras seemed to be working properly. They all went out into the corridor, expecting to see a huge hole developing somewhere that would quickly suck out the atmosphere and end their days. Nothing, they saw nothing, however, they did feel a very smooth vibration. Now close by the airlock, it felt like something was on the other side, vibrating against 'Comet' or trying to come in. Without cameras to see, they could only speculate.

Geoff wondered, "Could it be the rocket down to take us all back home?"

"They would have told us," said Henry, "they would have found a way, besides it is a long trip and it's much too short a period since we were having problems with the laser comm for a ship to reach us. I'm suspecting a small comet is smashing against the hatch and has damaged the connections to the cameras."

They stood in front of the airlock waiting, totally unsure of what they could do. They just had to see what followed. Any moment the hatch could be ripped off with dire consequences for them. It seemed like they could all be sucked out into space with about 30 seconds of life left in them, yet nobody considered trying to get a spacesuit on.

For some reason the little window into the airlock was very dark. There seemed to be movement behind the thick glass, although it was hard to judge. They had no defence against whatever it might be out there, and the only hope they had was that the thing doing the damage would work itself loose and go somewhere else. The gentle vibration didn't stop at that point, it continued, suddenly rising in pitch for a brief moment after which it came to an abrupt end.

Geoff was thinking nice thoughts towards Thelma, when the inevitable happened and the force in the airlock finally pushed the inner hatch fully open, propelling them all back against the opposite wall. William was the first to spot what was happening and made a dive for the comm's room, to send off a message. It was vital that Cambridge knew how they had met their end.

The three other inhabitants of 'Comet' just stood there, not quite believing this was happening, as four black figures rushed into the corridor and pushed what looked like pistols into their faces. They stood there very still, expecting some violence to be used against them. If these were aliens, then they were humanoid in shape. They were totally in black, save for a red emblem on their backs that could have been a dragon or a dinosaur. With everything happening so fast, and the three fearing for their lives, they took little attention of detail. They just backed themselves up against the wall nervously, not knowing what to expect next.

They could hear that William had made it into the comm's room, telling Cambridge, "We have been boarded. Aliens ripped airlock op..."

That was all the time he had to say anything, for the alien that had followed him into the comm's room had shot him in the back at point blank range and he fell as a crumpled rag on to the floor.

Henry put up his arms to show surrender and that he wasn't armed. He hoped they were not all going to be killed in such a casual manner. Richard and Geoff followed his lead.

Pointing their guns at the three, the intruders indicated that they should go in the same direction as William, who had not moved since being shot. A gun was pointed at William, after that it was pointed towards the three of them, until they got the message that they were to carry out this unconscious man. When they picked up William, they were relieved to see no blood, and could feel his heart still beating.

The intruders gestured with their weapons for them to go through the hatch. The airlock had been severely damaged, ripped open in fact and was now totally useless. There was no lack of air though; they could still breathe as they were led across the edge of the broken hatch door into the bowels of what looked like another vessel, very much larger than their own.

They walked in almost pitch dark, the floor beneath their feet smooth yet firm to the feet, not slippery. The aliens moved them towards an arch that was well lit, where they got their first look at the inside of their abductors' ship.

The four men in black removed neither their head coverings nor anything else. They were as tall as them if a little slimmer, more agile, perhaps. Henry started to say something but one of the black clad intruders cut him short by raising his hand with the weapon in, as if saying that he would use it if they did not remain quiet. They were moved on up a wide corridor that gave no clue to their fate. It could have been a corridor from any place on Earth. There was nothing significant about it save that it was a mottled green in colour.

Looking back through to the blackness, the way they had come, Geoff noticed that 'Comet' was sitting inside a vast empty space, a huge internal hangar, still looking like the proverbial spiky potato, but now with a forlorn look to it. This alien ship had literally swallowed their rock as though it were a tiny pebble. Considering all of this, he wondered just how big this ship was, "double huge," he concluded to himself. The airlock door had been cut off at the wide hinges that normally held the door in place, and there was a deep gash on the other side, through the locking mechanism.

They were urged along until they came to a narrow crack in the wall that went from ceiling to floor. One of the black intruders touched a small device on the wall with three fingers and the crack opened up to allow them to enter into a small room.

Once inside William was put gently on the floor, with Henry checking to see how his breathing was. That seemed to be reasonably smooth as though he were just sleeping, which was a relief all round. There were no obvious signs of permanent damage to his body, so they straightened him out on the floor into a better position.

One of the black figures indicated some bunk beds on the side wall and put his gun hand up to his mouth to suggest they would not take any questions.

They all sat down together on the floor, next to William and looked at each other with dread in their eyes. "What in heaven's name just happened?" managed Henry.

Richard's voice was croaky and indistinct. "Kidnapped, hijacked, we've been taken prisoner by aliens, possibly pirates."

For once Geoff could think of nothing to say, and he wasn't the only one in shock. It had all been so rapid, and came as a great surprise, considering none of them had even thought aliens possible until a very short time ago. They looked around at the walls, at the entrance, and the beds set into the wall, for some image or something they could relate to that might give them a clue as to their future. On the main, longer, wall was symbol similar to that on the backs of the four aliens. It could be a big animal like a dragon or it might be a dinosaur, hard to tell, so that gave them no clue as to the reason why they were attacked.

"That was brave of William to get that message off to Cambridge," said Geoff, "at least, hopefully, they will know what became of us. It seems that even in our own backyard there is danger from others. I really had expected if we were ever to meet any aliens that they would be friendly, not like this!"

"Yes," agreed Henry, "but they haven't done us serious harm, yet. They could have killed us if they'd wanted to, so unless they are collecting old fogeys to sell off as slaves let's assume they are not totally evil."

William started to stir, rubbing his shoulder and looking around with misty eyes. "What the hell just happened?" he managed.

"We have been abducted by aliens," said Henry bluntly. "We are in an alien space ship, with 'Comet' sitting in a large hold of this ship, and we are prisoners to a race that doesn't seem to like questions."

"They haven't been introduced to Geoff yet," said Richard with warmth in his voice. They all smiled, and helped William stand up.

"That was a good move to send that message as you did," Henry told William, "a shame they shot you. You don't seem to have permanent damage from the outside, but how do you feel? Is it wearing off?"

"Thanks, yes," replied William, "it felt something like a taser, if not so sharp. Made my back and neck go numb, while the 'putting to sleep' part was almost instantaneous. I just hope Cambridge pick up the message and understand it, as it would be the only clue as to why we just suddenly disappeared."

"Indeed," said Henry. "We might as well use those bunk beds considering that we don't know what to expect or when we will get a chance to confront these aliens."

As they each sat on a different bunk and raised their feet from the floor the lights faded to almost nothing. They quickly put their feet back on the floor to see if that made the lights come back on again. "Hmm, impressive," said Henry, when the lights returned.

While the others rested, Geoff couldn't help himself. He was restless and started to explore all around the room, touching this area or that to see if any concealed doors or cupboards, or anything else, presented themselves. He ran his hands against some cracks, attacking it from either side before he spotted a tiny hole. He held his hand over this and a small shelf opened up. There was something like a faucet, at nose level, and below that a small drain. He put his nose closer and was rewarded with a jet of water into his left eye. He lifted his mouth level to be in line with the jet, and pushed his face in again. This time he received a deliciously cool liquid into his open mouth. The others had been watching and now came over to queue up behind him for this little treat.

"Nice find," said Henry, as it came to his turn, "see what else you can find."

"I'm looking for a door back to my own reality," said Geoff, "although a water fountain is a good start."

A few more pokes and prods later and Geoff had a larger cupboard open. Initially he was not sure what to make of the contents that appeared to be firm light coloured biscuits without any aroma. "Can we have a scientist over here to evaluate this new find, please," said Geoff smiling.

The other three men came over. They sniffed the biscuits, even broke a piece off to look at the inside which provided no further clue as to what it was made of. William took the challenge and popped a tiny piece into his mouth. "Hmm delicious," he said, chewing on a whole biscuit.

They each ate a biscuit and agreed with William. "Tasty," they all said, "as well as satisfying." They only needed one to perk them up a bit.

The three scientists followed Geoff's example, examining each crack or hole they could see, pushing or prodding here and there, but nobody produced any more finds, except for Geoff. He now had a short drawer open that contained some blank paper and what looked like short ballpoint pens. Additionally there were a couple of magazines and quite a few colour brochures. The script on the material was of course totally strange to them, looking like a cross between Arabic and Egyptian hieroglyphics. They each took a pile back to their bunk; unfortunately, they were unable to look at anything because it went dark as soon as they tried to lie down.

"Check if there are any controls in the bunks," suggested Henry. "There should be some overrides for the light going off, or at least a light above our heads."

William was poking at the surface just above his head and by sheer luck hit something like a small button. "And then there was light," he declared.

The others also found the switch for their bunk, and all were soon flipping through the brochures and magazines, trying to make sense of them. "They could be travel brochures," suggested Richard, "some of these images are quite fantastic, although if they have to kidnap innocent people to make them see these sights they can't be that good, or there will be some nasty catch."

"Agreed," said Henry. "There is a nice shot here of a beautiful blue and white sun with a small white dwarf in the background. Now who can guess where that might be?"

"Woof woof," smiled William, "that sounds like the Dog Star."

"Hang on though, that is about 8 light years away from Earth," said Richard. "If they are Dogs, we should wonder why they were in our domain, but also just how long we might be cooped up in here. Even at the speed of light, which is nigh on impossible, we will be quite old and worn out by the time we get anywhere, not that I am not nearly there already."

"Too many unknowns," said Henry, "let's wait and see what they want from us."

They browsed the coloured pamphlets to see if there were any more clues and shared anything of interest, and eventually they settled down, turned out their lights and slept a solid sleep. It wasn't as good, or as comfortable as they had recently been used to, observed Geoff, even so it was almost satisfactory, now that they were convicts.

~ CHAPTER 5 ~

~ CONVICTS ~

They were disturbed as the main lights gradually came on, waking them to a brand new day of captivity on an alien spaceship, with little hope that they would ever see Earth again, or even be able to communicate with their captors.

"I'm busting for a pee," mentioned Henry, "hope they realise that we need to relieve ourselves every so often."

Very quietly, a part of the wall opened up to allow several alien figures to enter in to the room, standing against the one blank wall, hands on hips, or guns, they looked directly at the four prisoners. Now the captives got their first proper look at what their captors, dressed in a close fitting black uniform, were like in the flesh. There was a slightly scaly look to the skin on the hands and face, although otherwise they could pass for humans.

Their fingers were slim and the nails came to a distinct rounded point, their eyes were wider, with the folds of skin at either edge stretching further into the sides of the face, and the iris colour for each alien was a variation between emerald and shamrock green. Ears were narrower, almost becoming pointed towards the top. There was no facial hair visible except on their heads and this was either pitch black or different shades of orange that could have been carrot or flame. From the small rise in the uniform tops, where breasts might be, the aliens were all assumed to be female, although there were other clues, in the fullness of the lips and the shape of the eyebrows.

"Good morning," said Henry hopefully, putting on his best welcoming smile.

This was not an acceptable approach it seemed, for the females all frowned at Henry, and put a hand across their mouths as if to say, "Shut up." One issued a string of sounds that sounded quite rude, abrupt even. Henry remained quiet.

One guard who looked to be the most senior, she was certainly the tallest, pointed at Henry, indicating that he should follow her. She approached a corner of the wall, waved a finger at a certain point and the whole area opened up to form a short passage into a larger room, that Henry could see held various devices inside, and suspected that this could be a bathroom, although he lacked any understanding of many of the pieces of apparatus in there.

She gabbled something in a stern voice, clearly comfortable at giving orders that couldn't be translated, pointing towards one wall where some devices were partitioned off. Henry guessed correctly that they were toilets, but how they functioned was a mystery for now, without a full scientific investigation. Walking up the line, taking a good look at each, he would shake his head, until he came to one that looked like a water closet with an odd shaped seat. He examined this more closely, finally nodding his head at the guard to imply this might work for him.

She came over to the chosen toilet, and demonstrated its use by almost sitting down on the seat, using her hand to indicate a flow from her rear end.

"OK," said Henry, "I get the idea, now will you leave, so that I can use it?"

She ignored his comments and directed his attention at some other units, one of which looked like a normal shower unit enclosed in glass. Henry touched it and nodded towards the guard again to say this one might be acceptable. She revealed the controls to him, demonstrated how some push buttons issued soap, one for washing the body, and one for the head which was clearly a shampoo, after that she indicated the controls for the shower itself, followed by one which Henry assumed was to dry you off, as it sent out a flow of nice warm air. She had done all of this without getting herself wet.

Unfortunate, thought Henry. He would have been interested to learn what she looked like without the uniform, purely from a scientific viewpoint he reminded himself.

He indicated again that he would like to use the WC, but she hadn't yet finished. There was a wide cupboard which she opened to reveal some bright orange one piece jump suits, and below that some bags, which she indicated were to be packed with the clothes he was wearing.

"Well, alright, I've got all that," he signalled. He pointed at his beard, only for the guard to look blank; it would seem there was no way for him to shave. By this time the pressure was building in his abdomen. He strongly indicated that he would use the WC and went over to it. She stood watching until he signalled that she should leave, waving his hands for her to move back to the other room. She finally did so with a tiny smile on her face. Although there was no toilet paper in sight, to use the WC was a great relief. It had some additional features he hadn't been expecting, flushing automatically as he sat there. After a while, just as he was about to stand up, he got hit by several jets of warm water that cleansed him thoroughly, followed by a blast of warm air to dry him. "Very nice," he said to nobody in particular.

He found the shower exhilarating, strong and hot, just the way he liked it. He dried himself under the warm air part of the shower cubicle, "All very nice, modern, and pleasant," he told himself. Walking about naked, he felt a little embarrassed, and concerned that he might get disturbed by the alien coming back. He quickly took some jumpsuits out of the cupboard, and found one to fit, then packed his clothes into a bag provided, looking around to see what kind of a mess he might have made. He realised he did smell better, and felt refreshed, although being unable to shave and having no comb to put his hair in some sort of order made him feel extremely scruffy, while the brightness of the suit he was wearing didn't help his mood one bit. He ran his hands through his hair, attempting to shape it into something like the style he normally wore, failing miserably, before going back to join the others. The guards had left by this time, so it fell to Henry to explain the procedures to use the bathroom, after which each captive in turn completed their ablutions.

They looked at each other in their bright orange attire and confessed to feeling like convicts, which the suits suggested that they were now. "At least we won't be forced to dig roads being on a spaceship," suggested Geoff.

"I'm sure they could find equally distasteful punishments to throw at us if they are of that mind," said Henry, scowling somewhat.

When William, being last to come out of the bathroom, was all done, the guards came back and they were marched out of the room, along the bright corridor a little way and into another room, which could have been a canteen, or a dining room, having a big wooden table with chairs in the centre, and a variety of what looked like food in different containers.

A white jug held something akin to milk, while another jug could have held orange juice. The tall woman guard indicated they should help themselves, so they started with the orange looking juice, pouring a little into a vessel similar to a cup without a handle. "Hmm nice," William told the others. They sampled the small pieces of food in the containers, some of which looked like fruit, others were like small biscuits.

Geoff took a mixture of items that almost looked like the muesli he enjoyed at home, drowning it with the white creamy liquid, as he normally did, from the white jug. He announced himself well satisfied with his concoction and seemed to be enjoying eating it, using a rather broad spoon to get the bowl contents into his waiting mouth, a little at a time.

After the cereals were eaten, they were shown pictures of what looked like cooked food and they each selected something that from the picture at least looked not too unappetizing. The hot foods seemed to vary between thick wafers, to very bloody steaks. Only Richard was a little disappointed with his choice, which he said was oozing blood and extremely spicy. They had been given implements that were a combined knife and fork, yet they mainly got by using their fingers. They were allowed to wash their dirty hands under a running tap, and were shown how to extract a wad of soap for the purpose. Finally they were presented with a hot drink, in another handle-less cup which had elements of tea and coffee in it; it proved to be wholesome and tasty.

They were allowed to relax for a short time and talk amongst themselves, speculating, but without any plan of action, wondering what was next on the agenda.

They had agreed amongst themselves that the symbol on the alien uniforms was a raptor or more precisely, for the scientists, a Velociraptor. Did this suggest they were fearless brutal hunters, or was it just a memory of the past, when they had been more vicious? Nobody at this point could answer such questions, and they wouldn't know much until they could at least start a dialogue. Their thoughts were interrupted when a senior officer came into the room. He was clearly of a high rank as the four females stood up very straight and put their arms smartly across their chests. He came over to the captives with a half-smile on his face, and jabbered away for a few sentences of something. After that he seemed to switch to a different language, just a few sentences. Getting no response he appeared to try another ten languages. That seemed to exhaust his repertoire and he was about to leave when Henry asked, "Do you speak English? Parlez-vous Français? Sprechen sie Deutsch?"

He clearly didn't speak any language that Henry knew, and frowned at these people who couldn't even understand the primary languages of this part of the small galaxial arm. He was no doubt wondering which planetary system they could possibly be from, as he left the room, after giving some instructions to the four alien guards.

The guards took the four men through another opening into a smaller room. There was a large display console that was showing lines of script. Each one was very different, and Henry assumed they were all asking the question, "Do you speak…" whatever the language was called. He was shown how to scroll up and down the list, and he totally got the idea that he should search for his own tongue. There were over 97,000 lines of text all asking the same question in a different language, Henry didn't know that at this time. He was just aware there were a very large number of them. They all stared at the screen as Henry moved down, one line at a time, and were at it for a very long time, hours in fact. They swapped over to take a turn scrolling down, and looking, but still nothing vaguely familiar to the European alphabetic script came up.

At one point the guards indicated they should stop looking, and they all went into another room, clearly one for study, with books in shelving along one wall, and posters on the other walls. It seems that someone had decided they would have to learn the ship's language if they couldn't find a common one.

The guards pointed at posters lining the walls, which had some scripts on, clearly in their local language, although none of the four convicts could do anything with that yet, it did show individual letters of their alphabet. So, they went around the room, looking at the images shown, writing down the new scripts on pads provided, in the best fashion they could, adding the English word below where the picture was clear. After that they were presented with the alphabet in full, which comprised 37 characters.

Once they had written down the alphabetic characters, and that was not easy due to the complex way they were constructed, there followed posters and pictures of different quantities of a variety of items, with characters that could only be numbers. Henry was itching to ask if they used a base of ten or whatever, for he was able to work out the digits for one to ten. He was keen to work out how he could ask about this. Pointing at the alien numbers, he indicated the ten, then with a question on his face tried to get the idea across of what came next. Finally he was duplicated and the digits representing eleven were written on a board, which was just the first digit shown twice. He had made progress, and it was comforting to know they did use ten as base.

Further progress was interrupted as they were taken back to the canteen for another meal. This time they were given no choice, instead, waiting on the side table was a dish for each to pick up. There were some grains in a little sauce, some berries, with something which was a little more solid, dark orange in colour that was probably the protein component of the meal. After getting another cup of the same beverage they had drunk earlier, and given some time to relax, they were taken back to the room, now known as the bunk room, where they retired for the day after spending a little time relating what they had learned to the booklets in the room, which was generally limited.

They now considered themselves orphans of space and would have to make the most of any opportunity that came along, just to survive. Being well fed and educated was one thing, although they were also missing some daily exercise. One day William asked one of the prettier guards who smiled at him frequently, by a combination of mime and words he had picked up, if there was somewhere they could exercise. There was, and it turned out to be a proper gym, advanced alien style, yet nothing like an Earth one. Even Henry was unable to describe what the apparatus were or how they worked on the body, they just did in an invigorating manner. Even Geoff liked them. "Hey, this beats a rowing machine for a great workout; it actually seems to help you along. You might tell them Henry that we will take a few of these exercise machines in exchange for them smashing up 'Comet'," puffed Geoff.

So it was that another activity was added to their regular routine, although they did start to make real progress with the language, things were due to change again, soon. By this time Henry had reached the level of a three year old in being able to form simple sentences, while the others were still having general difficulties with the alphabet.

The routine went on in the same fashion each day, them constantly seeking their mother tongue on the big screen, with nothing coming close, followed by food, and, or, some basic language lessons, and, or, exercise. This went on for about a week.

Henry had made good progress, having acquired a small vocabulary, including: me, I, you, door, floor, hello, dragon and so on, which he constantly tried to build into sentences. He had always enjoyed learning languages, and wanted to be able to communicate with anybody that he met, even aliens that had abducted him. He was feeling pleased with himself when he could impress the guards with his first real sentence, even if the grammar was far from correct.

"Hello, I am Henry. What is your name?" He practised this over and over and did finally get to find out the names of the guards and a few others.

By now they could have travelled anywhere. For sure, 'Comet', if it could ever be made safe and space worthy would never be the same again, and it wasn't likely that they could ever communicate with their base again. If they ever got back inside 'Comet', given the great distance they were from Earth, it was doubtful that the laser link would still connect.

At no point had they felt any movement of the ship, and certainly no motion, the ride had been extremely smooth, but as they were eating breakfast one day, they had trouble keeping the food down. The smiley guard tried to explain that the ship was slowing down rapidly and they would land soon. Henry tried to ask, "Is it always hard to eat at such times?" The question clearly didn't come out correctly, for the blank expressions of the guards demonstrated they hadn't understood, meaning that Henry still had a very long way to go with his pronunciation.

In any case, their normal routine was continued until a senior officer came in to tell them to go with him. By now they knew enough words of Sirisian, as the language was called, to understand the gist of what was said to them, as long as it was kept simple. William smiled at the friendly guard on the way out and was rewarded with a brilliant smile, one he decided he would hang on to for now, and give back to her at the first opportunity he had.

They went through the hangar with 'Comet' sitting there looking uncared for, and pitiful, in its damaged state, wondering if they would ever see it again. Going through a set of double doors, they were quickly outside in fresh air, with the sky a woolly kind of white, although there was no sign of any sun. The complete lack of any blue in the sky was somehow depressing, and they sensed that this was an artificial environment. "After all this time inside, and not any blue sky in sight," said Geoff, voicing what the others were thinking. "What kind of a place is this?" Nobody had an answer.

After being caged up for so long, it came as a shock to realise they were out in the open. They found the gravity easy to live with, while a refreshing breeze was blowing that carried the smell of something like lavender, which had the effect of getting them all to breathe heavily.

Geoff had turned around to look at the ship, and he had to admit it was a beautiful sight. "It's nothing like the *Star Trek* ships from that well known TV program, still being repeated all round the world," he said, "it has a lot more grace, though."

The ship itself reached upwards from its base in a rounded, almost symmetrical way, with a doughnut shape sitting on the top of that, that Geoff imagined was the bridge.

They were encouraged to walk on by the guards; even so, they couldn't help noticing things, mainly similarities to back home. The ground beneath their naked feet was quite smooth, a little like tarmac without the small stones. The warm sensation on the souls of feet gave them a quick reminder, that they hadn't had any shoes provided, but were well used to walking around without them now, as well as being unshaven, not to mention uncombed. "We really must look like a strange scruffy bunch of criminals," mumbled Geoff.

They were moving now to what looked like a conventional door, with a handle to pull it open, and a glass panel to see if anyone was coming through from the other side. "How quaint," Geoff smiled to himself. They passed other aliens walking across the big yard, who generally ignored the four prisoners. Geoff suspected they were maintenance men, each with their little black box of supersonic screwdrivers, ready to repair a broken hinge, invisible door, or something of that sort. It was still about twenty paces to get to the door, and Geoff thought that while the ship had been big they could probably park half a dozen of them on this huge yard.

Now they were going inside, up some very normal looking stairs to the left, up to the first floor. *What*, thought Geoff, *not even electrically motivated to move you up or down with less physical effort, how disappointing?"*

The officer looked round to make sure he still had his four detainees, then dismissed the guard and stepped very smartly into an office that could only be that of a very senior official or officer. They passed a woman, sat at an imposing desk, that was clearly a secretary or personal assistant to this important man, and she just waved the party on. They were expected. Another few steps further on was an open door that led into a rather plush large office. A man sat at a desk with a screen in front of him, with some things that could easily pass for a telephone and a small keypad. Behind him was the most beautiful three dimensional map of what Henry guessed was the local star group.

"Jabber jabber," went the man who had brought them here, totally unintelligible to the four from Earth. The seated man replied, clearly asking some questions. Geoff whispered to Henry, "What did they say?"

"Didn't catch a word of it," admitted Henry, but the man behind the desk had caught their quiet conversation and he dismissed the officer at that point, waiting for him to close the door before speaking directly to the men that were stood around his desk. Henry expected more jabber and strained himself ready to pick out any words that he knew.

The officer came from behind his desk standing directly in front of Henry, looking him over, evaluating him. Henry decided to open the conversation, "Hello," he said in Sirisian, "my name is Henry. What is your name?"

The man smiled broadly and said something Henry didn't get. Much more slowly, he repeated the words in Sirisian, "Hello, Henry, my name is Kirk."

Instinctively Henry warmed to this friendly man and wanted to make physical contact with him. Holding out his right hand, and smiling broadly, he took Kirk's hand and shook it warmly. The alien returned the shake in an appropriate manner, with a big smile.

They smiled at each other as though they were friends already. Kirk approached the other three, asking each in Sirisian for their names, after which they also shook hands with someone who was clearly weighing them up.

Kirk wondered how long he could spin this all out, without letting on that he was very familiar with their English language. He decided to be abrupt about it. "Well, gentlemen," he said in Oxford English, "nice to meet you. Welcome to Sirzero, the primary moon in our system which we call Sirisia."

Four mouths fell open. "You speak perfect English," said Geoff. "On the ship nobody could understand us."

"Yes," said Kirk, "I am one of only twelve officers that have been permitted to learn the tongues of Earth. On the ship they have translators for many languages from this sector of the galaxy, only the popular ones though. Until now, we have never had visitors from your solar system!

Still in confusion, Henry responded with a blank look, finally managing, "Well that is interesting. You must tell us how you came to be so fluent."

"Indeed I will," said Kirk, "I have a lot to tell you, but first we really must do something about the clothes they gave you to wear. You look like damned convicts. To be honest, I didn't know you were from Earth until I heard you speak. I just knew you hadn't been matched to any known language. The study of alien speech is one of my specialities, as I deal with aliens from far and wide, so I need to be conversant with many languages."

"How many languages do you speak?" asked Geoff.

" Ninety-three almost fluently, if you count Sirisian."

"Amazing," said Geoff, "you don't have a robot brain by any chance do you?"

"No," said Kirk laughing, "I learned these over a long period, I must admit though, the first ten were the hardest. English came easily to me I'm glad to say. Now please follow me," he added, as he led the way out of the office.

Kirk gave some instructions to the secretary. After that he took the four ex-convicts downstairs and exited the building by different doors to the ones used previously, into a small green attractive park, with grass, flower beds and some ornaments. "Very English, don't you think?" asked Kirk. They all agreed and followed him into another building, down stairs to the basement level. "Now we will get you something more appropriate to wear." He spoke to the man behind a little counter and indicated the four, and the man went away. "I told him to find you something nice and casual to wear. You can change behind that screen. That will do for now and later you can go shopping for a complete wardrobe."

"Thanks," said Henry, "it will be good to wear something that doesn't make us feel like prisoners."

"Never prisoners," said Kirk, "guests without the ability to leave, maybe, friends also."

They liked the sound of that and all smiled back at Kirk. Things were looking up, somewhat, although how their lives would work out from here was still a worry as they certainly had no ability to leave, nor even make decisions for themselves.

The counter man came back with something for everyone. A pair of briefs, t-shirts, jogging trousers, and a zip top. While they changed the man went in search of some footwear having taken a measure of each pair of feet. He came back with something that was a cross between sandals and trainers, in a comfortable dark blue; they fitted very nicely. Instead of bright orange they now wore dark blue trousers with a black top and a white t-shirt with a dragon on the back. They certainly resembled the natives of Sirisia now.

More stairs, up to the second level this time, and onto a narrow walkway. Kirk pressed a button and very shortly a train carriage arrived. They went inside and it moved off. It could be described as something akin to a London underground train except that it balanced on a single rail well above the ground, yet that would make it a lot less than it actually was, for it was clean, fast, smooth, and best of all had a nice smell to it. In the space where mind numbing adverts were placed on London underground trains, there was a continuous moving image of the moon. As they moved along it seemed to be showing the area, at some distance, that they were approaching.

It took mere minutes to arrive at the next station, which resembled the previous one, almost exactly. They followed Kirk once more, down some stairs through several buildings into a park like courtyard. The smart sculpted building surrounding the courtyard would not have been out of place in a plush area of Kensington, being most pleasing to the eye.

They went to the top level of this building, using several flights of stairs.

Kirk approached an entrance with the sign of a dragon sitting on something white, with some characters underneath, and he pushed a bell. A young woman came out and greeted them before getting into conversation with Kirk. "Remember this door," he said to his four new friends, "Manya will be your contact here. She knows a few words of English so she will help you with learning our language and anything else you need." Manya led them down an elegant corridor to some impressive heavy dark doors.

"This is where you will be staying," said Kirk, "these are the VIP rooms we reserve for important visiting officials, so I hope you will be comfortable."

After looking inside the first plush one, with its deep pile carpets, large round bed and a bathroom that had more contrivances than they could imagine, the four agreed that the suites would probably be adequate for now. Smiles all round. There was a keypad beside the door, and Manya showed them each the key sequence they needed to use to open the doors.

Kirk was keen to move them on, so they didn't get a chance to explore their new apartments, he told them to find Manya when they got back and she would do the full tour.

Instead, they went back out of the building, towards something that looked like a driveway, with Geoff noticing how Kirk communicated remotely with others. He touched a spot close to what would be an ear bone in humans, and started talking. He touched the same spot again when he'd finished. *Interesting*, thought Geoff, *I wonder how much one of those costs?*

Outside on a patch of tarmac a car was waiting for them, although as they piled inside Geoff noticed there were no tyres or wheels even. He was just about to mention this when the car moved forward, and suddenly upwards, going over the buildings they had passed through. "Anti-gravity car?" asked Henry.

"Almost," answered Kirk, "it uses a form of energy from black hole technology that creates a kind of reverse thrust, but if you were silly enough to be under a car as it was moving you would certainly feel the energy, strong enough to cut a man in two."

"Oh," said Henry rather surprised, "I sure would like to learn more about that."

"That can be arranged," said Kirk.

Looking out, they could see that they were passing over a landscape that didn't change greatly. It seemed to be a repetition of clusters of buildings of different shapes and sizes, sometimes linked by a railway, yet always there was what looked like roads, even if apparently not in use. *There will be a reason for that design*, thought Geoff, locking that question away for future use behind at least half a million more important ones.

They landed at what looked like a festive area. The buildings were brightly coloured and had big signs outside. "This is the commercial area where goods are obtained and hungers satisfied," said Kirk, indicating their destination was a small building to their right that had a yellow and purple sign, whose wording at this distance seemed indistinct from other signs. It took a couple of minutes to reach what they had all worked out was a fancy restaurant.

"I've brought you here," said Kirk, "because they do a big variety of food, besides which I missed breakfast today, and I'm starving." William said he wasn't that hungry although he still managed to enjoy and wolf down a delicious meal of something he wasn't sure he could describe. Before that, they talked, during and after the meal they talked, and they all learned a lot.

Henry started, "While we really appreciate this great hospitality after being illegally boarded and taken prisoners, you need to tell us what was happening and why."

"OK," agreed Kirk, "that was the main purpose of this meal, apart from filling our stomachs."

"Good," said Geoff, "and it's nice to know that food wise we are compatible."

"Oh yes," said Kirk, "we are closely related in many ways. So, why were you boarded? We were actually looking out for Earth. That is one of the things we do as our combined history goes back a very, very, long way. One way we help is to stop your resources being plundered by pirates and thieves from other systems. When we find one in your system we put them in the hold of our big ship, confiscate their plunder and send them back home with their tails between their legs."

"We were neither plundering nor doing anything bad, why pick on us?" asked Henry.

"Yes," said Kirk, "you were a strange one, and at first the captain didn't know what to do about you. While we were aware of some artificial satellites coming out that far from your planet, we might have expected a ship, but never a carved out lump of rock. It looked as though your intent was to remain invisible, and that suggested espionage, so the captain had to act."

"It was all purely scientific investigation concerning what was possible," William interjected.

"That I do not doubt, now," said Kirk, "I trust you can see our logic?"

"I can," agreed Henry, "although, if you are our friends how come you haven't announced yourselves. As you perhaps know, the consensus on Earth is that space aliens do not exist."

"Along with fairies, and God, until proven otherwise. Yes, I was aware of that level of thinking," said Kirk. "We are not there to nurture you, for we have pledged not to influence you, too heavily, in the way you go forward politically. As harmful as some elements can be on your planet, we are not allowed to interfere. Even so, we can and do protect your space against intruders, invaders and purple Rhino."

They looked blankly at him over the last part of his sentence. "Can you elaborate on those last three please," requested Henry.

Kirk started to explain, "Intruders. There are always small traders or conmen, sorry con-aliens, who want to move in and take over what is yours. We police them and escort them far away. Invaders, yes there have been two attempts to my knowledge of large forces attempting to steal your planet and your gold, both within the last 800 years. We stopped them."

"Fantastic," said Geoff, "I'd love to study some of your history on this, but purple Rhino?"

"It's our pet name for a group of nutty scientists that developed some crazy ideology on keeping the body alive indefinitely, yet being alive and being able to function are incompatible with the purple Rhino's methodology. They like to sell their potions to anyone silly enough to trust them. They approach a planet as a superior race, without giving any secrets away, live off the hospitality of the target planet for a few years while setting up deals to sell their evil potions. When they finally leave, much richer, the population of the planet is often in a state of mental decay. They are really bad news."

"OK," said Richard, "let's get back to the main part of this. You are stopping the scum of the universe from harming and infiltrating our system although morally you are unable to intervene meaningfully, politically, in our affairs or in the way we advance as a race?"

"That's about it in a nutshell," agreed Kirk.

"Fair enough, already," said Geoff. "However, if your ships spend so much time in our domain why don't the crew learn our languages?"

"Good question," said Kirk, "the main answer is that most of the Earth languages have been around in their present form for less than 2,000 years of your time. It's not worth our while trying to keep up with the prominent languages until they have stabilised and you are not so divided socially. You are not the first developing civilisation from Earth that has ventured into space. The last one thought they had conquered all cultural ills, and still managed to blow themselves up along with one pretty planet."

Four jaws became slack and for a moment nobody could say anything.

"Oh my God," managed Richard. "You mean the asteroid belt between Mars and Jupiter? So that's how it came into existence, I take it?"

"Yes. Bit of a shock that last revelation, I take it," said Kirk. "Stand by for another one. One hundred and twelve million years ago, Earth had an empire that included ninety-six star systems. The planet was united and it had the most beautiful crystal buildings. It ruled well, and gently. Ninety million years ago, Earth was part of an empire that stretched almost the length of this small galactic arm."

"It sounds like Earth has an amazing past. I could not begin to imagine all of that, and how dramatic it must have been," said Geoff.

"We were always close allies to Earth," persisted Kirk. "They, you, helped us many times, saved our bacon countless times. We look a little different due to the influence of our suns, although our physiology is similar, as are our peaceful intentions, fundamentally, as neighbours we look after each other as best we can."

"Totally incredible," muttered Richard, "who would have suspected that when everyone on Earth imagines that mankind is somehow unique."

"Far from unique," suggested Kirk, "wherever you travel in this, or any other galaxy, no matter what type of star, you will find sentient life, mainly humanoid. One thing we are good at is persisting and spreading our seed."

Several minutes passed in silence as this news was digested and long held racial concepts were blown away. At that point the waitress, no different from the waitress one might find in any decent London restaurant, came over to take the used dinnerware away and offered a nice big smile to the now sullen four who had a lot to think about.

"Let's get out of here now," suggested Kirk, "I will be at your disposal each day for a midday meal, and we can continue these chats. I'm sure there are lots more questions, eh Geoff?"

"You bet," smiled Geoff.

~ CHAPTER 6 ~

~ NOT SO NASTY ~

After lunch that day Kirk took a little detour before taking them back to their assigned living quarters. "There is something I will show you, just to dampen the idea that we are a pushover or soft as a race," said Kirk, "we can be quite nasty when necessary."

"I think we have already seen your tough and nasty side when they shot poor William and herded us into your ship," said Henry.

"That was pretty mild actually," said Kirk, "what you might call the standard procedure with those not fighting back; however, we do use force, readily, to protect ourselves."

"Hmm, OK," said Richard, "I'm glad we are friends, by the way."

They stopped outside a large grey building that had tiny windows and metal bars lining the walls, going from below the surface to the roof. There was static electricity on the metal bars suggesting that they might have a heavy voltage going through them.

"This is our secure holding prison for unwanted aliens that have caused us trouble. Trust me, most of them are not a friendly crowd," claimed Kirk.

Going through the big double doors reinforced with a thick light blue alloy, they found a high wooden desk blocking access, and three mean looking guards who greeted Kirk by name. A brief conversation followed, after which one guard made a wide panel draw open, permitting them all to go inside, one at a time. Henry noticed various pieces of equipment that were measuring and recording details of their physical build and face contours, and probably other security options as well.

Walking down a long corridor escorted by a guard, Kirk said, "They asked me if you were the latest alien prisoners, and what level of discomfort should be applied."

"Oh no," said Geoff, a little concerned. "I hope you told them we were non-violent and friendly, as well as now being VIP guests?"

Kirk smiled back, leaving them in a little mystery as to what he had told the guards.

They went down some stairs and the surroundings got gloomier. Towards one side of the wall was a glass front and movement was seen within. Next to the glass was a set of metal doors that allowed observation of another part of the enclosure, with straw and other material littering the floor.

They all stopped to look in at this point, and Geoff, for one, wasn't sure what he should expect to see, a humanoid type, or some angry frustrated alien creature that was more than a little wild from being held in captivity. He didn't have a long wait to find out, for a figure had been watching them, and just as William and Geoff put their noses close to the door a figure leaped towards them snarling and spitting. It was about as tall as they were albeit very slim and it had a dark streak of hair running down its unclothed back.

"These," said Kirk, "are some of our more unwelcome intruders. They broke in to a hospital on the planet below and attempted to steal a vast quantity of something we call a regenerator. It helps to grow fresh skin over wounds, though these little scoundrels wanted it for a very different purpose. They were intending to use it on themselves, and a lot more of their fellows, to fool us into thinking they were Sirisian, with the intention of storming an outpost and holding it to ransom."

"Bad boys," said Geoff, "good that you have them locked up securely."

"Yes, they will stay locked up until the Shamack confederacy pays us a nice ransom," said Kirk. "Don't get too close as their spit can be venomous, and they are like wild monkeys when they get angry."

"Humanoid, if not quite human," suggested Henry with a half-smile on his lips. "I guess these are more like the aliens we expected to find out here far away from our world."

"Trust me," said Kirk, "they get a whole lot more strangely alien than this little monster, however, I won't scare you off too much, for there are some amazingly beautiful and peaceful alien humanoids out there as well. We just happen to live too close to Shamack for our own good, and they are like jackals, having no qualms about stealing anything, or even picking bones clean like vultures."

"I think we get the picture now," said Henry, and we do appreciate you keeping us safe from these little nasties. When we as a species do finally get out here, we are going to need a roadmap of the different civilisations around. I don't imagine I can get something like that from the console in my suite, can I?"

"Take a look under local system species," suggested Kirk.

After that little visit they went back up the stairs to the top level. "Now these fellows are much less bother, they got caught in a restricted area, although it was a case of high jinks rather than anything malicious against us. I will be taking these boys home in a few days' time, to hand over to their government, who have promised to slap their wrists."

This time the guard opened the door, and they all went into a fairly cosy looking cell with several bunk beds, and a number of humanoids inside a very clean environment.

Kirk greeted the very alien group. Explaining to the others, "They are called Toothies, and are different from other species in that their skin is almost see-through, apart from that they could almost pass for a human."

"An anaemic one," suggested Geoff, looking at their pale features.

"That effect," suggested Kirk, "is likely due to a time before their second star became a white dwarf. It used to be a very large white, almost blue sun, which means they would have been treated to specific rays from two giant white suns. Just as our Sirisian sun has affected our skin, so the people from their system have had their bodies seriously modified by the suns they lived under."

"Anyway," he continued, "I said they would be going home shortly, and what you saw with those raised lips, was two things. One, it was an attempt at a little smile, and two, it also meant a grateful acknowledgement. If you wave and stand on your left legs as we go out, to say goodbye, they should all do the same." They did as requested, raising the right foot a little off the ground and waving with the right hand. Kirk smiled as the Toothies copied them.

"Now come on, Kirk," said Henry, "that cannot just be a simple case of saying goodbye. I have a nasty suspicion, as I'm beginning to detect your deep down sense of humour is quite wicked, that you told them to copy us when you had us do that gesture."

Kirk laughed hard, feeling found out, but denied it anyway, "As if I would pull such tricks on you all."

"If you hadn't recognized our language, I guess that is where we would have ended up?" butted in Geoff, looking unhappily at what was almost an attractive building on the outside, yet not so nice inside.

"Yes, most likely," agreed Kirk. "You would certainly have gotten to know the guards very well that run this prison. First we would have done more work to find out where you came from, after that you'd have been interrogated, and trust me, that is not a pleasant experience."

Geoff groaned at the thought, asking, "What if you still couldn't find out which planet we came from? What if we only spoke Turkish or some other Earth language that you, nor anybody in your planetary system, knew?"

"You really would have been in trouble at that point," said Kirk. "You'd have been placed in the middle levels of our little jail and encouraged to learn Sirisian. Every so often we would have come to talk with you to see if you could tell us anything to identify yourselves, otherwise you'd have stayed there till you died."

"I don't like the sound of any of that," said Geoff, "thank goodness for your Oxford education."

"Amen," said Richard.

"For the time being," continued Kirk, "while we are deciding what to do with you, we will provide comfortable lodgings and food. Let us know if you are in need of something."

"You could always take us home to Earth in one of your big ships," suggested Geoff.

"That's not an option," said Kirk firmly, unwilling at this point to elaborate.

They looked at each other, now feeling glum, which Kirk noticed. "That doesn't mean we are going to keep you here indefinitely or that you will never see your home planet again, but we have to consider all angles and all options, and to be honest, it is not my decision. You actually have presented us with a unique challenge, so please be patient."

They found their way back to their apartments. Kirk had an appointment so he told the four that they were free to roam. What he didn't say was that they would be watched wherever they went. Before he left them, a short walk from the VIP apartments, Kirk gave them each a plastic card with some writing and other detail on. If they were lost or had any problems they just had to show the card and someone would get in touch with Kirk. Additionally, if they needed something, they could use the card to purchase it.

They went inside to look for Manya who was only too keen to learn a little more English and show them around their suites. She did a very good job and they soon knew how to use everything, even the console which was linked into a system wide web in a similar fashion to the one back home.

While they'd been on 'Comet' there had been one thing they hadn't been able to control properly, which was their grooming. Each of them had at least shoulder length hair, and their appearance was that of tramps rather than scientists, given that it was also uncombed, if reasonably clean. Looking at himself in a mirror, Henry asked Manya, "Can we do something about my hair? It looks so horrible."

"Horrible?" queried Manya.

"Yes, horrible," said Henry, "not tidy, a mess, not nice, not combed, very horrible."

"Ah yes," agreed Manya, lifting some of Henry's hair and snipping it with her fingers. She spoke into her personal ear phone, then said, "Just a moment, we will fix it better."

A knock at the door was answered by Manya, who let in a young woman of similar age and appearance to Manya, however she was carrying a bag full of cutting tools and a red cloth with a hole in the middle.

Henry was instructed to sit down, and the cloth was placed over his head, while Manya asked him how he wanted it. Henry quickly discarded the automatic response that came to mind, and simply said, "Like Kirk."

A few more words from Manya, and the woman got to work. Very soon she was done, and Manya went to find Richard, who also got the same treatment, followed by William and Geoff. They were supplied with combs and wet shavers, so they all took themselves back to their rooms for a hot shower, a great shave, and then they were more than ready to face the world again. "I feel like a new man," exclaimed Henry, and they all thanked Manya.

Geoff had his opening question ready for Manya. "You speak some English, did you learn from other visitors coming here?" To this she screwed up her face and Geoff repeated it slowly annunciating each syllable.

"Oh no," she said, "I learn with my brother Kirk, he practices at me when he has new language. You are first with English here."

"I don't know about any of you," said Henry, "but I don't enjoy wearing the same clothes constantly as well as in bed. Now that we are less scruffy, I think we should go shopping and get a proper wardrobe, as it looks like we will not be leaving here very soon."

"Good thinking," agreed Richard. "Manya, where can we go to get some nice clothes, so that we do not always wear the same things?"

She took them to her personal console and pulled up a map showing different buildings which she printed and gave to Henry. "This is a good store here, but they won't know what you want. Perhaps I should come with you?" She pulled up some pictures of people wearing different styles of clothing, leaving the four of them confused.

"Manya," said Henry, slowly, "we would need some clothes that are not horrible, not too formal, but not scruffy."

"Scruffy?" queried Manya, shaking her head.

"He means clothes that are not too casual, not too bright, or too young for us," translated Richard.

"Ah, OK, I think I know what you mean now," said Manya, "nearly smart, not too very smart."

"I think you understand," said Henry. "Will you come with us and help us?"

"Of course," agreed Manya.

Manya led the way out of the building, with Geoff noticing how she touched the bone above the left ear before talking quietly. He didn't have the courage to ask who she was talking to.

"Well it doesn't look like we need overcoats or any special gear to stay here," said Henry, "so several tops and trousers, and so on, in different colours should do the trick."

An anti-gravity car was waiting to take them shopping.

"This is exciting," laughed Geoff, "I've never been out shopping on an alien world before." They all laughed with him.

The store they came to, some 20 minutes ride away, had a rather small glass window front displaying what looked like a very formal dress suit. Inside the store was massive, with lots of changing rooms, and many rows of garments. Manya explained to an assistant what was required, and he went away to get a selection of suitable clothing. There were no major surprises. One outfit which looked like a casual suit, in dark blue that had a soft almost velvety touch to it, was liked by Henry and Geoff. Other possibilities included some tops with muted colours and dark grey trousers. They each selected four combination outfits that suited their tastes and tried them on to get the correct sizes, after getting a sign from Manya that they were suitable. The assistant brought out underwear, socks and shoes in different styles. All told they were in the store for about 4 hours, and finally just when Geoff's patience was at an end, the assistant brought out some pyjamas, which pleased Henry at least.

More than a dozen large bags were loaded into the car and they headed back to their accommodation zone. "I'm starving after all of that," said Geoff, "any chance of a snack anywhere?"

"A snake?" questioned Manya.

"No," said Henry, "Geoff was saying he is hungry, and can we get something small to eat?"

"Ah, you want a take it away food," stated Manya.

"That will do nicely," said Geoff.

Manya spoke to the driver and they stopped at a small building displaying a round green and purple sign. The food available was similar to hamburgers or pizzas, with one variety merging both into one meal. "Let me use my card for this, for the experience," said Geoff, as Henry was about to pay. "You used yours to buy all the clothes."

"OK," said Henry.

After enjoying that take it away meal, they were deposited back at the large attractive residential building and they retired to their own rooms to settle in, put their clothes away, and try out their consoles as well as the gorgeous beds. One thing bugging Geoff was that he had no concept of time here. If there was a clock in the rooms he hadn't spotted it. He liked to know how long he could sleep. He considered time a vital element of making any plan, even if it was just for breakfast. Finally he settled himself in the soft comforting bed and dropped off. He awoke some time later unable to discern how early it might be, not knowing if he should try to sleep some more, or not. Looking out of the window didn't help at all; the sky always seemed to have that same bright white cloudless look. He got dressed and went to see if anyone was about. Finding everything quiet, he tried the door for Manya who was very sleepy eyed when she opened up.

"Sorry if I woke you, Manya, I have a problem with the time. I have no way to tell when morning has arrived. Are there any time pieces?" He repeated that twice more until she perceived what he was asking.

She allowed him in to her bedroom, which was so feminine and smelled so good that Geoff was a little taken aback at the attractiveness of it. He felt he could very easily fall in love with someone in that room, especially with Manya; however, he controlled his thoughts and concentrated on what she was showing him. It was something he must have missed when she was explaining how everything worked. A tiny square button on a side cabinet by her bed, when pressed, illuminated some numbers. Just a single set, with no colon or anything to separate hours or minutes. He was none the wiser even though he was able to translate the numbers as '423'.

"Here," she said, "we measure time in single units. One unit is equal to a child counting up to one hundred. Our day goes up to 3499 units, and breakfast is at 1160. I will let you work out the rest for yourself," and showed Geoff the door.

He got into bed and displayed his time piece, now he could relax. He estimated lunch at about 1950 and dinner sometime after 2800 that is if they ate in similar time periods to Europeans. He still didn't know how their 3499 unit day related to Earth's 24 hour clock, although he'd made a good start in understanding local time.

Henry had awoken about the same time as Geoff, but his concern was in relation to where they were physically in the galaxy. The journey here had been less than 2 weeks he estimated, maybe one, and travelling at 186,000 miles per second, the speed of light, which was impossible according to Einstein's theories, that would take them only a little way towards Alpha Centauri. His mind was perplexed with the idea that they might have travelled much faster than light or used some type of worm hole. He would certainly have plenty to ask Kirk about at their next lunch.

When morning came, Manya escorted the four to breakfast in a military style canteen. She didn't have enough English to explain what all the dishes were, even so, they each found something to enjoy and sustain them.

The scientists were keen to see a local star map to work out for themselves where they were. After eating they all went into Henry's room and Manya showed them all how to bring up a map and move it around.

"Are these actual star colours?" asked Richard.

"No," said Manya, "if you want real colours and approximate sizes we need to go into this other map." She showed them.

Sol was easy to spot as a bright small yellow dot towards one corner of the screen; it had several red dots around it indicating small red stars. Right in the centre of the screen was a large blue white star. "Dog Star," muttered William.

"Agreed," said Henry. "What I want to know is how did we get here so fast? It's over 8 light years away from Earth."

"A good question for Kirk," said Richard.

They were able to zoom in on the centre star, to see the accompanying white dwarf. Further in, they found the primary moon that they were told they were on. A little more zoom and they spotted three other satellites of the large green and blue planet now in the background. Exploring around they found another three planets, each with its own atmosphere, prompting a question from Richard, "Are all of these planets being lived on?"

"Oh yes," said Manya, "and all the moons as well, nine in total."

Lots of what appeared to be statistics appeared at the bottom of the screen, and Henry wanted to know how it could all be printed out. Manya showed them how to get a print, after which they went to the end of the corridor where a printer had faithfully copied out all the required detail.

"Fantastic," said Henry, "now that will keep me busy all morning attempting to translate it all." Richard said he would lend a hand.

Geoff and William were keen to explore a little and got Manya to print a map of the local area, showing the walkways and the main buildings. On top of that she was asked to write the names in English over the words printed. She did this for those that she knew, some she couldn't translate. "You are here, and that is the name of the building. I would say to you that you go through this park, after, take the road towards the commercial area. That way you can't get too much lost."

"Don't bet on that," said Geoff, "I can get lost just going to the front door." Manya didn't get any of that even though she smiled politely.

They both, Geoff and William, felt excited to be outside, alone, on an alien world, exploring. Most things they saw didn't seem all that strange. The windows and building designs all looked recognizable, if very specifically sculpted, and the grass, well that was just grass, very green and totally free of weeds, though it was still grass, as they knew it. The signs were totally alien, not just in the script, their shapes and colours seemed to be at odds with those on Earth as well. They did a lot of walking, looking and surveying, finally ending up near the restaurant area that they had been at yesterday. Suddenly a happy face caught the eye of William. The female from the ship that had done a fair amount of exchanging smiles with William came over to greet them. The clothes she wore were such a contrast to the black uniform they had seen her in before. Now with tight dark purple slacks and a colourful white, yellow, and red woolly top, she looked amazing. Geoff gave a brief wolf whistle, while William was looking her up and down in total approval, saying, "I think I'm in love."

Not knowing what William had said, she got the idea that it was something nice about her. The girl smiled broadly, babbled a bit while William tried to tell her, mainly by telepathy, which he still hadn't quite mastered, that he couldn't speak her language. That didn't seem to matter much, the smile remained. William repeated the Sirisian phrase that Henry had made popular, "My name is William, what is yours?"

This all got repeated many times until she understood he was William, after correcting his pronunciation several times. Eventually William duplicated her name, which sounded awfully like Pudding. Geoff was getting a little bored by this time until he was rescued from further pain with Kirk, Henry and Richard approaching them.

William told everyone that this was Pudding from the ship that had brought them here, and she was invited to lunch as well, with Kirk doing some translating for her. She was on leave for 8 more days, which wasn't enough time to get home and back to base using the regular shuttles, so she was relaxing here. Seeing that Pudding and William were clearly very attracted to each other, Kirk put a few words into his silent mouth and told Pudding that William needed to learn Sirisian and she would be a great teacher. She readily agreed, welcoming the opportunity to spend time with such a handsome alien, especially now that his hair was tailored so well.

After the formalities of choosing and ordering food, Henry opened the discussion with, "How on Earth did we get here so fast from the edge of our solar system to this big moon? It is about 8 light years, and according to an eminent Earth scientist it is not possible to exceed the speed of light. Even approaching light speed you have to use so much energy to go just a little bit faster that attempting to do so becomes progressively more resource hungry, and unachievable."

"Ah yes," said Kirk, "we have heard about this theory, and we always have a good laugh about it, because you see, while you were on the ship you were travelling at just under one light year every day, that is how you were able to reach our Dog Star in less than 6 days."

"Are we talking Earth or Sirisian days here?" Geoff wanted to know.

"Sirisian," replied Kirk, "our standard day is about 5 hours longer than an Earth day."

"That's even worse," said Richard, "I make it we were travelling at approximately 7 trillion miles per day."

"That's hard to believe," said Henry, "almost impossible, in fact that must be at least half a million times faster than we have calculated light can travel at."

"I hope you won't take it badly, Henry, if I tell you that it is possible to go much faster than that even, with the right propulsion."

Henry still had trouble believing what Kirk had said. "So no worm holes?"

"Sorry, Henry," said Kirk, "worm holes are another figment of that wild Earthly imagination."

"That is really travelling," said Henry, trying hard to accept these new facts that cut across a major component of his scientific knowledge. "What do you use to generate such power?"

"I will take you over and show you after we have eaten," said Kirk.

"Just to change the subject," said Geoff, "how come you can speak such perfect English?"

Kirk answered with, "I wondered when you would get around to that. From your accents I'd say you were all British born so you will fully understand the implications when I say that I went to Oxford, at Corpus Christi College to be precise. I did my basic English here of course, some little while later I signed on, in Oxford as a foreign student. They mostly thought I was from Japan. I was never challenged as an alien and ended up with a history degree, which to be honest was very limited, only going back about 5,000 years, but it gave me some insights, and allowed me to perfect my English."

"I always thought aliens were amongst us," Geoff joked, "now we know it for sure."

"OK, another question," said Henry, "why can't we see space, stars or planets from here?"

"That is because of the way we've constructed the moon's atmosphere. To hold in a complete air pocket we had to seal it effectively with a special kind of thick heavy gas. Objects can pass through it, after which it seals any gaps, keeping the air where it should be. The atmosphere ends quickly, a matter of a few hundred feet above the tallest buildings, and we do have to refresh or top up the oxygen levels. There again this method allows us to work on our moon and make the best use of the land surfaces that we have."

"How old are you?" Geoff wanted to know. "You look around 30 Earth years, but it's hard to say."

"In Earth years I'd be celebrating my 88th birthday shortly. Locally I'm 35, and yes we do live a lot longer than you guys. I put it down to the pure atmosphere, exercise and real food, as well as a more sensible attitude to life. Our planet takes about two and a half of your years to go around our marvellous white and blue speckled sun."

"How far does your history go back?" Geoff asked, happy to have someone around that was older than he was.

"Well over 400 million years," answered Kirk. "We were truly independent after the Voluelleta Empire collapsed, 186 million years ago, and it took a long time to rebuild our civilisation. Earth first had some of our people living on it around 300 million years ago, when there was but one continent, and before some vandals ruptured the crust, which resulted in the tectonic plates forming and moving about."

"So," said Henry, "we wouldn't have had all of those volcanoes and so forth, if those vandals hadn't broken through the crust of the single continent?"

"Correct, and they were quite meticulous in how they cracked open the hard soil, right down to the magma of the mantle, in multiple locations," said Kirk. "That one activity changed so much concerning how your world developed."

"Any idea which planet these vagabonds belonged to?" asked Geoff. "When we get our big spaceships built, we can go and bomb them."

"No idea," said Kirk, smiling at the thought.

"Where can we read about all of this, is it available through the console?"

"Yes," said Kirk, "you will have to be able to understand our language very well to fully get it all. Now that gives you an incentive to learn Sirisian. Ask Manya about getting on a beginners' course. It won't take long as they have found ways to really speed up the learning process."

After lunch, William and Pudding took their own route back, while the others were taken to their lodgings in the car that had picked up Henry, Richard, and Kirk. They spent the afternoon on the console, finding their way around it, with Henry enrolling on the intensive language course while the others browsed their own consoles and bugged Manya about various things, so they all had plenty to talk about when they met for dinner.

Some days passed in the established fashion, William was coached by Pudding, and Henry really got to grips with the intensive language course, while Geoff and Richard mostly relaxed. Kirk kept all of his promises and shared some advanced technology with them including the faster than light engines and how to avoid having to use a lot of lubricants on heavy machinery, as well as many other little innovations that made the Sirisians an advanced space culture.

It was at breakfast one day that Kirk came to join them, saying, "We have the clearance to take those naughty Toothies back home, so I was wondering who wanted to come along. Henry you can continue your course while we travel, if you would like to briefly see another planet that is?"

"I'd love that," said Henry.

"Me too," chorused Richard and Geoff.

William was looking a little unsure. "Of course I would like it, except that Pudding has arranged to show me the tall mountains on the other side of this moon, and it wasn't easy for her to get permission for me to go with her there. I would be letting her down if I didn't go as planned."

"Best not to upset Pudding, I heard she is pretty hot on self-defence," smiled Henry.

"Understood," said Kirk, "in that case it will be just the four of us. We can go once you have eaten; the Toothies are already on board in their holding cell."

The cruiser was a fraction of the size of the ship that had brought them to Sirisia, although it was even prettier, Geoff acknowledged, and comfortable, despite the fact that they had to share cabins, Richard and Geoff together, while Henry shared with Kirk.

When Henry wasn't consumed by the console and his language course, he and Kirk had some fascinating chats about the state of science on Earth. Meanwhile Richard was trying to orientate Geoff to approximately where they were within the galaxy; Geoff was having trouble with some terminology, and spent a lot of time watching stars go by.

One quiet spell when Richard was attempting a conversation with a crewman, Kirk found Geoff in his usual perch, and said it was time to switch roles and for him to ask Geoff some questions.

"Fire away," said Geoff, "just don't make it technical, I'm no scientist."

"That was what I was wondering about," said Kirk. "What is a non-scientist doing on such a mission, you must be terribly bored, and I can't believe they had you along just because of your inquiring mind?"

"No," said Geoff, "I wasn't even selected for this mission, well not initially. I mean I had no involvement with it when it was being set up and indeed no knowledge about it at all."

"Yet you became involved, clearly," said Kirk.

"Yes," said Geoff, "even though it was not with my consent. I was press-ganged into joining Henry and the others in the most horrible way possible."

Kirk frowned, wondering what was to come. "Spit it out, Geoff, you have me even more curious now."

Geoff carried on, recalling the initial feeling of horror when he found himself inside 'Comet' millions of miles from home. "It was not as though anything had been planned. Totally out of the blue they had me inside the 'Comet' and there was nothing I could do about it."

"Sounds very harsh," admitted Kirk, "tell me how it happened. Did they come and drag you from your home one sunny day?"

"Yes," agreed Geoff, "one partially sunny day, I had just had something to eat; we were in the kitchen minding our own business when it happened. One minute I was beside the sink, the next I was sat in a chair, held in place by huge straps, unable to move, and inside the 'Comet'. It was truly a gruesome feeling, being helpless and immobile, in a very strange place."

"I can imagine," said Kirk, frowning even more. "You didn't say how they got you into that chair, or why."

"The why is easy," said Geoff, "they totally screwed up, taking me rather than someone else, yet I couldn't possibly explain how they transferred my spirit on some kind of beam all the way out to the edge of the solar system."

"Wow!" exclaimed Kirk, mouth dropping open a little. "Let me see if I have this correct now. Someone was clearly due to have his spiritual beingness transferred from Earth to 'Comet'. Somehow the beam missed the intended person and hit you, so that you were transferred into this body?"

"That's about it," agreed Geoff.

"I'm still amazed at the whole thing, Geoff, we have dallied with such things for military operations, however, it's not something we use often, or have great skill in. I will check with Henry later to see what information he has on the mechanics of this transfer device. I can see you were pretty traumatised by the whole process?"

"Oh yes," agreed Geoff, "I thought I was losing my mind suddenly thrust into this strange environment. It was just fortunate that they had a problem with the mainframe computer that allowed me to focus on it and gradually orientate myself to a new life."

"Couldn't they send you back?" asked Kirk.

"Shortly after I arrived there was all of this turbulence that pushed us to a different orbit within the Oort Cloud, and base at Cambridge just couldn't get a proper lock on 'Comet'."

"Amazing," said Kirk, "I can see that you have a propensity for being kidnapped. Glad we were able to do it for you as well."

"Cor, I've never been hijacked in my life before," said Geoff.

"Maybe a previous one then," suggested Kirk smiling.

"The odd thing is," said Geoff, "that the problems they were having with the computer were exactly the sort of thing I did before I retired from work, so at least I was able to get that all working for them, meaning raw observational data could be processed before being streamed back to Cambridge. They had been expecting a software expert, they got me instead."

"What a lucky accident, for them," said Kirk, "I can imagine you felt pretty shook up about it all, it would certainly give me the willies finding myself in a different body, without warning, so far from home."

"I think I need a drink after relating all of that, any chance of a beer with our late meal?" asked Geoff.

"Let's go find one, I'm in the mood now for a couple of beers myself," said Kirk.

Over dinner Kirk had Henry explain what he knew of the mechanics of the transfer chair, which wasn't much, leaving Kirk with many questions. "Do you mind if our technical people take a look at it?" asked Kirk. A surprised looking Henry said that was OK but wasn't sure why Kirk was asking as they'd already confiscated their rocky ship.

Kirk announced that they would arrive at the Toothies' home world by the early hours of tomorrow, local time, which was similar to Sirisian, "That will give us time to shower and eat breakfast. After that we have an appointment with our ambassador, who will escort us to the Toothies' court of justice where we hand over the prisoners."

"We know this star as Procyon Alpha," Henry mentioned, "it's much brighter than our sun, about seven times the luminosity, so it will be hot and dazzling. If I'm correct their large planet orbits well inside the inner boundary of their Goldilocks zone?"

"Correct," agreed Kirk, the natives call their system after this main planet, namely Dogshoo, at least that's how it is pronounced."

"What distance will we have travelled to this new planet?" asked Richard.

Kirk replied, "It is about 6 light years, and we will do that in one and a half Sirisian days.

"I've asked the captain of this ship to make the journey a fast one as I have several things I must do urgently when I get back, so we go well above cruising speed. By the way, the ship that brought you to Sirisia, name of Frenchair, normally runs at the same cruising speed. If we had a race though, this little ship would win."

"Oh my gosh," exclaimed Geoff, "that speed must be a real big number in miles per hour."

"Roughly two trillion," suggested Richard, "very approximately."

"OK, I can live with that," said Henry, whose considerations of speed out in the galaxy was still wobbly.

"I'm not sure I can," said Geoff, "those speeds just become unreal to me. Maybe I should stick with light years, miles per hour are alright on a planet, out here they are meaningless."

"Agreed," said Richard, "OK, that becomes something like 0.0017 light years per hour, although I'm not sure that is any easier to get your head around. Does that help, Geoff?"

"Not a lot," said Geoff a little more sullen.

"Let's look at it in terms of days," suggested Henry, "I make that 2.8 light years per day on this craft."

They all agreed that this number would suit their purposes for now and went off to their bunks with plenty to think over. Geoff was thinking that despite all of this fancy travelling around space at high speeds, visiting alien planets and watching the beautiful stars, he'd give anything right now to be back home, cuddling Thelma.

Kirk was busy thinking on how the spirit transfer could be put to military ends, while Henry was still arguing with himself, and protesting the Brobdingnagian speeds at which they travelled.

The details and ceremony of handing over the juvenile Toothies to their authorities, kind of passed Geoff by. He was paying attention, but wasn't much interested. What held his attention was how the world looked, as well as the formality of the way the people dressed. The ground was almost a golden colour, interspersed with blooms of dark purple, and yellow, or gold coloured one storey buildings. It was hard to describe them as buildings for they appeared to be more like African huts linked together, rather than bricks and cement, although they were substantial enough when they went inside, as well as being quite extensive. They were all happy to be inside, away from the glare of the too bright sun, and despite the very dark sunglasses Kirk had provided, they found the light from the sun overpowering, and the heat from the sun's rays almost too uncomfortable.

"So this is what it feels like to live on a planet under a big white sun," said

Richard, sweating heavily.

Kirk mentioned that Sirisia also had a bright white star that was much further out than the Toothies' main sun.

"Kirk," asked Geoff, "how come these people stand in groups of three? It looks like a female with a chunkier male either side, but always the male to the left is a little broader and shorter."

"That can only be explained in terms of evolution," Kirk replied quietly. "The female needs two males to fertilise her eggs, or no baby results."

"Oh," said Geoff, "like a threesome?"

"That pretty well describes it," said Kirk, "the female is genetically different from Earth women in that she has two openings, with each male attacking, so to speak, one each."

Geoff's mind started to mock up the possibilities, but he quickly decided he would be better off concentrating on the Toothies being fully clothed rather than what was creeping into his thoughts.

After the handing over ceremony they were given a brief tour of the facilities and ended up at what was clearly an exclusive eating establishment. Along with descriptions in Sirisian there were small pictures of the food. Geoff expressed everyone's feelings when he said, "These all look very similar and so much like dung beetles or cockroaches, probably cooked in different ways. Talk about spam spam spam." In the end Kirk ordered something for them all that didn't look as though it had previously been employed in rolling excrement into balls.

The tour was a short one, and they were thankful for that. Nobody, not even Kirk could imagine wanting to live there, although as Kirk mentioned, "Humanoids live where they can. You can't always choose the planet you get to live on, and you adapt to the conditions. You either do that or become extinct, like the dinosaurs on Earth."

As they stood on the landing field about to board their ship Kirk reminded them of the formality for the occasion, "Now wave and stand on your left leg, raising the right foot." The Toothies did the same, ending this diplomatic mission where Earthmen were first introduced to a second alien species. Henry noticed that Kirk had not made the same motion.

~ CHAPTER 7 ~

~ GETTING NASTY ~

As the captain of the ship went through the formalities of making sure that everything was in working order, they all got seated in the soft beige lounge seats. "These are nothing like the economy seats I normally get when I fly," said Geoff, "these are so comfy. You just sink into the fabric, they support you so well, and I can stretch my legs!"

"I agree," said Henry. "When we sign our first Sirisian trade deal I will make sure we get a fleet of these."

The ship quickly gained altitude and they broke out of the brightness of the planet into the deep darkness of space. Kirk wanted to know how they had liked their visit.

"They were a bit strange," admitted Richard, "I'm not sure I could easily get used to dealing with them. Odd customs as well."

"Yes," said Kirk, "although they liked the quaint way you said goodbye."

"Oh you bugger," said Henry, "I knew that was a wind up, now whenever the Toothies meet any of us from Earth they will expect the same gestures. I hope you didn't introduce any more little formalities for us to follow!"

"No, no, that was it, for now," admitted Kirk, "it was quite funny though, and you didn't really look like idiots, honest."

Henry threw a cushion at Kirk as they felt the ship pick up speed, turn slightly and head back towards Sirisia.

"Getting back to the Toothies," said Henry, "I can't help wondering why they don't do something to make themselves more comfortable. They could surely create bigger underground accommodation, or control the weather to some degree, or even move planets."

"I concur, partially," said Kirk. "You have to admit though, that you normally get used to the climate you are living in and don't think of altering it until you experience something different. Besides, controlling the weather to make a difference here would take a lot of resources; I think it could be done, with the right scientific brains on the job. I shall mention your suggestion, Henry, next time I speak with the Toothies, and we'll see if we can get you seconded there for a couple of years to implement it."

"Not bloody likely, thank you very much," scowled Henry.

Kirk smiled at his own little joke and they all followed his lead.

"I have another issue to take up with you, young man," exclaimed Henry. "What were you implying earlier on about dinosaurs becoming extinct? According to our analysis they were wiped out by meteors. A subtle difference," he continued, still trying to hang on to some Earthly scientific theories. "Now don't tell me we got that wrong as well?"

"Only a little," replied Kirk, smiling broadly and throwing the cushion back. "No amount of rocks could cause that much devastation. It was ash from a dozen or more volcanoes that polluted the atmosphere and effectively smothered all life. Very few animals survived well, some did of course, but they had to initially adapt to very poor conditions, which took over 2 million years to clear up. After that we reintroduced some more animals to bring the planet back to life again, however, we stopped short of reintroducing the big beasts."

"Another theory trashed," grumbled Henry, "next you will tell me that humans didn't evolve from apes."

"I'm not sure you can take any more home truths, Henry, I don't want to make you feel that all Earth science is wrong, it isn't, but in the case of evolution it is wrong. Apes are a very different genetic line. You have to ask yourself, why are there still apes on Earth? Why didn't they all evolve into humans?"

Henry was about ready to put his hands over his ears and whistle loudly, but he was still a scientist, still a searcher after the truths of life.

"So why didn't you just colonise Earth and make it part of your empire?" asked Richard.

"Politics, old boy," replied Kirk. "We don't hold the deeds to it, and would have been quickly kicked out."

"Oh boy, life isn't easy out in the bigger universe, with all of these rules to follow," said Geoff.

"Well where did we come from?" asked Henry. "If we didn't evolve from the mudflats of Africa, where did we come from?"

"It's a good job you are sitting down," said Kirk, "are you sure you are ready for this?"

"I will close my eyes," said Henry, "and open my ears. Just get it done quickly; this is almost as painful as going to the dentist!"

Kirk continued, "You've often wondered if aliens have visited Earth, what if I told you that you were bred from aliens? The whole bloody planet is full of aliens."

"How?" was all Henry could say.

"Let me answer that by asking you a question," said Kirk. "When a certain fish or animal dies out in an area on Earth, what do you do to repopulate that group of creatures at a certain location?"

"We would take some of the required creatures from an area where they were flourishing, and move them to where they were scarce," replied Richard.

"Exactly," said Kirk, "and that's what we did with Earth. We took people from different planetary systems who were willing to live on a raw planet with no luxuries and no societies, with nothing as regards decent implements or devices to help them survive, just their wits and their desire to create a brave new world."

"Amazing that they survived at all," said Richard, "also that they were able to develop into the societies we know today."

"Amazing, yes," said Kirk, "it was no mean feat, although not unique by any means. It has been done before in different sections of this galactic arm, even. Sometimes a new sun will be born, wherever that be, and it can be a while before anyone discovers its fresh new planets. If it's close to another system then it will be taken over, colonised, all too often though, it's a case of survivors who have crashed on this new planet forming the basis of a new civilisation. On odd occasions people migrate to a planet with limited resources and no backup, then start to work the planet and make it habitable for themselves and others. It's a great feeling to start such an adventure on a brand new world. You'll not believe it, but somewhere within high command's secure offices, there is a blueprint for establishing a society on a new planet."

There was silence as they took in what he was saying.

"Can I open my eyes yet, or is there more to come?" asked Henry.

"Not much more to say really," said Kirk. "Different species were used in different parts of Earth to suit the climate. If we had time, I'd show you where the Chinese people came from originally, or the native people of Africa, or even the American Indians. As it was a good number of tribes, as we could call them, a tribe coming from a specific planet, died out. Only the smartest and toughest survived the fight against the competition and the ice ages."

More silence, even Geoff couldn't think of anything to say.

"Did any migrants come from Sirisia?" asked Richard, who was accepting these new ideas better than Henry.

"Oh yes," replied Kirk, "there were five groups each with 100 people established in what was to become Western Europe. They formed a circuit around an area that was good for food and shelter. As they expanded outwards they knew in case of major problems they could always retreat to a safe welcoming place. They traded with each other as they developed different skills and methods to create the basic requirements for life and as you can see they prospered, as did several other groups."

"Would we have the same DNA as you?" Geoff asked Kirk.

"It would be a pretty close match," said Kirk.

They retreated early back to their bunks to grapple with the earth-shattering information Kirk had given. Henry in particular was examining each set of data and relating it back to what he had previously known to be facts, realigning it all, questioning other related sub-topics, going backwards and forwards, until the new data sat a little more comfortably over the old data. After that he slept deeply as his mind worked overtime, filing the freshly received data into the correct places within the right subject area, followed by a re-indexing of it for future use.

Over breakfast Henry wanted to know more about the real facts of life, just what else didn't Earth people know or understand, or what other surprises were out there.

"Oh, where shall I start?" exclaimed Kirk. "Certainly the general reality level of Earth thinking will require a major shift if you as a species are to survive. To a degree it will be up to you three here to help change assumptions and expectations. Your leaders are inward looking, and I say not often willing to make the right choices. If they lean any more towards socialism then your future will be grim and short."

"I realise our politicians are pretty awful at times, however, that puts a new slant on life," said Geoff.

"Not sure what we can do to be honest," said Henry sullenly, "we are no politicians."

"You are much better than politicians, for as scientists you deal with the truth," replied Kirk. "By publishing scientific papers you will be able to change perspectives, and you just have to persist at that."

"Hmm, OK," said Richard, "we can do that."

"Here is something you will not be aware of," continued Kirk. "We have been observing the extent that environmental politics are affecting the shape of your society. Those trying to stop use of carbon producing fuels have got it all wrong, and deliberately so. There are elements from the Seventh Star system on your planet dishing out misinformation about the way the climate behaves, and you need to counteract this with real science."

"You mean," said Geoff, "another alien civilisation is actively planting lies and fuelling the idea than Man is about to destroy Earth? As if it were not bad enough that we find out we are aliens, now we have more aliens amongst us trying to ruin us."

"Exactly, and yes," said Kirk.

"My head is beginning to spin somewhat with this change in my reality," said Henry, "I can appreciate a little more how you felt, Geoff, when you found yourself suddenly in 'Comet'."

"While I must say I had suspicions about the alleged science of climate change I never really questioned it because so many other professionals had accepted it," said Richard, "but who or what are the Seventh Star system aliens, and why are they interfering?"

"Good question," said Kirk. "Henry will no doubt be doing some research on them, and they are not nice to know. They have a vicious society that crushes the weak and empowers the most ruthless. They are underhand and basically after your gold, or anybody's gold, come to that."

"Dirty thieving aliens," said Geoff.

"Going back some millions of years," Kirk continued, "Earth was a part of their empire, just before those volcanoes erupted and wiped out much of the life on Earth. There have been rumours that laid the blame for the exploding volcanoes with the Sevens, but it's impossible to prove. Now they want control of the planet back. They can't just take it over as that would get them trouble from all their neighbours. They allowed it to go fallow for so many years, meaning ownership reverted back to the natives of the planet; those natives have to speak with one voice on how their future will look. The Sevens have infiltrated your society at all levels to prepare you, by making life very difficult, stirring up wars and hatred. The idea being that when they appear out of the blue, on the White House lawn probably, as an advanced civilisation, welcoming you into their empire, the people of Earth are bound to want to join them. It will mean that all the people of Earth would be asked to agree to be part of this empire, and very few could resist, I'm sure. So you see where the propaganda comes in?"

"It just gets worse and worse," muttered Geoff.

"That would certainly be the case if that vote was won by the Sevens," said Kirk, "you'd be slaves before a year was out."

"OK," said Henry, "we need to attack the propaganda so that things do not get so bad, yet even if things were not as bad as you make out they could be, many people have a romantic idea about aliens, and would likely vote yes anyway."

"I agree," said Kirk, "it will be an uphill battle. You can use your celebrity status and your new science to gradually change opinion."

"Isn't all of this against the rules of engagement?" asked Richard. "Surely someone could put a stop to it?"

"Not a chance," said Kirk, "we know what's going on, proving it is another thing, and by the time we had enough support to do anything, the game would have moved on, and those behind the lies would have vanished with no way to say who they were working for."

"It's going to be a big task for us three to change opinion," said Henry. "On behalf of Earth, can I make a request that Sirisia also pursue this matter, with all means at your disposal? Even if it only caused the Sevens to change course, it would help, by giving us more time."

"I promise to speak with my superiors," agreed Kirk.

"Is there any way to recognize these damned Seventh Star system aliens?" queried Geoff.

"Not always obvious, although, yes there are some signs you can watch out for," said Kirk. "Their home sun is a red dwarf, which means most of them have very light blue or even grey irises. Additionally, they frequently squint because of the brightness of your sun compared to theirs, and their skin can often be pale."

"Interesting," said Richard, "how long have they been doing this for, it suggests they are well organised?"

"Very well organised," agreed Kirk, "and the front men are usually native to Earth, bribed or influenced to peddle the lies. This has been going on for well over 100 years."

"Is there anything else you can tell us about how they structure themselves, is there any way we can spot them or take some action against them?" asked Richard.

"That's a very tough question," replied Kirk. "I'm afraid they pose too well as natives to stand out in a crowd and they are very secretive about their organisations, mostly one or two men cells. I've mentioned the characteristics I know of, another common trait of Seventh Star system aliens is that they sometimes lisp. It goes without saying that they not have any of the characteristics I've mentioned, and have others. The thing that will show them up is their conviction and determination to spread lies and misinformation at every opportunity."

"Not a lot to go on," said Henry. "How many of them are there on Earth?"

"Several hundred, at least," replied Kirk.

"How do they get back to their planet or receive new orders; is there a place where their ships land?" asked Geoff.

"These people rarely leave in a ship," said Kirk. "It's deemed a lifetime's work to infiltrate your society and to do their dirty jobs. They generally only take orders from one person on Earth, so no; they do not go forth and back. They are there for the duration. They go back to the Seventh Star system when they die."

"Is there any way to stop them," asked Geoff, "that doesn't involve shooting them dead? I mean if we confronted one, how should it be handled?"

"Again, not an easy one to provide a real answer for, Geoff," said Kirk, "they could just deny your accusation and make trouble for you. They certainly won't come out quickly with the truth. I would say that if you spotted one you should observe what he does. If he enters into the environmental argument do what you can to disrupt his message and invalidate whatever he says."

"How different is their DNA to ours?" asked Henry. "I just wondered if we could use that in any way."

"It is very similar to your own, and from memory, I don't believe there are any significant differences," said Kirk. "I do recall something that helped one of our people when a situation arose off planet with the Sevens. They get heavily brainwashed, at least the reluctant ones do. Their government makes sure that when they send their people on a mission that they operate within certain guidelines. Now this brainwashing affects these operatives very heavily, sometimes to the point that they become almost robotic. Some of our people discovered that certain keywords can turn on or turn off this programming. I will attempt to find out what it is, and I will let you know."

"With so much intrigue and nasty business going on, I'm not sure if Earth would be safe joining this interstellar club," said Henry. "Perhaps it would be better if we just stayed ignorant."

"Join it or become a disastrous effect of it," responded Kirk.

"Is the whole galaxy like this?" Geoff wanted to know.

"By and large, Geoff, yes. Remember though, the galaxy is a huge collection of different societies and civilisations. Just look at Earth and the way different nations have organised themselves, some more rational or friendly than others. Multiply that degree of cultural and ethical differences by 200 million. That might give you a clue as to how varied things could be in this interstellar club," said Kirk.

"Oh my goodness," said Geoff, "talk about a loss of innocence. If only I'd known by washing up the dishes that day that all of my feeble concepts of outer space would be so easily shattered. Talk about Adam and Eve sharing that apple; this is 200 million times worse."

Even Kirk enjoyed that analogy, and they all had a good laugh.

"There are many civilisations out there that would knock your socks off," said Kirk, "in terms of futuristic stuff, for example, castles in the sky are just one feat some can still achieve. Some systems have incredible things going on that would make you imagine they were a mini version of heaven, and most of these are run by decent governments. That notwithstanding, don't forget that basic humanoid aberrative nature will always impinge on the most worthwhile societies when times are difficult. What I'm saying is that the possibilities for superb living are endless, but look below the surface and no matter how advanced, the society still has its own particular problems."

"I'd love to see those castles in the sky," said Geoff.

"You'd need to go pretty close to the galaxy centre to see the really amazing things like that, Geoff," said Kirk, "for the planetary environment changes so much with the effect of gravity when solar systems are close together. I'm afraid we have nothing like those castles on Sirisia, we are down-to-earth types that do what we can to help ourselves, and others where possible. We are pretty well, run of the mill, for space civilisations, damned boring really, but with the occasional excitement disrupting our calm."

"I like your kind of boredom," said Henry, "please do not talk yourselves down, you actually sound like a beacon of hope in an otherwise crazy cesspit."

They smiled at that description, all going quiet, thinking hard about life in the wide galaxy.

Still about half a day away from their destination the ship began to slow rapidly, and then it came to an abrupt stop. They bounced a little in their seats as gravity exerted its power over the occupants of the ship. Remaining firmly in place, they started to wonder what had happened. An urgent babble came through the intercom, clearly intended as a warning for Kirk and the security people that were on the ship, who all went to arm themselves. The guards took up different positions opposite to where the airlock was situated, while one hid behind a curtain.

"Big problem," said Kirk to his guests, "we have a dangerous situation developing and it is likely to become very serious, please remain seated for now."

The ship's captain came out to talk with Kirk and after more babble stood next to Kirk in silence, waiting.

"We are about to be boarded, and the captain is unable to send a sub-space distress message out as it is being blocked."

"What about a radio message?" asked Geoff. "I know you use that too, and it might take a while to get anywhere but eventually your people would know what had happened to us."

"Good thought," said Kirk, and told this to the captain who went back to his cabin to relay the fact that they had been stopped by a large battleship, on his radio.

"Who are they?" asked Henry.

"Not totally sure, they could be Sevens," answered Kirk. "When a big battleship commands you to stop or you will be shot to small pieces, it's normally a good idea to comply, we've no idea what they want of us, and no we were not trespassing."

They felt the battleship connect to their ship via the airlock with a bit of a bump, waiting until the hatch opened to see what their fate would be.

"Haven't we experienced something like this before?" mumbled Geoff.

"Indeed you have," agreed Kirk with a wry smile, "however, this one is a real hostile situation, trust me."

Kirk and the guards moved to defensive positions close to the hatch, weapons ready. Almost silently, the hatch opened up and three figures stepped into the brightly lit lounge, almost dazzled, squinting at the effulgence. Looking through to the inside of the battleship, Richard could see three other figures standing ready at the in-between point, though it was almost in shade, the light level from the other vessel very low, gloomy even. He realised, as Kirk had, that they wouldn't see much of what was happening in this ship as they would effectively be blinded by its bright lights.

One of the intruders babbled something to Kirk, causing him and the guards to drop their weapons under the seats. The leader of the intruders came into the centre of the cabin, taking a close look at the passengers, Geoff in particular.

Kirk started to say something, but was rudely shut up by the bigger trespasser. They didn't look like soldiers, they were not in uniform, and what they were wearing didn't match. One had brown trousers, the others green, while their tops were each a different colour. They were not even clean-shaven and looked rather scruffy against the Sirisian guards. The one with brown trousers moved closer to Kirk in a threatening manner. "Let us start to use a language that your guests can understand," he said in stilted English.

Several mouths went wide open.

Brown trousers turned towards Geoff, saying to him, "We want you to come with us, now."

"Me?" demanded Geoff. "What have I done?"

"It is not what you have done, it is who you are," said the alien.

"In that case you have the wrong person," said Geoff, "I'm nobody of importance. I'm not in any government, and I'm certainly not a spy or an invader. You have the wrong ship!" Geoff stood up to better confront brown trousers, moving inwards towards the pilot's door, giving himself some space.

"No mistake; we know what you are. They call you Geoff."

"How do you know my name?" Geoff demanded.

"We know all about you and your three friends. Don't worry it is all on the Sirisian information system, and we have access to it." Kirk looked totally shocked at this news.

"That still doesn't answer what you want with me," said Geoff, raising his voice a little, and edging in towards the seats, forcing brown trousers to move away from his companions.

Kirk realised that Geoff was trying to position the intruders so that they could be attacked more easily. He signalled the guards to be prepared to act, with a very secret Sirisian eye movement and wormed in Geoff's direction, saying, "You won't get away with abducting people like this you know. Your ship will be disabled before you get safely away into your own space."

The abductor smiled, "That is where you are wrong. The rest of you will not live long enough to give an account of this." He turned back to Geoff, telling him to go to the exit.

As if to demonstrate how ruthless he could be, the scruffy unkempt alien with clothes that didn't go together, raised his gun towards a Sirisian guard, and shot a blast towards him, shattering much of the column the guard was standing next to. The guard didn't flinch.

Kirk shouted something in Sirisian that not even the intruders understood, and brown trousers waved his gun around, demanding to know what was said. "I just told everyone not to overreact, to be careful, as we have a crazy man aboard." The man smirked at this, satisfied that they now understood him and would do as he told them.

For a moment Geoff stood still, unable to decide what he could do. Brown trousers was getting serious, aiming his laser gun at the seat next to Geoff he blasted a hole through the seat padding, and ripped a big hole in the metal below. "Now move," he said quietly, with a threat in his tone.

"Am I supposed to put my hands up?" asked Geoff.

As brown trousers was about to answer Geoff started to move his hands up, deliberately hitting the hand holding the weapon very hard in an upward motion, forcing the alien to drop it. At the same time, Geoff barged into the would-be abductor with all of his strength, knocking him off balance. Kirk was quickly onto the man, hitting him so hard that he fell unconscious to the floor. Meanwhile the three guards had taken on the other two intruders and had rendered them also totally unaware. The three people in the airlock could see little of this, which was fortunate, because it allowed a Sirisian guard the time to very quickly hit the emergency release lever, to separate their ship from the battleship, and close the hatch.

Even before the hatch started to close, the ship was moving away. There were a few hectic moments as air was sucked out of the cabin, before the hatch closed fully, creating a strong wind that would have pulled the guard through the open hatch had he not been prepared. Kirk wasn't so worried that the three in the airlock would likely get sucked out into space, "That was the price pirates pay when things go wrong for them," he muttered.

The captain had been watching everything on the internal monitor, and as soon as his control panel showed separation from the battleship, he turned the power thruster full on and guided his ship quickly away.

Kirk said, "It will take them a short time to realise what just happened. There will be a little time for us to get clear, as there will be some confusion on their side. They will not have been expecting us to take on their bully boys," adding, "they will not be able to start up their ship from a standing start to high speed as quickly as we have, so we have that advantage."

The ship gained speed, as Kirk advised, "All we have to do now is evade their missiles, for once we get out of range of their sub-space blocker we will have sent a message far and wide, identifying our assailants. At that point they should slink away."

That's just what happened. The captain raised the speed to absolute maximum, and very shortly they were in Sirisian space, within the bounds of their solar system.

The three intruders, still unconscious, were stripped of their outer garments, searched thoroughly and deposited in the holding cell, with a guard outside to keep an eye on them.

Kirk sighed deeply, shaken by the action, and sat next to where Geoff had retired to. "We were lucky they were so sloppy. If I'd been doing the invading I would have had several more troops inside and around the airlock. There again, if they'd had more people around the airlock it would have meant that more would have been lost," he said with half a smile fighting against a frown.

Geoff was breathing hard and holding his hand, exclaiming, "I was not going to be abducted a third time for God's sake, better that they shot me down, for I've heard enough about the Sevens to know I would not want to visit them under any circumstances."

"That was a smart move you made there," said Kirk, "I'm really impressed and thankful, you saved our lives and this ship, for they would surely have blown us up when you had left."

"I agree," said Geoff, "they were real villains and not to be trusted further than you could throw them. I did hurt my blooming thumb, though, I may have broken something."

"Better a broken thumb than a big hole in your head," suggested Henry solemnly, coming out of his mortified state.

Somebody gave Geoff some ice and he nursed his injured thumb, saying, "I still can't believe that they wanted me. What the heck did they pick on me for? I can hardly spell 'Seventh Star system', and Richard is much prettier than me."

"Who knows," agreed Kirk, "we will question these three and maybe we will get the truth out of them, but this needs to be a warning to us all, that the Sevens are turning nastier than usual."

"How could they have known that Geoff was on this ship," Richard wanted to know, "and how did they tap into your information centre?"

"That, I promise, we will find out," answered Kirk, sitting back into the chair, closing his eyes and sighing deeply again.

They were soon back on Sirzero, taking lunch at their favourite restaurant, and discussing recent events, including the shocking news Kirk had hit them with. The good food made them all perk up a bit, and afterwards Kirk said he had some urgent business and was not seen again for some days.

Richard wanted to know what adventures William and Pudding had had on the other side of the moon.

"Well," said William, "it was quite fascinating. It was fairly easy to climb up the sides of these moon-mountains, and there was also a ski chair like device to bring you back down again, or this enormous slide that went round and round the mountain sides. We came back down on the slide. It was totally exhilarating and great fun as we landed on this huge cushion with a few dozen other people who were also a little giddy, and trying to move off the cushion. At the very top of the mountain the air starts to get a little thin and we were pretty close to the limit of the false upper atmosphere. We could almost touch the white fluffy stuff. The mountains were a natural clay, so it's a good job there is no heavy rain on Sirzero otherwise they'd be washed away along with literally hundreds of little pieces of very artistic graffiti in the walls."

"Sounds nice," said Richard smiling, "clearly not a scientific expedition."

"Absolutely leisure," agreed William, "and not a scientific thought anywhere, well hardly, I did learn a few interesting words though. The inside of the mountains were hollow at ground level, and that is where they kept a lot of space vehicles, and some weapons, just in case they get attacked. The peak of the tallest mountain was hollow as well, and it poked well above the fluffy stuff. They have equipment to scan the space around the moon and major planets. Seems like it was a way to keep an eye on any suspicious activities around their solar system."

"I've heard say," said Pudding in slow Sirisian, "that there is also a missile launching capability within that mountain peak, to shoot down any unwanted visitors or stray comets." That made everyone frown once William had translated it, with some help from Henry.

They all met up for dinner 2 days later with Kirk joining them, looking rather pleased with himself.

"What news?" asked Henry.

"Not much," said Kirk, "we are still working on the Sevens, although one chewed a poison tooth and he is no longer with us. We managed to stop the others doing the same, and they are getting the worst of what our interrogators can throw at them. Enemies like that are shown no mercy. The Sevens's ambassador was summoned by the high command and given the third degree. Of course he denied knowledge of the offence, suggesting it was a rogue element pursuing its own interests. He was told that one more such act of piracy would be in effect a declaration of war, and it was up to his government to root out any rogue elements before they could cause trouble, if indeed they existed."

The discussion turned to what was happening on Sirisia and what preparations were being made in case of more trouble. "You wouldn't notice the difference," said Kirk. "I've been thinking though, I have to go down to see my senior, face to face, to give him my verbal report, why don't you all come along and see our big planet?"

"I won't get squashed by gravity will I?" asked Geoff. "Your planet is much bigger than Earth, so I'd be worried that I couldn't even stand up."

"Not at all, in fact gravity is very similar to this moon, for various reasons," answered Kirk with a smile, "so you will have no problems with being squashed."

William immediately said that he didn't want to miss out again, so he and Pudding asked to go along. Henry wanted to devote some real concentrated time to his language course and other research, so he declined. He told the others he felt a strong need to consolidate as much information as he could about Earth's relationship with its nearest neighbours. So it was just the five of them that met early the next day, with Kirk, for this fresh trip to another world.

"We won't stand out as aliens, will we?" asked Geoff. "With everyone staring at us?"

"You'll get one or two long looks from curious individuals," said Kirk, "it's mainly your eyes and skins which are different. You'll have some people try to touch the smooth skin on your faces, generally though, most of our people tolerate foreigners quite well. You won't get any trouble, that's for sure."

William was making great personal gains in understanding Sirisian, written and verbal, all thanks to Pudding, while Geoff and Richard had a fair smattering of words and phrases, now having picked up a few choice curses they'd heard Kirk use. While William could almost hold intelligent conversations, Geoff was at least able to ask for the nearest toilet or restaurant.

The planet Sirisia was a great revelation, and so much more like home than a recent planet they had visited. It was mostly a lovely green and white from space and utterly beautiful, especially as the travellers got closer. It was so much bigger than Earth, but the gravity didn't weigh them down as the inner core was no more dense than Earth's.

Kirk took the ship in fairly high at first so that they could all see the layout of the land from above. "Beautiful," said Geoff, "and just look at that deep turquoise sea. Why, it looks clear enough to almost see the ocean floor below."

Kirk took them lower and they really could just about see the floor of the ocean below the gentle waves, in parts, and all Geoff could say was, "How super clean is that!"

Kirk started to explain some of the features of his home world. "There are two continents, each about double the entire land mass of Earth. One is called East, one called West. The inner core is molten, yet there are no active volcanoes, earthquakes or sliding tectonic plates. Logically, the two continents are almost exactly the same distance apart whichever way you travel, although not quite the same size and shape, they are very similar. There are maybe two dozen large to small islands dotted around as you saw when we came in, with the largest called Sirntrum being the administrative centre and official government home location. Interestingly with four satellites, the single salt ocean is reasonably calm. Both East and West are self-sufficient in terms of food, while they equally supply resources to Sirntrum."

Now they approached a small outpost some way from any habitable areas on one of the continents – it could have been East or West. Kirk told them this was his own private interchange area, in fact it was some land his family owned and from here they would go on by anti-gravity car.

Kirk parked the space shuttle in a small hangar, and they walked across a yard towards some garages. Inside one of them an attractive woman was bending over the engine compartment of something that looked like a boy racer's car. Kirk walked over and gave her a kiss on the cheek, telling her that he was with off-worlders and had an urgent appointment at Sirntrum. She was curious about the off-worlders, and walked across to greet the strangers.

Richard immediately fell in love with her. She was tall and slim, seemed younger than Kirk, had a lovely mop of red hair, clear white, almost soft skin, and very long legs. For a change, Richard was the one to step forward, using the phrase Henry had come up with, and smiling broadly. "Hello, I am Richard. What is your name?" She blushed slightly at the attention he was giving her, and told them all that her name was Joovie, and welcome to their home world.

"This is my other sister," said Kirk, a few paces behind Joovie. "She lives with my parents on this plot of land, and they earn their keep from having guests to stay in cottages. This area has some interesting geology, so they get plenty of paying visitors." He told his sister that these people were from planet Earth, and had just begun to learn the language. When she heard they were from Earth Joovie became all excited, having heard so much about it from history lessons, and approached Richard, looking more closely at him.

"Perhaps you can come visit us over the next few days, I'm taking them to the hotel Floral in Spontins for a few days," said Kirk.

"Oh, I'm much too busy," she said, giving Richard a small wink of the eye.

"Shame," Kirk told her, "we'll be leaving on the fourth day. If you decide to come down I can get you a room for the last night. Call me." Her eyes lit up at the prospect of a short stay in a luxury hotel; however, she still wasn't sure she could take the time off.

Brother and sister made their goodbyes, after that Joovie said goodbye in Sirisian to the others.

"The weather," Kirk continued as they took off in the car, "is fully controlled, with rain programmed at certain times, mainly in the early part of every other day. It is required to keep the atmosphere clear and the ground moist enough for food to grow, also to wash away the dust that accumulates."

They were still a little way out of town so Kirk had enough time to complete his monologue before they reached their destination. "If we were to go to the far north, there is, at least to my way of thinking, an interesting way to extract salt from the ocean and provide plenty of natural clean water that can be extracted from the ground or reservoirs. A rather large machine pumps seawater to the top of the mountain ranges, in the far north, after this the water makes its way south, filtered through the rocks of the mountains to meet the needs of the rest of the continent. The salt is easily collected when the stream of water from the sea is directed at a different high point. The mountains and crevices below are clearly very salty but it's a great way to get pure water, and plenty of pure salt."

"I really fancy a nice glass of cold mountain water now," said Geoff.

Kirk smiled and carried on, "There are plenty of fish in the sea. Large forests hold game like deer and rabbits, as well as cow-like creatures. Sheep with their woolly coats, along with goats, are allowed to freely wander in the highlands close to the mountain ranges. Cow's milk is only ever used to feed calves which grow large quickly; we do not milk animals for our consumption. Broad areas in the south of each continent are used to grow grains and vegetables in cycle, for the seasons do not exist as Earth knows them. Temperatures vary only slightly, day to day, more so north to south, for it is the south that needs the growing power of the very warm blue white sun."

Richard nodded his approval.

"Almost there now," said Kirk. "Towns are scattered around, chiefly in the central lowlands where the climate is most reasonable. At the poles no land exists, they each have a fair amount of thick ice, though."

The car was parked and registered in something like a pay and display board. As they walked on, Kirk concluded with, "The towns tend to spread upwards and downwards instead of outwards, with many levels of buildings and transport facilities. Even at the coast the towns move down and out, often submerged below the sea enough to permit ships to travel above them. Even so, they still dig deep into the continental rock surrounding the coastal area to provide yet more accommodation, so some live below water level, some at water level, some above, and some well below the clay that lines the seabed."

Geoff gave a short clap for that data, and added, "There must be a limit on how much land, or sea-land, that you can use in this way. I notice here most buildings are a maximum of three levels, so it is clearly a design feature you aim for. What happens when you reach a critical level, with too many people and not enough space for them all?"

"Yes, there are limits," replied Kirk, "we like to keep most building at a low level, with some exceptions of course. At some very busy areas we have had to build many levels to accommodate our needs, but we have planned out areas that we can expand, and when a limit is reached we look for a new solar system in order that we can migrate half of our population. After that we have plenty of room here and on the new world. We would develop the new world on similar principles as here. We have done this five times to my knowledge."

"Interesting way to deal with the problems related to over population," agreed Henry, "it must take a large effort to find a suitable new world?"

"It does," said Kirk. "We are always watching for new stars to be born, and we keep track of any suitable planets so that we can register our interest. Sometimes the migration is very far away, even at the speeds we can travel, and we cannot always provide as much support as we might to the new world."

"Does that mean you have a fair sized empire in planets?" asked Geoff.

"Oh, not at all," said Kirk, "for as soon as a planet is fully established they become totally self-governing and truly independent from us. We remain friends and allies, and there is plenty of travel between the worlds we have spread out to, but no, we do not rule them."

They had arrived at a holiday town on the east coast of East, by the name of Spontins. It was clearly designed to be of interest to tourists, having been designed or based on many different styles and colours from several historical periods including what looked like some British concepts. Trinkets were openly displayed in a variety of little shops, along with an adequate supply of refreshment parlours. There was also a double pier that went way out to sea, allowing those hot and bothered to cool off in the refreshing sea breeze half a mile, or more, out.

While the others were booked into a luxury hotel, where they enjoyed all sorts of rejuvenating spa and body treatments, Kirk took Richard somewhere else, saying, "I couldn't help noticing you have trouble with your torso and knees. Let us see if our specialists can help you."

Richard was pleased that Kirk had taken the trouble to think of him but was at first reluctant to go, having been inspected and prodded so often in the past by British doctors who always ended up telling him he'd have to live with his conditions. Kirk finally persuaded him, based on the logic that he had nothing to lose. While Richard was examined and treated, Kirk went off to meet up with his senior officer to give a full report of the incident with the Sevens.

Kirk headed for Sirntrum by way of the underground railway, as even he was not allowed to take his own transport there. The track was deep in the bedrock of the continent, meaning access to it was through a large shaft, which housed twenty big passenger carrying lifts. Once on the train the journey was extremely fast, and within a matter of hours Kirk was discussing the attempted abduction and boarding of their ship with two senior figures in the high command. Still, they had no idea why Geoff was singled out by the Sevens, although one thing was for sure, the Earth people would be a magnet for trouble if they stayed. "You have to get them back to where they were as a matter of priority," Kirk was told by his immediate senior.

Three days after Richard reluctantly checked into the Sirisian special clinic, Kirk came back to pick him up. Richard was jubilant, he could barely contain his excitement, hopping about and running on the spot to show the difference in him. He could never have run before, or bent forward. Previously, whenever he even walked hard, never mind trotting, he would get a thump, thump, in his brain, now even that was quiet. He felt that he was as agile as a young man, and so happy to be free of pain. Even the pain lines in his face had eased, taking years off his appearance. He couldn't stop thanking Kirk, as he drove Richard to the luxury hotel to catch up with the others.

They would stay one night at the luxury hotel, with the other four, who had been having a great time, exploring and losing themselves in the newness of exciting things around them. Everywhere was so clean and attractive; it would be difficult not to fall in love with the place that raised one's spirit up so high.

William and Pudding had taken off on their own every day to enjoy the sights, meeting up with Geoff for dinner, and sometimes breakfast. Geoff had a great time wandering the streets, buying little things, even doing a spot of sunbathing on a superb yellow sandy beach. He lost count of the times he had gotten lost, always expecting his sense of direction to get him back to the hotel. Several times now this sense had failed him, and he had ended up having to ask someone. He used the same lines each time as he approached someone that looked as though they might be helpful, and would say in his best Sirisian, "Hello, my name is Geoff. I am lost. Where is Hotel Floral, please?" Always the helpful person would babble on, trying to explain where Geoff should go, and always Geoff would hold up his hands and look blank, by holding his ears he hoped he was indicating that he hadn't understood anything. After this the person would simply point, and Geoff would take off in that direction, smiling a big, "Thank you."

One time Geoff had gotten just beyond the street traders and small shops into an extensive park. He took his time to meander around, matching any plants to names he knew, but after a while his stomach told him it was getting close to dinner time, and he didn't have a clue as to which way to go. He noticed two women, of a just past ready age, walking lazily by, so he approached them with his phrase, "Hello, my name is Geoff. I am lost. Where is Hotel Floral, please?"

They gabbled a bit, eventually realising that Geoff just wasn't getting it. Very slowly one said, "Hello, Geoff, my name is Gracefur."

The other woman said something similar, "Hello, Geoff, my name is Goshma."

He shook hands with them both, although they were a bit reluctant to indulge in strange practices. They did, however, each take one of his arms, point ahead, and said, "Hotel Floral." They slowly marched him forward down some side streets until his hotel was right in front of him. He thanked them both, and even kissed their hands. They wouldn't leave him there though. They went into the hotel with him and finally waved him goodbye in the large lobby. Geoff assumed they were also staying there.

~ CHAPTER 8 ~

~ DRAGON WORLD ~

Richard didn't say anything about his treatment as he met up with Geoff at the hotel, he wanted to demonstrate his new self, somehow, and he found the perfect opportunity in the hotel where a dance was being held that evening. They all sat down around a big square table, William, Pudding, Richard, Kirk, and Geoff, watching the action on the dance floor, with Richard recalling that once, long ago he had been a fair dancer. He was sure he could duplicate the movements of the dancers he saw, some of whom were not so perfect. He looked at Pudding, then at William, asking, "May I borrow your young lady for a short while?"

William was a bit surprised, not to mention curious, although he quickly said, "Yes, of course." Richard stood up, inviting Pudding onto the dance floor. The first few twirls were a little out of coordination but soon the couple synchronised their movements and their twirls were magnificent. They made several circuits of the room after which they came back to the table where Richard thanked Pudding, saying he hadn't had so much pleasure for so many years. The others looked at him in awe as he explained how the specialist clinic had worked major miracles on him, and in such a short time. His eyes had filled with tears, and they dropped happily down his face. "Oh excuse me," he said, and went across to an open window to breathe deeply of the invigorating air.

He returned to the table as Geoff stood up and started to clap Richard. The others joined in, so happy at the change in their friend. "Stop, please," he begged, "you'll have me crying all night."

They did stop clapping, after which they kept asking questions about his treatment and how his body felt now. He was very happy to tell them everything until Geoff suggested he should get back on the dance floor as Pudding and William were clearly enjoying themselves on there. Geoff checked with Kirk on the correct phrase and etiquette for asking a woman to dance. Armed with the correct words, he went with Richard across to two rather attractive females with whom they were soon twirling. Geoff didn't last too long; he enjoyed the challenge nonetheless. Richard stayed with it for a while longer, now thoroughly enjoying the freedom of movement he had lost so long ago.

After taking a well-earned rest, Geoff spotted two familiar faces on another table. These two faces smiled back at him, so he felt he had to go and say hello. "Hello, Gracefur, hello, Goshma."

"Hello, Geoff," they responded.

As he had reached the limit of his Sirisian vocabulary, pretty well, the only other phrases coming to mind involved asking where something was, or what time it might be. He knew where he was, and had a very good idea about the time, so there was nothing else to do but to ask the ladies to dance with him, using the appropriate etiquette. They did so, one at a time, smiling with him, enjoying his company briefly, as they twirled around. After that, feeling a little breathless, he escorted Goshma back to her table, thanked them both, and gave them one of his big smiles before walking back to his own table.

"Did you have a good time, Geoff?" asked Kirk.

"Yes thank you," smiled Geoff.

"I really don't know how you do it," said Kirk smiling back, "you can hardly spell your own name in our language, but you manage to chat up and dance with not one but two nice looking women, not to mention the earlier dance you had with that younger woman. Tell me your secret, Geoff. How the bloody hell do you get these women interested?"

"It's all down to my little boy lost demeanour, old boy, you've either got it or you haven't," laughed Geoff, who was well ready for his bed now.

Geoff noticed that Kirk received a call on his ear phone, causing Kirk to excuse himself. Two minutes later Kirk was back, with a very beautiful woman with very long legs, wearing a bright gown of red and white. Richard immediately recognized Joovie, his eyes lit up, wide with pleasure. They all said their hellos again, as the woman sat between Kirk and Richard. Kirk told them that she had come visiting for one night only and had a room in the hotel as well. She had been so busy she nearly didn't make it. Richard was especially glad that she had.

Geoff announced that he was done in from all the dancing and would fall asleep in front of them if he didn't go to bed straight away.

While Geoff was making to leave, William passed a notebook across to Richard, his friend and colleague. "You will find some useful words and phrases in there," he said, raising his eyes towards the redhead sitting next to him.

As Richard opened the book, Joovie leaned close, looking at what was written. Very soon she was helping along his pronunciation of strange words that he suddenly had a great desire to learn.

William and Pudding took to the dance floor once more, and Richard could not resist asking Joovie to dance. They made a great couple, moving together as if they already knew each other very well. Richard had never smiled so much, and Kirk watched him with a new fascination, for Richard was like a new man, with so much vitality. When the pair came back to rest and take a drink, Kirk told them that he'd had a pretty busy day, and said goodnight.

Joovie and Richard sat there for a very long time, talking, just talking, sometimes not even bothering if the words were understood, or not, but somehow the meanings were received. The world around them ceased to exist for a while, as they laughed and asked questions of each other, with Richard using the notebook constantly. Soon he knew more Sirisian words than he had thought possible.

Finally they noticed the music had stopped and the hall was almost empty. It was time to go to bed. They went up in the lift one level, turned up the corridor, walking slowly to her room, still laughing quietly. She opened her door, turning towards Richard with a deep longing in her eyes. He took her hands, felt them warm and so alive in his, he leaned forward a little, looking into her beautiful deep blue eyes and pressed his lips ever so gently against hers, feeling the passion rise in both of them, his lips lingering against hers as she moved her lips against his. Then he was pressing against her soft warm lips once more, lingering some more, then slowly releasing. They opened their eyes together, both sparkling and happy. Their hands slowly parted and Richard gave her one last look as he made his way down the corridor, dancing a little dance to some tune he had in his head. She smiled happily at this nice man from Earth, finally closing the door and jumping into bed, still thinking of him. Richard floated to his bed, happier and more content with his lot than he'd ever felt in his life before. He was so alive, really alive for the first time, for everything had changed so much for him, and he just didn't want to stop thinking about Joovie. He dreamed of nothing but floating around a dance floor with the alien of his fantasies in his arms.

They met briefly for breakfast, after this she was quickly gone, out of his life; even so, her sparkle had awakened a desire in him that would never lie down again.

On the journey back to Sirzero they took a little detour to another moon. "This one is called Dragon for obvious reasons," said Kirk. "By the way did you know that in our language dragon is a synonym for dinosaur?" They hadn't known that, although they were interested to see this small moon.

They had to use a special bus on a triple rail system that took them through the canopy of a jungle. In places the jungle was very thick, which made it hard to spot any creatures below. It wasn't until they'd been travelling for 10 minutes that they came across two small creatures that looked like sloths, just below them. Geoff, who had never been too keen on zoos, was impressed that they had allocated a whole moon to preserve wildlife and allow them to live free of interference from humanoids. A little further on they came to a clearing and Geoff couldn't believe his eyes. A giant tyrannosaurus rex was feasting on the remains of a creature with a long neck. "Oh my God," he declared, surprised, not just at the way the large creature was able to rip away the flesh so easily, but also at seeing a real live T-Rex. Just at the edge of the clearing a bunch of raptors were jumping up and down, angry, as though their prey had been stolen. At this point Geoff checked around himself to make sure the rattly old bus was safe and secure.

"Don't worry," said Kirk, "they've never lost a passenger yet!"

They saw more unusual creatures as they went on, dinosaurs long extinct on Earth had been preserved here. "There is a stegosaurus," said Richard.

"Oh boy, just look at that triceratops," shouted William as the beast started to move over towards them.

Above them a small shuttle started to circle around, looking as though it might be in trouble and seeking somewhere safe to land. It moved out of sight behind a small forest of trees, moments later the sounds of it crashing noisily filled the air. It didn't look good for the aliens that had been inside the craft, for they could all see a plume of smoke starting to rise in to the sky. The bus driver had already used his radio and it was assumed that he was telling the control tower about the crash. Starting up again, the bus went on quite slowly, with everyone hoping there had been no damage to the rails ahead that supported the bus. A few minutes further on they saw two men running into a small clearing. The men had seen the bus and began to run towards it, but, even before they were halfway across the thick grass, a predator came out of the heavy foliage, smelling their scent, seeking them.

"That looks like a yutyrannus with those feathers," suggested William.

"Doesn't look like any bird I've ever seen," said Geoff, "he's fast and what a size."

The body was about 12 feet long, although with the large tail he was over 24 feet total in length, and the creature was moving quickly towards its prey. The man closest to the bus had reached the edge of the clearing and was looking for some way to climb up to the bus which had stopped for him. The driver had started to lower a rope ladder for the men to climb up, however, the man with the gun, now in the middle of the clearing realised he was really in trouble and turned to face his fate.

Putting one knee down to steady his aim, he took a shot at the beast only feet away now. The projectile hit the yutyrannus in the side of the head, although it didn't seem to notice, it just kept on charging, picking up the man in its open mouth. Slowly, the shot seemed to be taking effect, the yutyrannus seemed to be moving sluggishly, almost in slow motion. Before collapsing on the ground, plainly using all the strength and energy it had left, it swung its mighty head from side to side, flinging the man ten or more feet towards the left side of the clearing. The man either dead or stunned didn't move. Afterwards the beast lay still, as well.

By this time the first man had managed to climb up to the bus and had clambered inside with a great deal of relief. He sat down heavily, in front of the Earth party, saying some things to the driver as he recovered his breath, that William didn't pick up.

Pudding told William in plain Sirisian, with the others listening, what had happened. "Their engine had not been working well and they were unable to land at the control centre, however, the ship just kept on going, with the pilot having no way to stop it. As soon as the ship crashed they were attacked by some small dinosaurs which ran off when that beast appeared. It was not safe to stay inside the ship as this yutyrannus was jumping on it, smashing it."

William translated that for the purpose of Geoff and Richard, as best he could.

The bus still hadn't moved on, it seemed the driver was waiting to see if the man recovered, also as Kirk said later the bus would be used as a marker by the rescue party that soon came to pick up the injured man. The rescuers, in the form of a hover truck sledge, slid down towards the body. Four men quickly lifted the crumpled man from the bushes into the truck, after this they hovered off quickly at tree top height. Once the rescue was complete the bus started to move off as well, just as the beast below began to stir. There was blood on the teeth of the yutyrannus, meaning this one certainly had had a good taste of man. The bus proceeded quickly onwards with William counting nine other dinosaur species before they made it back to the control area, fortunately no more aliens were at the mercy of any of them.

"That was a jolly good morning on your wildlife moon," said Geoff, "it was really fascinating to see real live dinosaurs, and somewhat different from the images we have been shown. What an experience," he concluded. He was pleased though that it hadn't entailed any walking in the jungle.

When the party arrived back from Sirisia they all met up in the compound near to Kirk's office. Henry was so excited at what he had learned, and the others were even more excited trying to tell Henry what he had missed that nobody could understand anybody else. Eventually the excitement dimmed to mild elation and that gave Henry the opportunity to be heard. "Had the most awesome time reading up on the history and local geography of this system. Trust me this is no backwater off a seemingly small galactic arm, there have been some awesome things going on. There have been more conflicts and treacheries around here than you could possibly imagine. Certainly more than all the wars on Earth put together."

"Never mind all that," said Geoff, you have missed the most stupendous sights you cannot even imagine. We have seen real live dinosaurs!"

Geoff let that sink in with a moment of silence.

"No," gasped Henry, "real live, bloodthirsty, huge, dinosaurs?"

"In the flesh and blood," said Geoff, "and Sirisia wasn't at all bad either, we all had a fantastic time, especially Richard."

Despite what he had found out in his studies, Henry now felt he had missed out, but said, "Never mind, I had a great time on the console, there really is nothing I couldn't inquire about and it's all very comprehensive."

"Nothing?" asked Geoff in a serious voice. "Is there no security at all, no data unavailable to unauthorised aliens?" Turning to Kirk, in a questioning manner he asked, "Is that right, Kirk that all of your data is available to anyone that can get onto your network anywhere within the system?"

"Well, yes," agreed Kirk, a little alarmed at the seriousness in Geoff's voice.

"We don't believe in keeping anything secret, we are as transparent as we can be in allowing everyone access to the databases."

"Bad mistake," said Geoff, "not from a transparency aspect, but do you really want your enemies to have access to everything you know?"

"Different question," said Kirk, "but no, and currently there is no way to stop anyone who can get onto our network from stealing the data we have."

"Not wishing to lecture an advanced race," smiled Geoff directly at Kirk, "the Sevens have already infiltrated your network, and I'm amazed that you haven't done anything to protect your vital data and yourselves. Just look at what the Sevens were able to learn, never mind what one of your dastardly enemies could do if they were intent on taking over this moon, or downloading all the important stuff you have, including any command sequences for launching battleships or missiles."

Kirk had gone visibly grey and frowned back at Geoff, "You are right, now why haven't we done something about it before now?"

"On Earth we have so many people trying to steal or corrupt data that a protection industry has evolved. First of all you have to categorise each stream of data. Following that you assign all users a logon name and password, and limit their access to what they need to know about. After that you will need to watch out for bugs introduced to corrupt data or destroy it."

"Here of course," said Kirk still looking unhappy, "we are not fighting against different groups, we are all one in terms of identity, so we've never had the need to develop sophisticated data protection, but I really do see what you are saying, Geoff, and I agree with you, now."

They walked up to Kirk's office, with Richard almost jumping up and down, telling Henry what a super place Sirisia was, and hoping he would notice how he was now moving, but for some reason Henry's mind was split between his own discoveries and tales of the dinosaurs, totally failing to cotton on to the differences in Richard.

Once in his office, Kirk came straight to the point. "We have to discuss your future. You have been here now for some weeks, having fun and learning about us, as we have been learning about you. It is possible that you could all stay here, and that would mean taking up a position in our army, although I fear you would not qualify for a very high profile role, and while you are fundamentally scientists we would have to fully retrain you for you to be productive here. Or we can take you back to where we found you, and to be honest that would be the best solution from my perspective."

They all went quiet, realising their great holiday was at an end.

"I would say going back home would be the best option," agreed Henry, "however, 'Comet' was in no shape to live in, and indeed was far from space-worthy last time I saw her."

"We have fixed those small issues, which is one reason we didn't have this conversation before, as the upgrades have only just been completed," said Kirk. "The plan is to avoid any unnecessary questions from your home base; we would put you in exactly the same position and trajectory as when we found you."

"Sounds reasonable," they all agreed, forgetting that they had been headed for almost certain oblivion.

Geoff added, "We have had an amazing time here, and for that I thank you sincerely, Kirk, but there is no place like home."

"I hope we can stay devoted good neighbours," said Henry.

"Absolutely!" Everyone in the room agreed together.

"Good," said Kirk, "the ship departs in 200 units' time." Then he repeated it in Sirisian. "Pudding, you had best get on board now, the ship departs in 200 units' time." Pudding dashed from the room to comply.

Kirk continued, "We have repaired the damage we did to the rock's airlock, and made some enhancements so that the next time we board you it won't mean we have to break in. Please get that airlock design used as standard in your ships and any new rocks you carve up in future. Someone laid an image of our dragon motif on the airlock to identify you as being under our protection.

"Super," said Henry.

"Not finished yet," said Kirk. "All of this and the VIP treatment was to make up for what happened and we truly hope this has been an experience you will treasure."

"You were fantastic, true friends," said Henry, "I for one will never forget this amazing experience."

Geoff piped in, saying, "I'm running out of superlatives to describe the incredible time we have had since you abducted us, and I'd just like to say that you can do it again any time you like. I won't offer any resistance."

"Yes," said Richard, "I personally cannot thank you enough. I am rejuvenated."

"Good to hear that," said a smiling Kirk. "Oh and if you bump into any ships from any other planet, you will get scanned. We've put an automatic response mechanism in so that the ship doing the scanning will get informed you are protected by Sirisia. It is a small red box in the comm's area, and it will save lives. It doesn't need any maintenance and a scan will trigger a response, you don't even have to touch it. We have left full details of how to replicate that, and full details of the enhanced airlock, in some drawings showing all the improvements I'm mentioning, plus a few surprises I will skip for now. Again, be useful to include the features in any new ships. There are half a dozen spare red boxes as well."

"You've more than made up for any trouble we had," said Geoff. "You are a most generous host. I hope one day we can return the favour."

"You are very welcome," said Kirk, "as innocent explorers you didn't deserve to get taken prisoner, so the enhancements I hope will make your trip back home a little easier. Besides, this gave the trainee fitters some training in retrograde technology, so it was useful." He smiled and they laughed. "Take a look at the new water creation system we have installed, it literally takes oxygen and hydrogen from the ether and constantly tops up your water tank. I'm not sure how you managed to capture such a small water comet, yet even with very effective filtering you were likely to be drinking too many heavy minerals." He paused to let that sink in.

"Fresh water, that will be nice," said Geoff, still wondering how much water was actually recycled.

Kirk continued, "Of course, if for any reason the water tank goes low your old system will kick in whereby any used water is cleansed and recycled."

Yuk, thought Geoff, *I knew it!*

"We've also introduced a better way to provide and use oxygen," said Kirk, "you will like it, and 'Comet' will smell fresher."

"Your people have been busy," said Henry.

"We like to keep our engineers active and give them challenges," Kirk said. "Oh, by the way those power jets that were fitted in different locations on the outside of 'Comet' were pretty useless, and didn't work anyway. If you were travelling at up to 200,000 miles per hour, as you were when we found you, they just wouldn't have slowed you down effectively. You'd have been the other side of the sun and back in the Oort Cloud before you came to a stop. We did some work on them and they are now fully efficient, more powerful, plus they use less fuel. We added a solution to stop the fuel freezing up as well, so you are literally all ready to go back to where you were picked up. Please, do tell your space design people to work out how to build a real spaceship. Asteroids really are for cave men." Laughter all round.

"Now," said Kirk, "one last thing in case I or some other officer ever comes to Earth, please write down your full names and addresses so we can find you."

They collected the small amount of souvenirs and clothes they had accumulated while in the Sirisian system and walked back through the doors below Kirk's office, onto the landing area where their ship was preparing to leave.

Kirk was there waiting to say goodbye, along with a group of officers that worked directly for him. "I have one final thing to say," he said, "excluding a final goodbye, and that is to congratulate Geoff for being awarded a medal for gallantry, in helping to defend Sirisia against the pirates of the Seventh Star system." He placed a metallic, colourfully engraved medal, around Geoff's neck and saluted him in the local tradition with a fist pushed towards the heart. The other officers gave him the same salute.

Geoff was choked. He'd never had an award for anything before, and could only smile like an idiot and gently fondle the engraved surface of the trophy he'd just received.

"With that you are awarded also the freedom of Sirisia, you will always be held in high esteem and that will give you the ability to travel and stay anywhere within our system."

For once words failed him, he could only mumble his thanks.

It was time to go, and they shook hands warmly, Earth style. They all thanked Kirk yet again and then reluctantly, they walked quickly across to the open door of the big battleship where the captain was waiting to take them on board. Turning around for one final look towards Kirk, they couldn't help laughing at the sight. Kirk had lined up the other officers to face towards the ship, all with a big smile on their faces, with their right foot raised off the ground and waving energetically with their right hands. William, Geoff, Richard, and Henry of course did the same, laughing at their own antics. Then they got on their ship, with Geoff thinking that Morecambe and Wise would have appreciated that little routine.

This time they had a VIP suite each on the ship, and were not asked to wear any brightly coloured jump suits. Henry had lots of time to continue to read the history of the local systems as well as exploring the ship which they all enjoyed doing. It had some amazing features, for example a room set aside for recreation where gravity was 40 per cent effective at the corners only. Two people used a short racket to hit a light ball into the centre point of the room where it had to stay there balanced for one time unit. Of course, if an opponent could reach the centre he could smash the ball away, which was not so easy in a messed up gravity field.

For the duration of the trip Pudding had been promoted to VIP liaison, so she was able to spend a lot of time with William, who kept mentioning the fact to the other three that our race was totally compatible with theirs.

Geoff never took off the medal, even when sleeping he kept it on.

The four were often on the bridge, watching how a real spaceship was run, and especially how navigation was performed. The first officer explained how pulsars are used to get the ship's position in space. All such stars have a signature that is recognized by the on board computer which effectively generates a three dimensional soft image of their location. Once the exact position is verified, the computer can determine the required direction for the specified destination.

The days passed quickly with so many exciting things going on. There was always a new food to try or a crewman to practice language skills on, but all good things must come to an end, and one day, after dinner, they were informed that after breakfast they would be leaving the ship. That night they slept well, too well perhaps. The lights had changed to a penetrating orange that made them feel heavy, and when they awoke feeling rather dopey, there was a musky aroma in the rooms, as though they were being fumigated. Right after breakfast, during which the four Earth men couldn't stop yawning, the captain escorted the crew of 'Comet' back to the hangar and into their personal asteroid. Once they were sealed up in 'Comet', the new airlock monitor signalled that it was airtight, confirming that it was properly closed. With some means nobody had explained, 'Comet' was ejected from the hold without anything touching it. After that, the ship adjusted position so that the bridge was level with 'Comet's' main observation window. They could see the captain and Pudding as well as some other friendly crewmen. They waved each other goodbye, and in two blinks of an eye the ship had moved up and away and was nowhere to be detected. They checked their cameras and just managed to see a large shadow fading away into the darkness of space.

Just to make sure everything was exactly the same as it was, more or less, the last thing that the big ship did before it became a vague shadow was to create a blast wind that accelerated 'Comet' to close on 200,000 miles per hour, the same speed 'Comet' had been travelling at towards the sun when boarded.

They had a good look around 'Comet', everything seemed to be functioning, and quickly checked over the enhancements Kirk had mentioned. The red box was sitting under a ledge in the comm's room, with the diagrams just above, on a shelf, but nobody had the energy to look too closely at anything.

Geoff summed it all up, "Ah well, looks like everything is back to what we might consider normal modus operandi, but that was one hell of an adventure!"

"Amen," said a happy, smiling Henry.

For some reason, nobody was able to concentrate on anything at all. Geoff was yawning away and announced, "I don't know about you but I can't stay awake. Unless I'm needed for something I will hit my bed."

The others agreed that they were in the same state and also went to their beds, sleeping for 14 hours and waking up with a ravenous hunger.

"Whose turn is it to make breakfast today?" asked Richard.

"I did it yesterday," said Geoff, "must be your turn, Richard." Richard went off to cook the bacon, while the others went into the comm's room.

"That was one heck of a deep sleep I had last night," admitted Henry, "first time for ages I didn't even dream."

Geoff and William agreed the same for themselves; they decided it was down to them having worked so hard lately, not to mention the stress at being blasted by that unknown broom.

"I've been meaning to ask you, Geoff," said Richard, "what is that plaque you wear around your neck, it looks very interesting, although I can't recall Dave ever wearing it?"

Geoff picked up the gong as though he'd never seen it before, and shook his head. "You know, I really don't know. Hadn't even noticed I was wearing it, and goodness knows where it came from." He removed it and placed it with other items of Dave's in their room.

"Looking around at the painting that we all did," said William, "it all looks a bit faded now."

"Just a little," agreed Geoff, "it's still far better than that dull grey, even if you can see some strands of broccoli and too many fruit pips."

"Perhaps we can improve on the paint formula," suggested Henry, "I for one would like to do some more."

Breakfast interrupted their thoughts on painting, and somehow it tasted wonderfully nice, yet different, as though they hadn't had it just about every day, forever, but they really, really enjoyed it.

Despite everything, the dull routine, being locked up together in a small space for so long, they were all remarkably jubilant, indeed quite happy. Even Richard, who often woke up grumpy due to his stiff neck, was adamant that he was feeling great and what a wonderful sleep he'd had.

"Strange," said Geoff, "I've sat here in this chair many times and it's like I'm seeing things for the first time. I don't recall seeing that small red box before. What does it do?"

"No idea," said Henry, "I've never touched it; Cambridge will have provided it for some reason." He looked at the activity log and started to make detailed plans for the day's activities. "We can try again at getting Cambridge a proper fix on our position, if we can work out the exact speed we are going."

Clearly they were still concerned about how their journey would end, now that they were travelling so fast, but as Henry said, "We carry on as normal, we are professionals after all."

"Any chance space aliens are behind all of this sweeping broom stuff?" queried William.

"Not a chance," said Henry, "we will work it out sooner or later, I'm sure, and it will be something logical like an unknown rogue planet. Besides, no evidence yet that aliens are out there. I will believe in them when I see one."

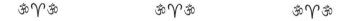

To everyone's horror, a Japanese amateur astronomer let it be known that there was a rather large comet heading in the direction of Earth. It was alone, certainly, which was odd in itself, suggesting something else was forcing a single comet to move, instead of the dozens they had been used to every few weeks. It would almost certainly wipe out more than one continent if it struck Earth, depending of course on where it landed. They had been unable to estimate when it would reach Earth due to the lack of clarity in the dusty images viewed. Different teams around the world took up that question to resolve, for it was almost certainly heading towards the only world inhabited by humans in this solar system.

Julie was just back from her daily rollicking with the boss and the PR guys, but for a change was in a good mood. "They were almost having a communal fit regarding this business of the sun going brown, but for a change they couldn't lay any blame with us. I interjected with, 'I'm not going to be a gobermouch, but shouldn't someone be taking this back to the zounderkite that first spread this idea around?'"

"Nice turn of phrase," said Mike.

"Yes, I prepared for that statement and spent half an hour online seeking out the appropriate descriptive words. Not sure they liked it much although it did create an effect. Poor old Jack Skinner from Client Relations really threw a tantrum. He couldn't even look at me. He stood up yelling something nobody could understand, and twittered on for a good 5 minutes about calming the situation. I swear his feet left the floor at least 10 times. He was wild. He yelled at Joe, his assistant, and told him to find out the source of this nonsense. For once the attention was off me. I made a suggestion to Samantha Gibbons that we should invite a friendly media hack in to show him the actual colour of the sun. She liked that and told me to get on with it."

"Cool," said Danny.

"I will start with someone I know at the *Daily Mail*. So, guys, we have to put together a convincing presentation showing the sun as it is. We can probably plug into a good telescope locally, the important thing is that we show that this is the sun now and it is still very yellow."

"OK," said Gary. "I'll schedule the use of an appropriate telescope."

"Good. Mike can you create an agenda for this presentation and start writing some slides, please? Doesn't need to be longer than 20 minutes. One thing we need to do is to emphasise what exactly a brown star is, and make sure they get it."

"You mean include some real science, like how brown stars still have their lithium while our sun used its supply up over 4 billion years ago? Or that a brown star can be detected as such by its own supply of lithium?"

"Yes, exactly," agreed Julie, "and add something about the temperature, brown stars are cool compared to our sun, 1,700 degrees Celsius as against 5,500."

"Indeed," said Mike, "molecules like methane or ammonia can only exist in objects cooler than real stars, so if a star contains these molecules, it can be classified as a brown dwarf."

"That's the idea," said Julie, "throw it all at them!"

ॐ♈ॐ   ॐ♈ॐ   ॐ♈ॐ

The solar wind had started to pick up some velocity once more and was beginning to blow patches of the metallic debris away from the Goldilocks zone towards the outer planets. If the particles kept moving they might end up in the Oort Cloud. Or again, with luck they could be collected by the gas giants and absorbed into their atmosphere. That wasn't an ideal scenario for most astronomers, as the implications for the planets and their moons were unknown, especially where some fragile unidentified life form just might be affected. Despite that, they had no way to affect it anyway.

Astronomers were happier that the space around the planet was becoming clearer, making observations that bit easier and more accurate. Everyone agreed this was a small step in the right direction, and that the sun was beginning to impose its control over the solar system, although it took a few weeks for the effects to start being truly noticeable.

As space became emptier of the dusty debris it was possible to see the constellations and much of the Milky Way again, and even the space in front of the moon looked like it had been thoroughly cleaned of the dust. Within 3 months NASA announced that it was all gone, no more of the instrument clogging dust remained within the Goldilocks zone, and it was also getting better for the outer planets.

Closer to home, in a radio interview, a Julie Banks from the British Astronomical Society announced that, "The space around the inner planets of the solar system was pretty much free of dust now, and it was expected that the whole solar system would end up the same pretty soon. Interestingly, many astronomers perceived the space to be a great deal cleaner than before the charged dust started to give them problems. Some reported that the space is so crystal clear that one can only assume that the purpose of the dust blown our way was a way for nature to clean up a little."

The brightest object in the sky now was not the moon, and it was soon realised that mankind had almost missed the sight of a lifetime as Betelgeuse came to the end of the main part of its life as a hot red giant. It shone a dozen times brighter than the moon and fascinated everyone for over 4 months until it finally got dimmer and shrank to its new life as a white dwarf.

With the metallic dust particles out of the way, the strength of the rays of the sun came back to normal, making for a much happier world population, save for concern of the last comet. All attention now was focused on the arrival of it, with many wondering how come it was some months behind the previous batch of comets. With so many uncertainties about its structure and final impact point everybody was making different estimates on potential damage. If the thing fell into an ocean we would certainly see enormous tsunamis that had the potential to drown whole continents, at the very least. If it hit a populated area it could destroy a lot more than several overgrown cities on impact. The collision itself could create a massive series of earthquakes, however, with so much of a comet's contents normally being dust and gas, many other problems could result. Dust thrown into the air could block sunlight and even pollute the air making breathing difficult. Such an impact has the ability to kill thousands initially killing many more as the weeks went by. So the speculations went.

There was a much talked about, big question mark, over the ability of the Russians to actually hit the comet, now on its way to us, as it came close to the outer atmosphere. That could just have been some Western prejudices creeping in, but the fact remained that it was technically challenging. Hitting a moving object shouldn't have made the task much harder, however, it was yet another parameter that had to be considered, and exploding the comet too low in the atmosphere could result in more problems as dust seeped into the stratosphere, with that causing a variety of problems related to weather and travel, as well as air pollution. Everyone crossed their fingers that when the time came the Americans would see off the comet, in the meantime they hoped that the Russians were getting in plenty of target practice.

ॐ♈ॐ   ॐ♈ॐ   ॐ♈ॐ

It was very hard to judge the speed at which they were travelling, but considering other data on comets that had made the same journey, it would take about 3 months to reach Jupiter. If the large planets didn't absorb them and they missed Mars and Earth, the chances are they would end up being swallowed by the sun. Not something Geoff wanted to consider, and he wondered if they could get the power jets working. If they could just slow the 'Comet' down, it might be possible to manoeuvre into a position close to Earth where *possibly,* they could be rescued from.

Geoff suggested this as an option to his colleagues but they just shook their heads as if he were mad. The jets had seized up almost as soon as they were installed, and the liquid fuel they needed was still frozen solid. Still, Geoff persisted, finally persuading the scientists to show him how it all was supposed to work so that he could at least see if he could fix it. For the next month and a half, with nothing better to do, Geoff fiddled and twisted this and that component attached to the jets, and eventually he reported that there was no physical reason why the jets shouldn't work. Even the fuel which had supposed to be frozen was flowing nicely. Henry took a fresh look and agreed that the jets should work. While everyone else thought about how to test the jets Geoff settled back to watch the Oort Cloud being left well behind.

While 1017 Kientsch had been drifting in its assigned pathway in the Oort Cloud, it had been relatively easy to communicate with the base at Cambridge, but now they were moving so quickly, the faster than light laser system was failing to connect to them from base. They could send messages to Earth because that had been plotted and the laser computer knew where to aim the very precise beam, they just didn't get much back. Very occasionally in their journey towards the sun they would catch a few words, generally making little sense, but they knew Cambridge was scanning the area for them, trying to fix the problem.

There was always the backup radio set, even if it meant messages took so long to reach them, although even that had been playing up lately, coming forth with more crackle than words. Real conversations were impossible at the distance they were from Earth via radio, and would be even after they did get much closer to home. What they did get however, was confirmation of their course, which would just avoid the outer planets and Mars. They were told that at their current speed they would hit the Earth on or close to March 12th.

As the sun grew to a larger speck, the radio stopped working completely. They still used the laser system to provide updates, and considered suggesting that it should be made public that people were inside the 'Comet' and that nobody should try to shoot it down, especially the Americans who had proved to be better shots than the Russians. After talking about it for a while, they wondered which death for them would be most painful, crashing to Earth as a fireball, wiped out by a nuclear missile or burning up as they fell into the sun? They decided not to ask, preferring to rely on the randominity of an unplanned death.

There was the option to use the space suits that were on board, which meant they had the option to eject themselves into space, although with a limited oxygen supply of a maximum 6 hours it was deemed they had just created another way to die. Rescue scenarios would be very limited for four people becoming dispersed in space, as they would not be easy to find, even tied together they would still make a very small target in the vastness of empty space.

~ CHAPTER 9 ~

~ SPACE ENGINEER ~

"So how are we going to test these jet thrusters?" Geoff wanted to know.

"You are correct to skip the question regarding should we test them," said Henry, "for we will need to confirm that they all work, and what effect they have, before we have to use them in anger, as to how, I would say very gently."

After some further discussion they agreed to give it a try.

"If all of the jets are turned on low for 2 seconds, at the same time, in theory this wouldn't alter our course too much," suggested Richard.

"Agreed," said Henry, "we really do not want to slow down the speed of passage just yet as there is still an incredibly long way to go and I for one would rather it all came to a fast resolution, whatever that was going to be."

Henry and Richard worked out a method to burn all jets at the same time and be able to measure any course deviation, as well as confirm that all jets were working properly. The test proceeded, and was deemed to have been a total success, with all jets working properly, and no perceptible change to their course. Geoff was told he was a great space engineer.

Henry had started on some calculations to determine how long the jets should fire for and which ones would turn the 'Comet' 180 degrees so that all the main jets would be facing towards the sun. As he said, "It would be silly to have the main jets pushing them forward when they lacked guidance and manoeuvrability, especially as they would be needed to slow 'Comet' down. To do them any good, the main jets had to be at the front."

Several days passed before he had anything concrete, then he had Richard check his figures very thoroughly. Another 3 days went by as discussion and clarification finally resulted in agreement. The laser communication was opened to Earth, to inform them of their plan, effectively to burn certain jets at one quarter capacity for 15 seconds to swing them around. After this they would use a different series of jets at one sixteenth capacity for 10 seconds to stabilise. They waited and waited, hoping Cambridge would confirm their calculations. Five days went by, slowly. Just as they were thinking of going ahead with the plan anyway, a short burst of words came over the laser link. Mostly it was words that didn't make sense, for the laser beam from Cambridge was still having difficulty locking on to them, but a distinct "YES" was heard, to smiles from all in the control centre of 1017 Kientsch. Richard sent another laser message, saying that they had received the "YES" and would be proceeding. In any case they waited for several hours just to see if a distinct "NO" might be forthcoming, which it wasn't.

Henry had William and Richard rehearse the intended plan twice, after which they did it for real.

"OK, let's give it some spin," said Henry.

The jets worked fine, except that they were a lot more powerful than expected, and Henry could see they would spin wildly if they kept the jets on for the full 15 seconds. After 5 seconds he had the first series of jets turned off, and also cut short the use of the second series to 3 seconds. This all worked better than anyone, especially Henry, had anticipated. Their back end was now heading directly towards the small yellow dot, and the observation window in the comm's room was showing the sensational view of the brilliance behind them.

"Thank you, Geoff," said Henry, "you not only got the jets working where three top scientists didn't have a clue, but you have made them so much more effective than they ever were. Very well done."

Geoff of course was very pleased to hear this. It validated him, making him feel useful and a part of the team.

The laser link direction finder to Cambridge automatically readjusted itself following the turnaround of the 'Comet', so they were quickly able to tell Cambridge that the manoeuvre had completed.

Henry said, "It would be good to know how this all looked to Cambridge and if anything has changed as a result, it's such a nuisance that the laser link is still dead from their side. I wish they could fix it."

"That's a real shame that we can't get anything realistic back from Earth," said Geoff. "Is there nothing we can do to make it easier for them to find us?"

"Not a lot," said Richard. "The actual synchronisation process took 3 days to complete when we first got down here, and for that we were pretty well motionless. It also helped that the ship we came down in could use its laser identification to help the link switch to 'Comet'. We had to be talking with Cambridge at the same time so that once the link had locked on we could confirm the status and get it completely registered on their mainframe."

That was when Geoff decided he would get the radio working, having had such success with the jets. Crawling under the bulkhead below the radio controls he searched for any unplugged cables or loose connections. Except for sleeping and eating, he was down there for 3 days, finally deciding that if it ever worked it was a mystery. Nothing was connected to the right thing as far as he could judge, and while there were components he didn't recognize, he assumed they were there to boost the signal. He took them all out, one by one to test them. All components were working fine and put back in place, but the radio was still dead. The only thing to do was to simplify the design. Geoff connected up all the basic components in one loop and turned on the power; the static nearly made them all jump out of their skins, in surprise. They had something. Geoff tried to dial into a number of bandwidths he knew and got nothing. Twiddling around with the frequency, he realised he had changed the way it operated, which meant, it was in reverse. Now he could calculate the bandwidths and try again. He heard a few words from his old ham-mate Ingor, and gave a loud "whoop" that woke up the two guys sleeping near the main consoles.

Now they could talk to Cambridge and get a response, even if it was with almost a two hour plus delay, but that was progress.

Having found Ingor's bandwidth, Geoff sent him a quick hello, and told him, "It's a bit complicated. I've been away; so far it will take a long time for your messages to reach me. Now on way home. Please send replies whenever you can. You are a lifeline."

That message would surely surprise and enthral Ingor, although it would be really nice to hear a familiar voice, once he replied, if he did get the message of course, and was able to reply.

Their journey had taken them well out of the Oort Cloud although it was not very obvious from looking out of the observation windows, even though Richard had mentioned that the density of comets in this area had lessened considerably. The next area of interest, that was indeed similar to the Oort Cloud in that it contained comets also, was the Kuiper Belt. It was different from the Oort Cloud because the comets were better behaved. They were on a similar plane to the inner planets and their trajectories were more stable.

Pluto, with its elliptical orbit, often travelled way out into the Kuiper Belt, and Geoff was keen to see this dwarf planet he'd heard so much about, especially with one moon almost as big as itself. He often sat in the rear, now the front observation window, trying to pick out the small planet, scanning the skies frequently, although it was some days before it was close enough to get a really good view of. It was within 6 million miles so the detail was magnificent from the on board telescopes, although much less so with the naked eye.

"What a sight," said Geoff to himself, and indeed it was. The small planet was mostly grey with a blue haze around its circumference. There were light and dark areas on the surface, as well as what seemed to be an orange patch near one pole. It has been described as having a snakeskin terrain, and it was easy to see why with the undulating surface and flowing ice sheets.

Just behind Pluto, in full view, was the moon Charon which really must have been an imposing sight from the surface of Pluto. Now this moon was something special, very dark red in places as though the many scars it had suffered had made it bleed. Geoff marked it down as one really battered twin, especially with its supersized grand canyon so much bigger than the one on Earth.

Looking out at the great expanse of open space helped Geoff expand his thoughts, away from himself, on to the marvels around him. It certainly increased his curiosity, making him more keen to discover new and fascinating sights, for it seemed that there was always something else to marvel at. One time he spotted a rock, not quite as big as 'Comet', far from any planet, travelling away from the sun.

"That must have been a comet on an elliptical orbit, having circled around the sun, it would have been going back out till it reached its aphelion, before coming back on a return trip," explained William.

When not gazing out of the large observation window, Geoff spent a lot of time getting different views of objects, near and far, using the equipment set up for that purpose. One monitor in the control room was used by all aboard to study the bodies of the solar system, and what was great about it was that it could switch from normal telescopic functions to the entire electromagnetic spectrum, including infrared. It was also possible to combine these to get a fuller image of whatever they were looking at. Any such image, no matter the subject, was always automatically recorded, processed by the mainframe and passed on to Cambridge for further analysis. Additionally a manual log was kept with specific details noting all sightings made. Geoff used this a lot to add in lesser detail for he knew he would never remember half of it when he finally made it back home. At least he felt convinced that he would somehow get home safely. He noted the names and some of the vital statistics of the other four Plutonian moons: NIX, HYDRA, STYX, and KERBEROS, "And what great names," he told himself.

ॐ ♈ ॐ   ॐ ♈ ॐ   ॐ ♈ ॐ

George Hanson was in his front garden picking up litter. It was not a job he enjoyed as it made his painful back ache worse and his legs quickly grew tired. The job was necessary on a too regular basis though, thanks to all the lazy individuals that walked by and threw their waste into this convenient place. The house was very unfortunately the first ideal place for dumping takeaway containers and wrappings, being just far enough away from the takeaways to allow the generally inebriated lazy souls, *(George used very different adjectives)*, to finish their late night snack and toss their garbage in.

George paused, straightened his back a little, looked up at the sky and wondered aloud, "Why me, what have I done to deserve this aggravation?"

Nobody was close enough to answer his question. There again, being pretty hard of hearing he wouldn't have heard it anyway. He looked up to the sky as if he was seeking an answer there, but what he was actually doing was looking to see if any comets were visible.

George and his wife Clara would have loved to have moved away, somewhere that litter wasn't a problem, where takeaways were a long bus ride away, and where no schools existed in the area. They kept playing the Lotto, but George was also wondering if a comet might help his dream along. If only a small one would land in his back garden and demolish some of the house so that it would need totally rebuilding, paid for by the insurance company of course. This would mean he wouldn't have to find the money to get new windows, replace the boiler and generally pay out a lot of money to make the house easily saleable.

Clara and George often discussed the options, and were not sure which would suit best, given the amount of clutter in the house. A comet would certainly help them avoid having to sort out and shift a lot of items of little value, on the other hand, a nice Lotto win would mean they would be able to afford a nice large bungalow in a good area, and they could pay someone to sort the clutter.

"Still," mumbled George to himself, "a nice little comet would cure a lot of problems, or even an alien spaceship. Now that would be something. I could sell it to the highest bidder. Now that could be very interesting!"

ॐ♈ॐ　　　　ॐ♈ॐ　　　　ॐ♈ॐ

With a lot of spare time on his hands, Geoff did a lot of thinking as well as watching the stars and the planets go by. He wondered how Thelma had taken it when they explained his spiritual self had been whisked away so far from Earth that he might never be seen again. They wouldn't have told her that though. They would have had a good story to reassure her, give her something to look forward to. He hoped she wasn't taking it badly.

Some months before he had been kidnapped, his daughter and small family had started off on a trip around the world. A low budget one which would see them mingle with local people much more than the tourists who went to the beach resorts, or stayed at the luxury hotels. It had to be a big challenge, and Geoff admired her for it, yet felt she was a little crazy for taking a brand new baby along. He could only wish her well and send his good thoughts that they had fun and didn't get into any trouble.

Pete, his older brother, would really chuckle when Geoff told him about his space adventures. His eyes would open wide, anticipating the story Geoff would tell, not sure at first if it was a wind up. When Geoff produced the evidence and it dawned on Pete that it was all real, he would laugh loudly and demand to know more. He was an inquisitive soul, just like Geoff, but had been born into an earlier decade. It had been interesting to see how things changed as the years had unfolded, growing up together. He recalled the sheer boredom of growing up in the 1960's. His father and mother both worked long hours to support the family and to give them a week's holiday in a caravan on the coast each summer. Then there was Christmas to look forward to. That excited feeling of having a pillow case full of presents sitting on the end of the bed on Christmas morning, was something special. In between there was little joy.

Birmingham was pretty dull though, especially Northfield, the suburb he grew up in. They had moved there, into a brand new council house, from a slum in the city centre, just as he was born, 2 days after, in fact. Birmingham as a whole, or in parts, lacked vitality somehow. He knew it, but Pete had said it many times as a lad growing up that life was pretty boring, not to say routine. It wasn't so hard, not really. Kids had plenty of free time away from grown-ups, and they used it well to discover places, play football in the road, build bonfires for Guy Fawkes Night, or just find a tree to climb or swing in. School homework was virtually unknown and Pete was a great brother, who would take Geoff exploring to different places, although he could never keep up and often got lost. It was a satisfying time though, finding things to do and making fun, often getting home just in time for tea, exhausted, and being told to, "Wash your hands before you come in here," by his mother.

Where the new council houses now sat had previously been farmland or open countryside, which meant the area hadn't been fully organised when they first moved in, and was so much better that way. A smelly pond, in a dip, in a wooded area was eventually "made safe" but until that time it had been an interesting part of the landscape. Eventually they made the open fields into a park, with long winding paths and a lot less trees to climb on.

The TV was also incredibly dreary, having only three channels and no handset to play with, or fight over, always there were so many chat shows on. "Yak yak yak," that's all they did. Saturday evening was better. The whole family sat around the box, snuggled up tight on the settee, watching some really funny shows. Pete would have been sent down the shops to get them all a few pennies' worth of sweets as a weekend treat. Magic.

Sunday night at 8pm was the Palladium show which always had too many acrobats and ballad singers on. Occasionally they would import a famous American comedian, well past their best before date; even so, they still did make us laugh.

The rest of the time they entertained themselves, even if it was only reading comics or scanning the patterns in the wallpaper, or drawing with chalk on the pavements outside the house.

Despite everything, that time had been remarkable as one where the rate of change in everyday life was significant. It seemed like life was coming out from behind a dark cloud. Gradually, even the music all changed. No longer were old crooners boring everyone to death with depressing custom-made melodies. They saw the birth of pop music and with that came such a feeling of hope for the future that was so deeply inspiring.

Financially, things certainly got better, there was more money about and the family even had a car. Dad had never passed his driving test although that didn't stop him driving the family to the coast a couple of years, still, whatever happened they always had to count the pennies.

Following the austerity of the war years and the country's long crawl back to economic health, many things started to look up and get better, with schools offering a fifth and sixth year for clever students. Even jobs were plentiful, with both parents changing theirs quite often. Geoff and Pete could even afford to go to the local swimming baths once a month or more irregularly, pay a trip to the cinema to watch a brand new film.

The underlying dullness in life was still there, yet people were more inclined to take little risks or do something different, for a bit of fun. Opportunities of all sorts opened up. Having left school just before his fifteenth birthday with no certificates to his name, Geoff took jobs that came to him. At that time he had no real interests or even much understanding of the world, didn't know what girls were for, not really, nor did he possess any self-determinism. Talk about a candle in the wind. Yet, surprisingly, one day he found an interest in computing, took a course and learned to program in basic, obtaining some certificates at the local college, followed by a job operating mainframe computer systems. One step at a time he advanced until he was elevated to mainframe storage. In between times, as his skills were portable, he got to see different countries and earned some good money, working in Germany, Belgium and even Saudi Arabia, while visiting many others in pursuing a career, before he ended up at CSC.

Now looking back on all of that, he wondered seriously how an idiot like himself had done so well for himself. How did an illiterate nobody, with no sense, make it so far? Perhaps others saw something in him that he didn't, or maybe even the others were just as dumb as him but acting the part so well. "Amazing fortune," he told himself, and here he was on an adventure so far-fetched, so utterly crazy, he just wouldn't have been able to imagine it to wish for it.

Henry and William came loudly into the comm's area, talking about the quantity of comets in the Kuiper Belt and whether 'Comet' would look like a real comet from Earth, "It would be really hard to judge, I'd say," concluded Henry.

This jarred Geoff back into present time, having been lost in his thoughts and imaginings, now it was time to check on Neptune as they were about level with its orbit, for they had travelled quickly through and out of the Kuiper Belt. He found a big beautiful blue planet about four times the size of Earth, just turning in its orbit towards the back of the sun, and while the hazy dust meant it lacked some clarity, it was still a sight to behold. The high winds and fluffy clouds of this ice giant were easy to pick out, although the rings were almost invisible. He found out, from Henry, that it is the methane in the atmosphere which gives Neptune the lovely blue appearance, as it absorbs red light.

After running out of fingers, Geoff found 14 moons around the blue planet. Triton, moon number one, stood out immediately due to it being so much larger than the other satellites of Neptune. He scanned the other 13, each being a little different, although none of them were exceptionally interesting to his layman's eyes. To him they were mostly odd shaped rocks with craters. He would leave it to the scientific world to make more of them.

Triton was a frozen world, spewing nitrogen ice and dust particles out from below its surface. Henry told him, "It is probably the coldest world in the solar system."

"Hang on," began Geoff with that question in his voice, "this moon is going the wrong way around the planet. How is that possible?"

"Correct and very possible," admitted Henry. "We don't know for sure why it is going the wrong way around the planet, but surmise that it was a free object at some time and got trapped by gravity, although gravity was unable to change its course."

"Hmm, oh," concluded Geoff, "some of these objects show no distress about doing things differently."

Geoff took a break from his scientific discoveries to get a coffee in the kitchen and met Richard there. Geoff told him what he'd seen, suggesting that moons were generally just large rocks.

"Mostly you are right," said Richard, "there are some amazing differences as you saw with Triton, its geysers and so on. As we get to Saturn, and Jupiter, you will see the effects that gravity has, and how a large body can squeeze a moon out of shape and make its very surface alter. Also of course, there will be some primitive life forms in frozen oceans, which are something we are keen to learn about."

"Now that sounds more interesting," agreed Geoff.

"By the way, have you been checking the speed of the satellites in orbit?"

"No, I thought those were all known and settled," replied Geoff.

"Yes, and no," said Richard. "It would be good to confirm accepted speed and distance to the planets, I'm also wondering if these huge blasts we have seen, one of which is blowing us to our doom, had any effects on any moons.

Have their rotation times changed, and are any likely to crash into any planet, or a passing asteroid?"

"I think I know how to do that," responded Geoff, "that will keep me busy and stop my mind wandering."

"Great," said Richard, "now let's have that coffee."

Over coffee, Geoff raised something he'd been meaning to ask about for a while. "Just to change the subject, I noticed that there are some really big cages in one of the rooms. They are empty, but I was curious to know what their purpose is, or was. Were you planning to hold prisoners, or were you hoping to find some real wildlife out here somewhere?"

"Nice question," laughed Richard. "I'm surprised we haven't filled you in on that as it is a big part of our story. There have been a lot of things going on haven't there?"

"Certainly has," said Geoff.

"Well," continued Richard, "yes, we did have animals in that cage. To be exact, we brought four tough looking gorillas along with us to do a special job, and they were perfect."

An urgent request from Henry for Richard to join him cut that conversation short, and left Geoff with even more wondering to do.

"What on Earth...?" He corrected himself, "What in the solar system would require a set of big apes to do at the edge of our known domain? Surely not as important a job as all that, even so, it must have been useful to go to all of that trouble."

Geoff decided that perhaps it was time he went to the gym. The guy whose body he was using would not be so happy to get it back flabby and really out of condition. He wondered how Dave, the other misplaced spirit, was doing with his decrepit old body, especially considering the lack of hearing. He was just hoping he wasn't sleeping with his wife, now that thought made Geoff really pedal a whole lot harder. He spent some time on the weights, after that he took a well needed shower, throwing his sweaty gym clothes into the washing machine. Actually, as he discovered, it was more than just a washer, it was a complete laundry. After the wash, the clothes were individually lifted out into a drying area and treated with hot air. Being in shape and hung as they would be worn, there was no need for ironing, well, not unless you planned to go somewhere special, like a nice restaurant. *Only problem being that any type of restaurant was pretty scarce in this part of the universe*, Geoff thought. They mostly wore a t-shirt and crease free trousers, so they didn't need anything fancy on a daily basis, just something functional. Geoff had been used to throw away paper tissues at home, for blowing his nose, but had to make do with linen handkerchiefs here as it would have been impossible to take too many paper ones along. These got laundered with everything else, quickly and without bother. Fortunately nobody had come down with a cold or flu, suggesting the internal air filtering and temperature controls were working fine.

He had a brief lay down on his gravity reduced bed. After a short rest he went back to the control room to get more data on the moons of Pluto. Pluto was a little way behind them now, and it would be interesting to see the mini system from a different perspective; interestingly enough, it seemed to be more active than before. He set about measuring the speed the moons were travelling around Pluto, as well as their mean distance from the parent planet. Comparing these figures against those in the database showed them to be reasonably accurate for distances out from the planet, except for the smallest moon, Kerberos. The four outer moons were all spinning a little faster making their trip around Pluto shorter, yet something really odd had affected Kerberos. Geoff took the measurements once more and had the mainframe recalculate the distance and speed again. There was no denying the fact that Kerberos now spun in the opposite direction and had moved further out from Pluto. He had Richard check his data, who was surprised, but he confirmed what Geoff had found. It seemed that Kerberos was in a different more elongated orbit around Pluto, now being outside and beyond the orbit of Hydra.

Kerberos was previously 36,660 miles from Pluto and taking just over 32 days to get around the binary Pluto and Chandra. Now it peaked at 73,320 miles from Pluto and was orbiting in 21 days.

Geoff took a break from his observations, all of those numbers made his head spin. Looking at the supposedly simple equations that Richard used to shortcut some calculations was like trying to read old German script, pretty well impossible. Time he collected his washing and put it away. Doing something mundane always helped to clear his head.

ॐ ♈ ॐ   ॐ ♈ ॐ   ॐ ♈ ॐ

The team were in a good mood for once, and were not averse to playing up Julie a little. Their analysis that showed the waves of comets was coming to an end, based on the lack of any debris moving out of the cloud for well over 12 weeks, was a high spot. The analysis had gone around the world and provoked agreement from all concerned. As Julie came in Mike started to sing, "Oh, don't let the sun go brown, don't let the..."

"What," snapped Julie, "who dares to sing that most perverse song?" They all went quiet.

Julie picked up the papers she was seeking, saying, "Let's not get too excited that all the danger is behind us. I've just had a brief discussion with ESA in Germany. It looks like moons are being affected now. I will know more after this conference call." With that she left the room, and immediately they all started humming that perverse song.

"I heard that," yelled Julie, "no overtime for a month," she joked.

She returned 30 minutes later looking concerned and deep in thought. "Several teams are working on this, although we need to do our bit as well. I should be getting the live data soon; in the meantime can we focus on Pluto please. Get the latest all spectrum analysis and do a check on changes to the moons of Pluto. Kerberos in particular."

Their work soon resulted in an image of the large comet they had been tracking, with the moons of Pluto some way behind it. "They have clearly got faster in their orbits, but that shouldn't be too worrying," said Gary.

"But look at Kerberos," warned Mike, "it has got a whole lot faster and it now has a very extended elliptical retrograde orbit. I fear some sort of collision."

They took some more readings and did the analysis on those. "Mein Got," declared Julie, "the smallest moon seems to have broken orbit and is heading straight for the comet. Now that is the best news I've had for a long time. It's a small moon at around 7 miles, but the comet is much smaller. We just might yet see that collision, Mike, and I wouldn't want to be that comet."

"Amen," said Mike.

"Hang on a bit, I don't want to burst any bubbles," said Gary, "if Kerberos, which is a damned sight bigger than the comet, is following this comet, won't that mean it will also impact on the Earth?"

Julie agrees, "Yes, although we have to see what happens with this collision. It could alter everything."

ॐ ♈ ॐ   ॐ ♈ ॐ   ॐ ♈ ॐ

"Geoff, how long ago did you take your last readings of Kerberos?" asked Richard.

"About 8 hours ago," was the reply, "time for another one I guess?"

"Yes," said Richard, "I'll do this one with you."

Two hours later they had the results, and more. "Henry and William," shouted Richard, "you need to come and see this."

After Henry and William had gotten seated in the control room Richard continued. "Kerberos has broken orbit as a result of the push. Pluto's other small moons have increased their orbital speed, although that doesn't seem to pose the direct threat that Kerberos does."

"What kind of a threat?" said the worried voice of Henry.

"The moon is headed in our direction and seems to be on the same trajectory as us."

"So it poses another bigger threat to Earth?" suggested Henry.

"Yes, but it gets worse," sighed Richard. "It poses a direct threat to us here in the 'Comet', due to the speed it is travelling at. We are moving at nearly 200,000 miles per hour. Kerberos has topped that and approaches us at 205,000 miles per hour. That gives us about 67 hours and 20 minutes to get out of the way or get smashed."

"Being hit by a huge solid moon like this at 5,000 MPH would be the death of us all," said Henry. "Let's do another observation to verify all of that, and repeat it every hour, just the important statistics including speed and trajectory."

Further analysis validated the details Richard had provided, and confirmed how long they had to do something.

It was possible Cambridge already knew about their predicament, they sent a laser message anyway, despite not expecting a real response as their link had still not latched on to the 'Comet'.

The only tool they had that would be any use at all was the jets which were now working thanks to Geoff. They all retreated into the working office where a myriad of scientific equipment was performing different tests. A big blackboard was used to scribble ideas on, while a white board listed the priorities of any actions performed.

PRIORITIES
SAVE THE COMET;
DEFLECT MOON AWAY FROM EARTH TRAJECTORY;
AVOID ANY REPERCUSSIONS.

After much discussion, blind alleyways and far too many cups of coffee, they ended up with a list of nearly credible options:

OPTIONS
USE JETS TO SPEED UP COMET SO ANY IMPACT WOULD BE LESS SEVERE;
POSITION COMET TO BLOW JETS AGAINST THE BULBOUS HEAD OF KERBEROS TO MAKE IT CHANGE ITS HEADING OR TO SPIN IT A LITTLE;
ALLOW MOON TO CATCH UP, USE JETS TO SLOW ITS APPROACH, ALLOW MOON TO PUSH COMET ONWARDS. ONCE WITHIN RANGE OF SATURN, MANOUVER COMET TO ONE EDGE OF MOON AND PUSH TOWARDS SATURN WITH JETS;
DO NOTHING AND SEE WHAT ELSE HAPPENED.

"Right," said Henry, "we need to start exploring the calculations to see if any of this is feasible. William please look at how we would use the gas pedal to equal the speed of the moon. Richard, if you can concentrate on the shape of the head of Kerberos, and where we would have to push from, I will do some work on trajectories. Geoff, keep feeding us the observational data on Kerberos, every hour."

While their deliberations had been going on, Cambridge had responded on the radio channel. They had seen all the data on the migrating moon, and asked that all updates be sent as soon as possible. Richard responded via the laser link, telling them what had been discussed and decided, saying he would welcome any further input from them.

~ CHAPTER 10 ~

~ KERBEROS ~

"Julie," yelled Gary, "where were you? The boss has been down three times to look for you."

"Another conference call," was the response. "What did that grumpy old so and so want this time?"

"Oh, he was in a good mood, we didn't tell him yet about that moon, he said something about going on a jolly to Frankfurt."

"Oh, that means a weekend away, while he plays politics and I get dragged in to talk dirty about comets and stuff," said Julie. "I'll pop up and see him shortly, but just to fill you in. Our observations and analysis agrees with what ESA and NASA found, and it truly is amazing. I will repeat it so I can get my head around it all because yours truly has to put out a report on this."

"Lucky girl," smirked Mike.

"OK, so we had the situation where the 8 mile long moon was chasing a comet of about a quarter of a mile. The moon, for unknown reasons, I might leave this out, took a lot longer than expected to catch the comet. It had been going a lot faster than the comet, oddly, the closer they came together, the more the speeds equalised. They ended up physically touching each other, with no damage perceived. As it stands, the pair has just crossed the Uranus orbit, still travelling together, and both due to smash in to Earth as previously indicated. One possible reason for the objects not crashing into each other is that both are charged magnetically, but that doesn't explain why they are still so close together. There certainly is something odd about this comet, nothing adds up, not the composition of it nor the mass. I'm sure it still has a few more surprises for us."

ॐ ♈ ॐ   ॐ ♈ ॐ   ॐ ♈ ॐ

"Hello, 'Comet', this is Cambridge," said Cambridge on the reserved radio frequency. "Only one suggestion regarding your attempt to change the direction Kerberos is headed. Do it from the top elevation. If you try to push it from the side facing the sun, it will come back and hit you hard."

William was sitting with Geoff as they came up to the orbit of Uranus. "It is," said William, "very important that we fully check all satellites as we move through the solar system, and review the systems behind us, in particular we have to take a backward look at Neptune's moons to make sure they are behaving themselves. More surprises would not be good for the heart."

They set about working out the distance each was away from the planet. After that they verified the orbital speed. Neptune had 14 moons, and they were all behaving well within normal parameters.

"It was fortunate that Neptune had been well out of the blast area," suggested Geoff, "so with luck it will be unaffected."

"Agreed," said William, "and the same thing should apply to the next gas giant. Uranus is the next planet in the grand order of things, and pretty close at only 70 million miles."

This world was a lighter blue than Neptune, and had a lot more moons, 27 in total, none as big as Triton. Even over the course of several days it was not easy to pick out the thinly populated rings of dust, ice and rocks around Uranus. After working through each moon in turn they concluded that the blast had had no effect on the speed or otherwise of Uranus's moons.

The thruster jets had been turned off as soon as 'Comet' had been touched by Kerberos, to save fuel, as there was no reason to keep them on once the two bodies had more or less stabilised their relationship. It wasn't so much a touch when they met, more like a railway wagon being shunted along the line, not a bone breaking jar, but not far off.

"Doesn't look like we suffered any damage," said Henry, after they'd checked every possible area for cracks. Just occasionally the moon would scrape against 'Comet' and they would hear that wherever they were within their little ship. There were vibrations that seemed to carry on for long moments, with occasional quiet spells; for sure Kerberos was making its presence known.

Henry had everyone constantly on guard to look out for any cracks or holes that might appear in the walls of 'Comet', which although they were pretty thick were also brittle. Any damage to the integrity of 'Comet's' structure could seriously impact on their survival.

"I've realised," said Richard, "that one thing 'Comet' lacks is a warning system to alert us if the structure was under pressure. That will need to go down on the wish list as a priority when 'Comet' is upgraded, refurbished, and made even better."

"Along with a proper coat of paint," laughed William.

Nothing untoward was happening in the Neptunium or Uranian systems, so they relaxed a notch, instead concentrating on checking the formulae and constantly going over their options in dealing with the large moon badly tailgating them.

Richard joined Geoff in the control room and asked what he was searching for so intently. "Just looking over the deep scars and gouges on Miranda, one of the 27 moons of Uranus. It was almost like someone had taken a ball of clay and scraped lines here and there, smoothed out some parts, before finally using a comb to gouge some stripes. A fascinating moon though, which must have quite a history, if only it could be traced back. It would be easy to imagine these moons as the backdrop to a real live space opera adventure, getting shot at, with ships crashing into them. You see that little series of lines? That would be where a ship came in and skidded, until hitting that dark shaped mountain side and exploding. Can't you just see Luke Skywalker flying his small ship between the peaks at the bottom and making that ear shaking zoom?"

"Not just solid rock of no real interest, eh?" smiled Richard, rubbing his tired eyes. "Gosh, I'm ready for some R and R."

"Fancy a coffee," offered Geoff, "or maybe a bacon sandwich?"

"If you're offering I'll take both," pleaded Richard.

"OK," said Geoff, "take a rest. I will shout when it's ready, or you will probably smell it." Geoff realised that the other two would come running as soon as the smell of bacon cooking permeated their awareness, so he made enough for four and a little extra. The toast always took the longest being deeply frozen, so he had to time it all properly so that the breakfast was ready as a single unit. He'd warmed and buttered the toast, and was just pouring the coffees, when all three men appeared hopefully, at the entrance to the kitchen.

They were not disappointed; Geoff made great bacon sandwiches, even in the depths of space.

After each man had taken several satisfying bites, Geoff decided it was time to learn about the gorillas. "I was asking Richard about the cages in the far room, and he started to talk about gorillas before we got into this issue with that ex-moon of Pluto. Were there really gorillas inside 'Comet'?"

"There were indeed gorillas on board," managed Henry between mouthfuls. "I'm surprised we haven't told you all about it, you know most of everything else I'd say."

"Indeed," agreed Richard, "you can't keep secrets from Geoff, but perhaps we should start a little earlier in our tale than what we did with the gorillas, for there was a whole bunch of thinking that went into this project. They called it Project BACKDOOR. Don't ask me why, Henry might know the background. Initially for us this project consisted of a lot of physical and technical training. They got us very fit and made sure we could operate the equipment. Clearly they skimped where the mainframe was concerned, but we did get a good grounding on everything else and what was expected of us." He took another long anticipated bite.

Henry continued, "OK, so a rocket left Earth, with four scientists, four gorillas, a three man rocket ship crew, and Donald."

"This is beginning to sound like one of those famous jokes about three men, one Irish, one English, and one Scottish," suggested Geoff.

"It may sound funny," interrupted Henry, "but it's no joke, and I'm not sure we can find a punchline to satisfy you. Anyway, Donald was a specialist, he looked after the gorillas, he was also an expert in several fields, including rock carving. I'm told that he was well known as a sculptor, as well having other artistic skills to his name."

"A shame he couldn't have done some painting in 'Comet', or left us with some works of art," suggested Geoff.

A swig of coffee and a smile from Henry, then he continued. "The first thing we had to do was to get hold of an asteroid that we could use as a base in the Oort Cloud. It had to be solid enough that we could carve up the inside, structurally sound, but not so big that it would be difficult to move. Several rocks had been selected as suitable by Cambridge from the asteroid belt, from just beyond Mars. We did some further mass analysis before selecting this one."

"That's when things got more interesting," added William. "The rock had to be attached to the rocket so that it didn't move about, slow the rocket down or make it wobble. A big rubberised hatch on the side of the rocket had been put there to allow easy access to the rock, and this became the comet's airlock, and where the carving out started."

"First," continued Henry, "we had to get the gorillas ready to do the work of carving out the rock's inside. Cambridge had already done a lot of work to find the best way to do this in zero gravity, and they found that the bodies of gorillas were best suited for this type of activity. Now you can train animals to do most things, but even with a good trainer, expecting an animal to follow a plan or dig out a specific area is just asking too much. That's when they came up with the idea of transferring human souls into gorilla bodies."

"So you used the thing that brought me here, to swap gorilla souls with human ones?" guessed Geoff.

"That's about it," agreed William.

"Except of course," went on Henry, "getting an animal to sit still in a chair while you do a personality swap is one heck of a lesson in animal behaviour. Donald struggled; we all struggled, even though the beasts were reasonably tame and otherwise friendly. We enticed them with fruit, smells, anything we could think of. We had no choice, we had to drug them to sleep, just enough to fall asleep. After that we were able to strap them in securely with even stronger bonds than we used with you and Dave."

"Gosh," murmured Geoff, "that must have been great fun."

"Errrmmm, no," said Richard.

"So what was it that made them so suited to this task of carving out 'Comet'? Was it worth it in the end, when men could have done the job just as well?" asked Geoff.

"As mentioned, it was mainly their agility and balance that made them most suited to the task," said Richard. "If you can also imagine how hard this rock is, it would have taken a man a whole lot longer to make the same progress as a gorilla, as they are much stronger than humans, with the added bonus that they are able to work for longer periods. Still, it took them months to carve out all the basic shapes and rooms."

"It was all time well spent," mentioned Henry. "It filled in the trip nicely, as it took about 8 months before we reached our target."

"You mentioned before that you were ready to install gravity as soon as you got to where you were going in the Oort Cloud. Did that make life easier and how did the gorillas react to the change?"

"Much easier," said William, "and the animals took it in their stride. Donald and his four guys completed everything they had to do, they did the personality swap in reverse, caged the gorillas again within the ship, and they all went back home leaving us four to live and work in the depths of space."

"There is a bit more to that, as well," interrupted Richard, "and this could be the punchline you might enjoy."

"Oh yes," said William, smiling. "We hadn't known it, but the smallest gorilla turned out to be a female, and it was following the transfer that Donald noticed she was pregnant. It could only have happened while the apes were carving up our little ship, so that will have been one surprised monkey when she got her body back."

"Dirty little devils," laughed Geoff.

"Ah ah," agreed Richard, "and that would explain all that noise and yelping during their rest periods. Could be they were all at it. Basic animal behaviour will prevail I guess."

They all laughed and finished off their coffee. "Time we got back to work," said Henry, "and no, that was not a pregnant pause." They laughed some more as they made their way back to plough on with what they needed to do.

Geoff sat back in his chair in the comm's area and proceeded to check again on the moons of Uranus. He would wait a few days before seeing what state the moons of Saturn were in as it was still some weeks' distance away. The Uranian system was still stable so he looked back at Pluto. Charon and Pluto were still doing their own little dance together in the usual fashion and within normal criteria. The other three moons had gotten a little faster in their orbits, which he mentioned to Henry, however when shown the specifics Henry suggested that it was not a problem, asking Geoff to do occasional checks to look for any big change.

ॐ ♈ ॐ　　　　ॐ ♈ ॐ　　　　ॐ ♈ ॐ

"Mike," Julie called out, "have we got the latest news on our comet, where it is and is it still attached to Kerberos?"

"Sent you an email update 5 minutes ago," replied Mike.

"OK," said Julie, searching through her huge email inbox. "Got it. So basically no change and about 3 weeks away from Saturn? Good, OK, thanks."

ॐ ♈ ॐ　　　　ॐ ♈ ॐ　　　　ॐ ♈ ॐ

Geoff stared out of the rear observation window at what was now the front, in terms of direction. The stars were bright as always, and the speck of a sun had grown to a slightly bigger speck over the last couple of months. He looked forward to seeing it grow, week by week.

There was still no change to the laser link from Cambridge. It was still not connecting. "It would be risky to do a transfer of him back to Earth considering the speed we are travelling," Henry mentioned one day, so it seemed like Geoff's fate was tied up with the other three guys in the 'Comet'.

Staring out at the space before him, Geoff allowed his mind to wander, back to earlier times, when hope for the future was the driving force that kept him going, day to day. It must have been late summer, one year, when it became dark by ten pm and the stars came out. With his friend Tony, they would linger around the side of his house, talking about things that interested teenagers, looking up at the wonderful view above, seeking shooting stars, often confusing an airline for a small meteorite burning up. Talking about aliens and spaceships. It was all so exciting to talk about such things, never imagining one day he would be up there, travelling faster and further than he could ever have imagined possible. One of their favourite thoughts went something like, "Just imagine, up there, somewhere, there are two girls looking back at us, wondering if there were two guys looking towards them..." as they scanned the heavens for inspiration.

Geoff moved back to the comm's room to chat with the others, but nobody was there. Still feeling nostalgic, his inward looking thoughts were disturbed as a shadow came across the window, blocking out a whole section of the Milky Way. In a degree of shock, he shouted as loudly as he could, "Hey, guys, quick, something is happening and I don't like it."

He could only imagine that the tailgating moon had started to roll across the front of 'Comet', and that would surely foretell disaster of some kind. Kerberos was more than big enough to mince the little 'Comet'; although even a little bump could crack open a wall and leave them exposed to the vacuum of space.

William was first to arrive, followed by the other two breathing hard. They immediately saw the shadow and came to the same conclusion as Geoff. They started to check their instruments to see how Kerberos had shifted. The groans and vibrations seemed to be the same, so they started to check for any damage to 'Comet'. Was it being crushed? That would certainly account for the shadow, no, they found no evidence that 'Comet' had suffered any damage, and the instruments showed only the normal relationship with the moon. So something else was going on. They scanned the areas all around their space to find out if perhaps some other moon was approaching them from a different direction. They found something, less than a few hundred feet away. Something quite huge was cutting off the starlight and leaving them in shade. If it was another space object, it was currently matching their speed which would be unusual for something that had seemingly crept up on them. The readings that came back from the instruments did not readily identify it as anything known. Light and other rays seemed to be absorbed by it, and that was the craziest thing Henry had ever seen, but they kept on probing, hoping to get a better clue. Without warning a light turned on at the red box under the little counter. Henry raised his eyebrows at this. "What the hell does that mean?"

Nothing happened for a while, except that the four men looked at each other, just wondering, unwilling to accept what this might mean. The red light went out and gradually a few stars showed to one side where the blackness had been. It had been still, compared to them, but now, whatever it was, was gently sliding to one side, gradually moving faster away from them. Suddenly, the shadow was all the way gone, having shifted very quickly away towards the edge of the solar system. They kept every possible instrument tuned to the shadow until they could no longer find it. At least the recordings would show they were not going collectively insane.

Henry was very calm under the circumstances, "Gentlemen, I do believe that was a close encounter of the second kind. I would count the recordings as scorch marks."

Nobody said anything for some time, they were open mouthed and still wondering if what they saw was actually what they thought they saw.

"William," said Henry, "please let base know that we had an unusual incident occur, and ask them to confirm what they think it might have been. Let's be diplomatic on this, for now."

Later, as he lay in his bed Geoff couldn't stop thinking about this shadow. If that had been an alien spaceship, they surely would have had advanced equipment to probe and analyse the solid little 'Comet'. They would know all about them, but would lack any concept of what they were doing or why. Almost certainly, they would be puzzled as to why a carved out rock was able to travel so fast and be in this empty part of the solar system. He could just imagine the captain reporting in to his senior when they got back. "Saw the most amazing thing on the way back. Never in all my days have I been so perplexed with those people that come from the third planet in the ZOT13 system. Never do they seem to do anything in a logical or normal fashion, and I'm only assuming it was them because this was most illogical. Can you imagine, there were people living inside an asteroid, not going out to explore, they were heading home? Now you will laugh. Behind them, pushing them back towards their sun was an even bigger asteroid. It was driving the smaller one. It could have crushed them at any stage; maybe they had some way to control it. Still, it was very, very, odd. Why do they do such things in the most complex way possible? Why don't they build a spaceship like normal beings?" Geoff laughed quietly to himself before dropping off to a deep sleep, dreaming of whizzing through the Milky Way looking for intelligent life.

The view of Saturn came soon enough. It was hard to miss as they seemed to be going directly towards it. The dot grew into a bigger darker dot, with the rings adding some dimension to it until they could just pick out some detail with the naked eye. The main telescope had been used of course to get a complete view of this gas giant, now with its rings edge on to them.

With 62 moons Geoff was kept pretty busy trying to find out if any had changed position or orbital speed. So far all were within normal range, although with some elliptical orbits that wasn't easy to judge. However, there had been nothing odd about any part of the Saturnian system that would cause him to raise an alert with Henry or Richard.

Titan was a wonder to behold. It was bigger than Earth's moon, also bigger than the planet Mercury. Geoff decided it would make an ideal companion to Earth if it could be towed to a position just opposite his planet and made to orbit. Now that was an interesting proposition, even if he had no idea whether life, as we know it, could thrive there or even if the atmosphere would or could be made to develop like Earth's. He would of course need superpowers to pull that one off, and his mind immediately started to wander off again, to days gone by, when as a very young teenager he would spend time browsing the new DC comics in the local paper shop. Such excitement as he read the cover, taking in the colourful artwork, escaping his dull existence while trying to pick one of that month's selection to buy for a shilling. Those naïve yet fascinating superhero comics had coloured his imagination, like so many other teenagers, it had also inspired him to want better things and more happy experiences.

"Titan certainly has a thick atmosphere," he told William. "Overall, it has a featureless orange glow and it looks quite volatile, with some fluffy areas that could pass for cloud." He spent a long time observing this satellite, in different ways, and would certainly recognize it again from all the other moons he had seen so far.

Another interesting moon was Pan, shaped like a walnut, a rather odd shape for a moon, Geoff conceded, and at only 14 miles across it was a baby compared to the others. Atlas was a similar shape to Pan except that the flattened part of the edge was wider. So they both must have had a similar history, but how they were formed was a complete mystery.

Generally, the moons of Saturn were somewhat chaotic to Geoff, some having a relationship to other moons, influencing them with gravity as Saturn did in its turn with all the satellites. The rings also featured in this relationship, but were not as fixed or as solid as Geoff had imagined they would be.

According to the database, there were four major ring groupings, and three lesser, narrower ones, although they were less easy to identify than the moons that often were inside a ring. After observing that the rings were made up mainly of ice and very small pieces of matter, or dust particles, not unlike comets, he lost some interest even though they were a spectacular sight; instead he started studying the planet itself.

"Saturn, the star of the solar system, the most attractive looking planet with a touch of romanticism attached to it. The planet everyone wanted to observe," said Geoff to nobody in particular. He checked the statistics, and they informed him that the planet turns on its axis once every 10 hours and 34 minutes.

Snappy, thought Geoff.

He could see, by selecting different images with the various instrumentation, how the upper atmosphere of Saturn is divided into bands of ammonia clouds, and below that largely water ice, below that are layers of cold hydrogen and sulphur ice mixtures. At the north pole he spotted what was said to be a hurricane-like storm, and although the outside is pretty chilly by Earth standards, the effective temperature of the planet is a frigid -178 degrees Celsius, while the core of the planet is hot, up to 11,640 Celsius.

Geoff was still staring at the colourful planet, showing mainly a beautiful pale yellow atmosphere with hints of orange, when the others came into the comm's area, at a bit of a rush.

"Right," said Henry, "the time is upon us. Let's put our plan into operation."

Geoff took a back seat while Henry read out the plan, line by line, with Richard or William executing it, line by line.

Without breaking impulse contact with the moon, they used the jets to slide 'Comet' very slowly, and very gently, up towards the roof of Kerberos. They stabilised that position, holding it and checking, rechecking that they were in the correct spot. Henry confirmed the distance now to Saturn, and it was within the window they needed for gravity to give them a helping hand. It was time to break away.

The line was read and the commands executed, and 'Comet' rose just a fraction above the long moon. Just as though it seemed that the moon would rush ahead, knocking 'Comet' for six as it went, Henry gave the details required to push the moon sideways and down into the gravity well of the huge planet. The jets were turned on at 100 per cent capacity to thrust the moon away from 'Comet' and downwards. The one fear, despite many calculations done on the concept, was that the moon would wobble or bounce back and hit 'Comet' with a great wallop. So far the push was working and the distance between both rocks was gradually getting wider.

They kept the thrusters working hard for what seemed like a short eternity, driving themselves and the moon ever closer to the planet. All the time Richard was watching the impact gravity was having. If they turned off the jets too early they would really get a good thump from Kerberos. They held their collective nerves until Richard announced that the moon was now in the pull of Saturn. Just to be sure of their own safety they performed an up and forward manoeuvre to guarantee they wouldn't be caught in any adverse reactions from Kerberos. All the jet power available was utilised to move them away from the clutches of this giant gas planet, and fortunately the jets were strong enough.

The moon was still travelling at high speed, and at first it looked like it was going to sail past Saturn and continue on towards the sun, albeit at a slightly different angle to them now. The calculations had been pretty accurate though, for Kerberos performed as expected, suddenly dipping in towards the equator of the planet. It would take some time for it to disappear into the depths of the planet, JWST-2, if it were turned this way would surely get a great view of it all. They too of course would follow the progress of this troublesome little moon. It was too soon to congratulate each other on the execution of the plan, for the moon could still start to spin and perform a bounce away from Saturn, however, they were hopeful they had averted an Earthly disaster, as well as stopping 'Comet' from getting smashed up.

They continued to monitor the moon until it hit an outer ring, driving a blank wedge through the icy debris, but that wouldn't remain for long. The rings were used to disruptions, and would soon form back to their usual pattern. Kerberos surprised everyone by appearing to twist and bounce in the middle atmosphere, before travelling back up above the outer ring, although its speed was slowing all the time. Its angle of travel was away from 'Comet', although it was difficult to guess where it would end up. It could bounce a few more times before settling down into one final fateful dive. They followed its progress until it hit the curve of Saturn and went behind it, their expectations being that it would drop towards the planet, before getting around Saturn, as so many earlier comets had done, to end their days.

ॐ ♈ ॐ   ॐ ♈ ॐ   ॐ ♈ ॐ

"Morning, Mike, you're in early," greeted Julie.

"Yes," said Mike, "I had my suspicions about what was happening with our comet, wanted to check it all out, and I was right. You will really want to see this. Make sure you are sitting down, and drink that coffee first."

What Julie saw was enough to make her almost speechless for the rest of the day. They watched a montage of images that JWST-2 had made earlier, enhanced with some spectral analysis. It wasn't crystal clear yet due to some dust that still lingered close to the big planets, although, it was clear enough.

They saw the moon, initially still pushing the comet towards them, then separation took place, with the gap in between the objects slowly getting wider, for no obvious reason. The moon went one way, towards Saturn, while the comet just continued on its course, as though nothing unusual had been happening, and that their parting had been by mutual agreement.

"But," spluttered Julie. "How did they separate just like that? It can't have been the influence of Saturn. They just upped and moved away from each other. This has got to involve intelligent life, somehow, somewhere."

Mike quipped, "I hope you're not suggesting that either the comet or our friendly moon have become sentient?"

"No, don't be so silly," Julie hit back. "What I'm saying is that this split took place because intelligence was behind it. That was no accident. Perhaps it was the hand of God involved again; he does seem to be quite active these days."

They watched on for some time, saw how the moon smashed through the top group of rings, and just as it seemed like the moon would disappear into the belly of the gas giant, it bounced around a bit, straightened up, and eventually followed a course almost in the opposite direction, working its way around the back of Saturn. That was all they saw of Kerberos that day. They both came in early the next day, a Saturday, to see what JWST-2 had picked up. There was no sign of the moon. Julie had been half expecting, half hoping that Saturn would capture itself another moon, it seemed that this wasn't to be. It looked like the adventure for Kerberos had ended in the depths of Saturn. Yet somehow Julie wasn't satisfied with that result, and went back to pick up from where the moon had moved behind Saturn, although she found nothing.

Each day Mike monitored the progress of the comet and scanned Saturn just in case Kerberos had gotten itself into some strange orbit. However, there was no sign, not until the twelfth day when he noticed a smudge moving across the surface of Titan. He watched with disbelief, confirmed his findings, letting out a very loud laugh that disturbed everyone.

"Now this has just made my week," he told everyone. "You know that moon that was pushing our comet before it fell towards Saturn?"

"Or was it pushed?" questioned Gary.

"Anyway," Mike continued, "we thought we'd lost it. It seemed to fall into Saturn, bounced around a bit in the atmosphere, and then we couldn't find it. But guess what I've just found?" He didn't wait for a response. "No, Saturn doesn't have a new moon, which is what we would have liked to see as the end result. We have something far more spectacular. The moon Titan now has a moon of its own. Now that is what I call stupendous!"

Julie of course wanted to see it with her own eyes. She did, eyes almost popping out at the way this had unfolded, after which she told the world. "There was no guarantee that this would be a stable relationship," she said, "for Saturn and the other moons of Saturn could so easily disrupt it. We will watch, wait and see."

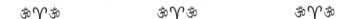

'Comet' just kept on going as though all the excitement about Kerberos was somehow below it. The occupants were in a different frame of mind, simply relieved that the small moon had not crushed them, and was now finding its own new destiny out of harm's way. As they watched it get caught by Titan, Geoff gave a loud "whoop." When it was scientifically confirmed that the big moon had its own little satellite, even Henry gave a quiet "whoop."

Henry said, "Can you imagine how scientists and astronomers back home will be reacting to this? The logistics of how it could happen will keep many active minds awake at night for some time to come."

"Once they all know it was us that did it," said Richard, "they will have more sleepless nights calculating the huge possibility for failure."

"And no doubt," said William, "there will be plenty of people who will tell us we got it wrong, and it would have been better if we'd done this or that."

"Absolutely," agreed Henry, smiling.

"Can you imagine what the newspapers will say when they publish this story?" asked William. "They will be talking about the impossible, while questioning many scientific theories."

"They will have a field day," agreed Henry.

"What about," said Geoff, "moon moves to a better, more exciting neighbourhood?"

William, "Moon leaves Pluto to set up home with a moon of Saturn."

Henry, "Moon of Saturn captures prize from Pluto."

Richard, "Bored with living on the outskirts, moon takes up new relationship with a Saturnian moon."

Geoff again, "When moving to a new neighbourhood, do it the Kerberos way, and hitch a ride on a passing comet!"

They were all in good spirits despite the stress of the last few weeks, but totally astonished at what had happened to Kerberos. They hadn't lost it to the depths of Saturn, which they had thought would happen, but the fight it clearly put up to stay alive followed by it attaching itself to Titan was almost an unbelievable event. It helped to inspire their own determination to see this trip through to a successful outcome. "If Kerberos can find a way to stay alive," added Henry, "then I'm darned sure we can at least do the same."

~ CHAPTER 11 ~

~ JUPITER ~

The British Astronomical Society was getting some good press, and that really pleased Julie's bosses. She led the team that had discovered that Kerberos had become a companion to Titan. As incredible as that seemed, the media were still speculating on just how it all happened. They were hoping for some fundamental scientific law associated with gravity to have come into play, but no matter how many times they asked they were always told the same thing by Julie, "There will be a reason the moon took a different course to that of the comet, but without data I can only guess, and by data I mean measurements of gravity fields in and around both the comet and the moon. As I don't have such detailed statistics to analyse we have to work with what we saw, which was that it appeared the gravity of Saturn pulled Kerberos down. Perhaps it protected the comet and allowed it to just carry on, but the thing to remember is that Kerberos is much larger than the comet and so more prone to reacting to gravity. As to why Kerberos ended up as a moon of a moon, it was a one in five million chance that Titan would be in the right place at the right time."

Julie and Mike had to give a number of media presentations, and always, after all the known data was presented, the question would come up about this being an unusual event but not unique. Is it possible that other moons have been passed from one planet to another? Julie was diplomatic as always, "No evidence to support that theory, but why not, as we have seen in the last 2 years, so many things we couldn't even imagine have come to pass. Who is to say what little tricks our home solar system can play when it wants to?"

The questions would naturally turn to the comet that was still travelling towards them at high speed. Julie suspected that the comet was not going to be the disaster everyone had predicted it would be, given the events she had witnessed so far, although she gave the official line on that. "The comet seems to have had variable speeds, perhaps influenced by other objects. It started slowly out of the Oort Cloud but was very much a late starter, being several months behind the last collection of comets. After that it got faster with Kerberos at its back, now it's slowed down a shade. It gets faster as it gets closer, yet, you can bet we will be keeping a very close eye on it." She wanted to say that she didn't believe it would be causing any problems, instead she said, "This comet is pretty unique in many ways, aside from being partially empty inside, its general behaviour pattern has been unusual, and we will just have to wait and see what it does next."

"Could it be an alien spaceship?" one reporter asked.

Julie flashed her small condescending smile at the woman and closed the presentation.

ॐ ♈ ॐ   ॐ ♈ ॐ   ॐ ♈ ॐ

Jupiter had just started to show. The sun had become brighter and somewhat larger than a speck, almost a spot, and they were just that bit closer to home. Richard announced that, "Jupiter has 67 moons at the last count according to the on board database and a beautiful red spot near one pole that keeps moving around slightly, driven by what passes for weather in the upper reaches of the atmosphere of this magnificent gas giant."

The planet was approaching their trajectory and at only 15 million miles distance meant that the telescopes could really pick out some great detail.

Geoff was looking over the different moons, noting how different they were to each other, although he was a little apprehensive at the variations in their behaviour. "Hey, Richard, how are you supposed to monitor all of these moons? They are totally erratic, with lots that orbit in the opposite direction to the planet, and there are so many of them buzzing around Jupiter," moaned Geoff.

"Don't worry," said Richard, "we will all have a go at checking these off, just be sure to mark your observations for the ones you locate."

"OK," said Geoff in one of his sombre moods.

"Have you noticed," suggested Richard, in an attempt to cheer up Geoff, "how big Ganymede is? It's not only bigger than our own moon it is bigger than the planet Mercury."

"Yes," said Geoff, "I'm surprised we don't steal it, tow it away and make it orbit Earth. We could do with another moon shining more light down on us."

"Nice idea," agreed Richard, "but can you imagine the gravitational effect that would create on the inner planets, Earth especially? It probably wouldn't be missed that much by Jupiter, but placed too close to Earth and we could see Earth, Venus and Mars, not to mention the moon, going through a rebalancing action as a new generator of gravity waves comes into their space. It has the potential for a great deal of chaos, and you simply couldn't just plunk it in there without expecting repercussions."

"Oh," said Geoff, "I'll be quiet, no more silly ideas from me."

Richard laughed at his retreat into self-criticism. "Don't stop having ideas, please. Your thoughts and reactions to our problems have done us an amazing amount of good, and don't worry if we kill off your good ideas with a sledgehammer; it's what scientists do to each other all the time. Just persist."

Geoff smiled, a little happier. "What about Callisto? That would make a good moon as well, or another planet."

"Yes," said Richard, "and I feel that as we become better at managing gravity you might just see some of your ideas come true. Although, have you seen how Io behaves?"

"Looks like mouldy cheese," said Geoff.

"Agreed," said Richard, "have you seen how the electricity moves on the surface when it cuts across Jupiter's magnetic field?"

"Wow, no," said Geoff, "I will look out for that, should be quite a spectacle." He brought up the image of Io on the big screen, waiting for the sparks.

"Any evidence yet of any strange movements from the moons, Geoff? If they are all there still that is a good start. I'm inclined to suggest it will be the small ones that could wander, if any do. The ones up to 3 miles in size."

"Haven't really checked in detail, they all look OK when you view them, however, with so many it won't be easy. I was just getting familiar with the way the moons went about their daily business."

"Fair enough," said Richard, "when you get a chance, do also check the moons with frozen water. We are expecting to eventually find life under the surfaces of some of these moons."

"Ah, okey dokey, I will be on the lookout for any faces under the ice," laughed Geoff.

ॐ ✝ ॐ   ॐ ✝ ॐ   ॐ ✝ ॐ

Julie and team were in the conference room with the video link to ESA in Darmstadt, Germany. She was just summing up what was known about this comet coming their way and checking if Darmstadt had any other data. It seemed not. She spoke to both her team and the German participants, "Given that something strange has happened at or just after the comet passed by a planet, I want to be extra careful in making sure we get evidence of anything else that happens. It may all be just a coincidence, or we could be seeing a brand new phenomenon in terms of what comets can be made of and what disturbances they can create. Who knows, maybe this comet with strange properties has been our problem all along! Now, Mike is going to update us all on where our object is and any other things he's been able to dig up. Mike."

Mike didn't have a presentation or pretty pictures, and just read from his notes. "Our comet is about 9 million miles away from Jupiter, which is probably an optimum distance to cause effects or disturb any objects in the area. Remember, it was pretty close to Pluto, as it passed by, after which Kerberos broke free. It was also quite close to Saturn when gravity appeared to steal the moon. It should in theory have taken the comet as well, as we all know, but that's a different subject."

"Yes," agreed Stefan from Darmstadt, "they were both going in the same direction at the same speed. There is no sense that only the moon became loose, it is almost like some intelligence is controlling some things here."

"Indeed," agreed Mike, "but I for one am not going to be the first to say that the comet is endowed with some kind of life force, even though we all have the same suspicion about this. For now I am working on the concept that nature alone is driving all of this."

"Thanks, Mike," said Julie, "and just to emphasise our position when we give briefings, we simply do not touch on the subject of intelligence in or on or around the comet. I assume it's the same with you, Stefan?"

"Yes, agreed," said Stefan.

"Can we all meet up again at 9.30am CET daily until the comet is well on its way to the asteroid belt. That will give us time to gather data and confer on any findings or observations?"

"Very good idea," agreed Germany.

Geoff was working with Henry to analyse the four inner moons of Jupiter. They lay at the outer edge of the main ring or very close to other rings so that material from these moons actually fed into the rings. "I can verify what you have worked out, Geoff," said Henry, "all of these four are performing as per the information we hold on them, which is good. Let's take the Ananke group next. There are 15 of these."

After checking this group Geoff informed Henry, "They all had retrograde eccentric orbits and were quite small, some as tiny as one mile in diameter, or across, because they were often far from round."

Henry agreed that no issues were found with these so they started on the 13 members of the Carme group, saying, "These also orbit in the opposite direction to Jupiter. They are unfortunately liable to change due to being pulled this way and that thanks to larger bodies around them, so deciding if any are now acting erratically is far from easy."

Geoff worked through the 13 objects with some help from Henry and they were able to tick off the box for that group, it had already been a long day.

"I'm hungry, what's for dinner?" asked Geoff.

"William was due to make chicken and roast potatoes I heard," said Henry, "in fact that smell is probably what triggered your hunger thoughts. Let's go and investigate."

During dinner, when Geoff had perked up a little, he mentioned how grey the 'Comet' still was despite the decorating they had done. "Before they send it on any other missions they should paint it some really bright colours. You know though, what I really miss is the greenery of flowers and grass. Be nice to have some trees and lawns on board."

"I'd fancy a grass tennis court," suggested William. "There is plenty more rock that could be carved out to create some recreational facilities."

"What if they created an orchard and a better way to cultivate home grown food? I really could fancy some tender new small potatoes. We only seem to produce big old ones. That was no comment on your roasts, William, they are very nice," said Henry.

"I'm surprised," put in Geoff, "that you are not doing all sorts of wild experiments, being out in here in deep space. Things to do with cosmic rays and fancy stuff like that."

"Well, actually, we are," said Richard. "We just haven't mentioned them. Almost forgot about them in fact. There is a room behind our office that was set aside to measure cosmic rays. We haven't needed to touch anything there since we installed the experiments. We will wait for the boys back at base to do the review and analysis on them."

"Indeed," said Henry, "at my last count we had 76 different experiments going on long term and another 34 just collecting data. That is in addition to any little experiments we get to think up."

ॐ♈ॐ   ॐ♈ॐ   ॐ♈ॐ

"Guten morgen," said Udo in Germany. "Stefan was not able to be with us today. There is a big issue with a third generation Meteosat weather satellite. I think they have lost the signal. Never mind, anyway, I am Udo, we can all do the usual discussion."

"Oh hello, Udo, guten morgen to you, let's make a start, as I have no major news and expect this to be short."

"Good, I like short meetings," said Udo.

"Right," said Julie. "The comet is making good progress and from our observations there has been no change in behaviour of any Jovian moons. Can you confirm that, Udo?"

Udo replied, "Yes, except for one detail, perhaps you can investigate it as well. One of the more erratic moons of the Pasiphae group, S/2003 J23 is giving us some difficulty. We have been unable to determine its outer most point in the orbit. It would be good if you could examine its statistics and help us to confirm if it is also about to leave Jupiter to follow this silly comet."

"Yes of course," said Julie. "We saw nothing on this when we checked earlier but better to be safe; we will review that one again. I will call you directly if there is an anomaly."

"Thank you, Julie, bye bye."

"Cheers, Udo," replied Julie, closing the video link.

ॐ♈ॐ   ॐ♈ॐ   ॐ♈ॐ

"I've completed the other groups and the small independent moons of Jupiter, but not the big boys," said Geoff to Richard and Henry who were lazing in their seats. "I've just looked back on some data for a small moon in

Pasiphae and it did have a bit of a wobble a few hours ago, although it now looks normal. What do you think?"

"Let's keep a daily check on it," yawned Henry. "These smaller moons of Jupiter are renowned for being somewhat random in their motions, so I'm not too concerned, however, of course, better to be safe than sorry. We should monitor them all on a regular basis to make sure none start to follow us."

While the other two went for some sleep, Geoff started to focus on the big boys. First was Europa, another moon almost as big as Earth's moon. The electronic database suggested that liquid water was just below the crust. He knew Richard, Henry and William were doing different types of analysis on the various objects that came into view, so he wasn't going to probe very much, besides he was already at his technical limit in assessing movements, and so forth, of moons. His maths had never been good. Always had trouble with percentages, and here he was working with formulae that would make him go blind if he stared at them for too long. Happily he could let the mainframe do the hard work. All he had to do was focus on an object to get certain information over a period of time, and then key in the appropriate set of commands. When the mainframe produced the statistics then he would compare these results against data held on the system. He looked more closely at Europa through the combined images of pictorial and x-ray. It was fascinating, and didn't those marks look just like a man's footprint? He took a printed image of that for his own personal collection, something he had been doing for some time whenever he saw something interesting.

ॐ ♈ ॐ   ॐ ♈ ॐ   ॐ ♈ ॐ

"Definitely had a bit of a wobble there," said Julie in her video conference with Germany, "it stabilised completely afterwards and it looks fine now. We have been watching it for 5 days without any quiver or shake."

"Super," said Stefan, "so I think we are done for today. Our comet is now nearly out of range of Jupiter to make more surprises. I suggest we have weekly instead of daily calls now."

"Yes, I can agree with that," said Julie. "Oh, by the way, just being nosey. What was the trouble with Meteosat the other day? Nothing to do with comets I hope."

"Possibly," suggested Stefan. "The satellite suffered a little bump from a very small piece of debris, we suspect. It pushed the satellite away, perhaps half a metre, which was enough to make it hard to communicate with. By trial and mistake we finally hit the command point and now we have it under control."

"Good to hear," said Julie, "in that case I'm closing today's call. I will send out email invites for further calls."

ॐ ♈ ॐ   ॐ ♈ ॐ   ॐ ♈ ॐ

Geoff allowed his amazement to wander over the fact that Jupiter had three moons that were all larger than our own, and could in theory have become planets in their own right. "How come," he mumbled to himself, "Jupiter was able to capture them, when they would have been much better off closer to Earth? In any case, Jupiter already has lots of worshipping pieces of rock circling it; it wouldn't miss a few moons."

He could not begin to imagine the great forces at work that created such a large family for Jupiter, spectacular as it was. If only he were Superman he would surely put them in a more prominent position within the Goldilocks region.

The next moon to get more attention was Io. Geoff had previously looked this over, and it still held his attention. Another for the scrap book with its pizza like face. It reminded him somewhat of that horrible little kid at school who insisted on poking him and being generally annoying. His face was often blotchy and yellow.

Callisto was bigger than Io, and what stood out most were its large bright scars. It seemed to have a surface fuzziness, other than that it was fairly dull.

Ganymede was something else. "This is the largest moon in the whole solar system," he told himself for emphasis, making comparisons between it and Mercury, weighing it all up in his mind, then saving that data away. The database told him that there was an internal ocean and a very thin oxygen atmosphere. "Surely," muttered Geoff to himself, "our wonderful Earth scientists could improve on that and make it a habitable world?" Nobody answered.

Richard and William were doing a final check on any Jovian moons that might have decided to leave home and chase after them, happily, they had to admit that everything looked pretty normal. The Jovian asteroids were now too far away to be a problem to 'Comet' but William had looked them over, one last time, to confirm they were behaving as expected, and they were.

They had about a week before the next objects came into view, and when it came closer, it was more like a sea of upturned lifeboats, with all being a grave danger to shipping. Henry was busy estimating if any large rocks were likely to be in the way of the path 'Comet' had decided to take. So far not, although, they might just need a little burst of their jets to get themselves around some of the bigger objects like Ceres, if they moved closer, but with so many objects, it was hard to plot each one's course, so they would make any adjustments to their direction once they got within range of any obstacle.

Despite being in the asteroid belt Ceres was called a dwarf planet. It was quite round, like a golf ball almost, and with a diameter of only 587 miles it was a lot smaller than Pluto. Geoff was keen to see its main features and took paper images of the two very bright spots inside a crater. The water vapour plume was harder to find, and he needed some help from Henry before he finally located that feature.

"Richard," said Geoff when just the two of them were alone in the comm's room, "I have a question about Jupiter, which I suppose applies also to the other gas giants."

"Go ahead," said Richard, "I will answer if I can. I'm all ears."

"Well," said Geoff, "if the atmosphere of Jupiter is very similar to a brown star and even our sun, before it became a sun, what is it that kicks it all off, and why hasn't Jupiter become a sun by now?"

"Hmm, interesting question," said Richard, "I can see you've been busy studying up on the birth of stars."

"Just a little," said Geoff, "the subject is somewhat confusing to an uneducated layman like me."

"You may not have excelled at school, Geoff, but you did in life, and your questions show you have abilities way above your own perceived level of personal intelligence."

"Thanks," smiled Geoff, blushing a little.

Richard continued, "There are several factors involved in a star igniting and being able to generate heat and so forth, and so much of it is down to our old friend gravity. If the internal pressure is not high enough, nothing will happen, and to a degree it depends on how big and how dense the core is. So the gas mixture can be just right, but without that pressure to jump-start the fusion process the object would remain as a gas planet or it might fizzle a bit to become a brown star, generating some heat but very little light, if any, because it is not able to fuse hydrogen into helium."

Geoff gave a little nod to show that he was getting it all so far.

"There is another factor which probably makes it all more conclusive," said Richard. "If you can picture a region where stars are born, lots of gas and matter finally succumbing to gravity and spinning around to form more solid objects. In our solar system the vast majority of hydrogen was collected into one specific point where our sun was born. Jupiter would have been created at a later point, having gotten some mass it attracted the left-over gases we see around it today, however, a critical aspect of all of this is the timing and accumulation of gases. If Jupiter had formed at the same time as our sun, then it would have ignited, and maybe would have ended up as a brown star which couldn't complete the process as it didn't have enough mass. If Jupiter had been able to obtain more of what the sun had, it too would have become a star. Most brown dwarfs are only slightly larger than Jupiter, but can be up to 80 times more massive due to a greater density."

"Wow," said Geoff, "that makes it a tad easier to understand. It's all about timing and mass."

"As with so much in life," agreed Richard.

"Would I be correct in saying that brown dwarfs look like planets but they form like stars?" asked Geoff.

"Close enough," said Richard, "just don't try to set foot on any brown stars you come across."

ॐ♈ॐ   ॐ♈ॐ   ॐ♈ॐ

"Mike," shouted Julie, "what do you mean you can't see the wood for the trees?"

"I mean," said Mike, "that we have temporarily lost our comet in a jungle of other rocks. It's passing through the asteroid belt and is hard to track."

"Oh, you should have said that," scolded Julie.

Mike continued, "I hope you have more people than we have on this small team trying to work out if our comet is causing any disruption as it passes through the asteroid belt. It's an almost impossible task to monitor so many objects, as you know there are fairly big distances between each, with all of them moving reasonably quickly."

"NASA," said Julie, "have the responsibility of tracking all asteroids. We are the extra team that does it effectively, best, and first."

"Yes, boss," said a melancholy Mike.

ॐ ♈ ॐ   ॐ ♈ ॐ   ॐ ♈ ॐ

"Hmm," said Geoff. "I hope nobody is expecting me to track and compare all the asteroids here. The database says there are upwards of 1.9 million of the buggers, and they move away too quickly."

"No," said Henry, "we do need to keep a backwards check. However, we do need to see if any start to come after us as we leave the asteroid belt behind."

"Just as well that there is so much empty space between the big chunks of rock. I always imagined they would be closer together and cause more problems for a spaceship. I suppose if it's a really big ship it could have difficulties navigating through these beauties."

"Indeed," said Henry, otherwise distracted.

"How will it work in future?" Geoff wanted to know. "Those big spaceships they will be building to travel to other solar systems will need something to clear enough empty space through the asteroid belt, or more specifically, the Oort Cloud to pass through. I guess though that they can't just push them out of the way as they could become a danger to Earth and other spaceships. Any ideas?"

"None," said Henry concentrating on the approaching rocks.

"Well," started Richard. "Interesting, but not a pressing problem. Glad we don't have to solve it on this trip, although I'd suggest there would probably be designated shipping lanes, whereby they keep comets and asteroids out of the way so that certain routes are always safe. It will depend on which direction they want to travel to of course, but that would be my approach."

ॐ ♈ ॐ   ॐ ♈ ॐ   ॐ ♈ ॐ

It was the Friday team meeting, where Julie checked over the progress of assignments, motivated the guys in her team and gave them any good news she could conjure up. She started with Gary.

"Gary, you were checking to see if any other comet waves had started up again, any sign?"

"From what I can see, and I've gone over three recent sets of data with very similar indications, no more waves of comets are coming from the Oort Cloud," Gary told his team. "It has all been quite settled for some weeks now, well, as settled as it ever gets down there. That makes it 16 weeks in total since the last wave was generated from the depths of the solar system. Now that Betelgeuse has fully settled down as a white dwarf I believe we should be able to close the book on the big comet push."

"Not yet," said Julie, "I personally will close this off when our comet completes its journey, one way or the other, and there will still be other repercussions. I have some other news that is likely related to the big push, and we can't even blame our special comet as it is still in the vicinity of the asteroid belt."

"Don't keep us in the dark," urged Mike, "what is this news? Can't be good from the face you are pulling."

Julie relaxed her face into a half smile, "NASA came through late last night and reported that Phobos, the larger moon of Mars, had shifted in its orbit. It appears to be more erratic, slightly more elliptical, and it's circling Mars in less time. It was close to Mars as we all know, only 3,700 miles above the surface and orbited three times every day. Now its lowest point is just 3,400 miles above Mars and it orbits four times every day. I should add that at its highest point it is 3,800 miles from the surface."

"That could be a disaster for anyone on Mars," pointed out Gary.

"Just as well we haven't colonised the red planet," suggested Mike.

"OK," said Julie, "our priority for this week is to get a full analysis and prediction on Phobos, while also keeping an eye on Deimos. It would be a real shame for Mars to lose a single moon, but how it would lose it is the important thing. At such a low orbit I cannot see it being ejected into space; even so, stranger things have happened."

"I think we should blame the comet personally," said Mike, "it may be some distance away but it is the common factor in all of this. I'm sure if we stretched our imagination we could even blame the comet for us receiving so many of its cousins in this vicinity."

"Nice try," said Julie smiling, "however, I have a hunch that our comet was the victim here, to a degree, as much as we were."

ॐ ♈ ॐ   ॐ ♈ ॐ   ॐ ♈ ॐ

'Comet' had entered the asteroid belt without any issues and they all got a closer look at the interesting near neighbour dwarf planet Ceres. It had no moons of its own, while the surface being so heavily cratered led to speculation on where it might have originated.

After passing by Ceres, another object came in to view, about 2 miles away on the port side. Moving to closely intercept them, was a small, but significant, asteroid well known to the trackers at NASA.

"Ah," said Henry, "they called that little rock Bennu. It was termed a class B asteroid because it was allegedly rich in carbons and as you can see it is very dark. The elliptical orbit of this little beast was expected to take it close to Earth in the 22nd century, so NASA has put a lot of effort into monitoring it very closely."

"That's right," agreed William, "whatever happened to that study project they sent up?"

"Oh, indeed," said Henry, "they did send up a special rocket to look more closely at Bennu and gather some dirt. The dirt got to Earth OK, however, it was an inconclusive result, and provided very little in terms of quantity, or quality. It seems the dirt returned was space hardened clay, with no sign of any liquid content, and very few minerals."

"Wouldn't it be wicked of us," suggested Richard, "if we dug into Bennu and got a really worthwhile sample?"

Henry thought about that long and hard. "Gosh, I would love to do that, the question is how to get a sample when you are travelling as fast as we are. We don't have any probes to send out. To be successful we'd have to find a way to get the dirt back on board. An almost impossible quest I'm afraid."

"Wait a minute," said Geoff, "if we have no probes then what is that set of controls over there for? It seems to show a live image of the rocks in front of us, and there are big letters that say "PROBE – TO COLLECT DIRT SAMPLES'."

"Well, I'll be..." mumbled Henry, "I've never seen that before, where did it come from?"

"Looks like another feature that someone like Donald installed for us, that somebody forgot to tell us about," suggested Richard.

"Blow me down, you are probably right," said a confused Henry. "Let's go for it." They waited a while until they got closer to their target. William turned the control nob to show Bennu in the centre of the screen. A number flashed up showing 200 feet, and a red light showed.

"That must mean we are out of range," suggested Richard.

"Ah that's better," said Henry, as the red light turned green and the distance went down to be 100 feet.

William hit the shoot button, and the screen showed a small double shovel-like implement jump out towards the black beast with a cable behind it. The implement opened fully when it was just a few feet away, and the cable went very slack.

"With luck," said Henry, "that will get well below the surface and dig up some real organic mud."

They watched as the two sides of the shovel closed, the image adjusting constantly to display the progress. Very suddenly the cable became really tight as 'Comet' moved quickly ahead, and the shovel implement released its grip on the surface of Bennu. They could hear the cable rewinding somewhere in front of them and a loud plonk as the shovel came back in. This was followed by a whirring sound, after which a message on the screen told them to investigate the treasure. They looked towards where the noises had been coming from and found a wide panel.

"That seems to be the only place it could have brought the stuff back to," said William. "I am assuming it won't suck out all the air in here if I remove the panel?"

"Everything else about this worked well," said Henry. "Can't imagine they would design something like this with a major flaw. Let's open it."

There was a large grey bucket behind the panel, about 3 foot square, and the dirt was heavy. It took three of them to lift the box over the lip of the place where the container had been sitting, and little roller wheels on the container's bottom allowed it to be pushed very easily after that.

"My goodness," exclaimed Henry, "now that is what you call a sample!"

Henry and William took the huge pile of compost smelling mud away to transfer it to smaller sealed containers to keep safe for analysis at Cambridge. They kept one good sized pot for their own tests to gauge the vitality of the organics and what elements of life it might hold.

"That will be a great coup for us, getting a real good piece of Bennu when NASA failed so miserably, relatively speaking," smiled Henry. "There were already some red faces at NASA when the almost useless samples came back, and this will make them even more red, I suspect."

"That will keep Henry occupied for several days," Richard told Geoff smiling, "and I would say it is time we updated Cambridge."

"Hello, Cambridge, this is 'Comet', Richard speaking, just to update you that we are almost clear of the asteroid belt without any issues. We will have a little present for the boys there that love to dig the dirt. We passed very closely by Bennu and decided that we would top what NASA were able to provide in the way of a dirt sample, so we grabbed a chunk of its hide. There is enough mud to keep a dozen analysts busy for months. Henry is doing some basic analysis, although there will be plenty of it left for everyone to run their extended tests on, once we get home. Nothing else to report. Over."

"That dirt should raise a few eyebrows at NASA," suggested Geoff. "Can anyone say why it is that an asteroid has a high soil content, and not stone, seems odd to me?"

"Agreed, we normally think these should be solid rock or stone. You know, there had been a theory from my old professor at university that at one time a planet had orbited the sun where the asteroid belt had been," said Richard, "which would mean of course that the make up of asteroids would be similar, so if one is mainly mud others will be too, of course a planet also has many solid rocky parts. We'd have to take a great deal of samples to verify the theory, and even so, if all the bits came from different layers of the planet it would be an almost impossible job to prove anything. Interesting theory though."

"That would be one heck of a jigsaw puzzle," laughed Geoff, "one wonders though, just how a planet could get broken up so badly into such small pieces?"

"That could be the question of the week," said Richard, "for which I have no data to work with, so I'll leave that to your imagination."

Geoff immediately thought of Star Wars, but didn't mention that.

ॐ ♈ ॐ　　　　　ॐ ♈ ॐ　　　　　ॐ ♈ ॐ

"Morning, guys, nice to see everyone in early. What's the latest on Phobos?" said Julie.

"Not good," said Mike. "The high point in its orbit is now 44,000 miles above Mars and it orbits five times per day even at that height."

"Mein Got," said Julie who had more than a little German within her. "It is going to hitch a ride with our comet!"

"Just like Kerberos," suggested Gary.

"Now that really would be pushing coincidences too far," stated Julie.

"Still think our comet is a victim?" asked Mike.

~ CHAPTER 12 ~

~ LOOMING DESTRUCTION ~

Mars was now a large dot in their comm's observation window. The sun had grown to a similar sized dot, although somewhat brighter and more yellow than the planet.

"What the heck has gotten into Phobos?" demanded Henry. "I thought we'd seen the last of misbehaving moons."

"It looks from here as though it has increased the height it orbits at," agreed William.

"Very strange," said Richard. "I've just calculated our trajectory, and the likely position of Phobos at the point it could break orbit."

"Let me guess," said Henry, "those two points will be very close together!"

"Spot on," agreed Richard. "I'd say we have 3 days to work out a feasible plan to avoid a nasty accident in the vicinity of Mars."

Geoff watched in awe as the three scientists drew series after series of computations on the blackboard, plotting their course as well as how Phobos was expected to behave. Geoff was asked to give hourly statistics on Phobos so that the rate of speed increase and height could be fed into the formulae.

During breakfast, Geoff wanted to know why Phobos had waited till now to perform its escape act. "The last wave of high level pressure from Betelgeuse was weeks and weeks and weeks ago. How come it's only now doing this?"

"The final push," said Henry, "would surely have passed by quite some time ago, as you say, Geoff. I suspect it generated a change in this moon that initially was hardly detectable, that change was slow to build, but build it did. It was the same effect that pushed Kerberos from its orbit; Pluto had much less gravity than Mars, so Kerberos left much earlier than Phobos. We are just lucky, I guess," he smiled a forlorn smile, "that our progress matched these two events."

"Yes indeed," agreed William in a solemn voice, "we've had nothing except luck on this mission!"

Their routine followed closely on other events where their luck had been challenged, with the three scientists formulating ideas and scenarios while Geoff supplied a steady stream of new data and coffee.

Finally the scientists came out of their room and they all sat around with their refreshed drinks and sandwiches.

"The weakest point on the orbit of Phobos will be at its peak," said William. "Our theory is that we need to get in a position just above that peak so that we can push the moon back to the ground. Not an easy thing to do considering we are still travelling at nearly 180,000 miles per hour. We've done our sums, worked out the odds, made peace with our Gods, and we are as ready as we could ever be."

"It will mean," added Henry, "that we have to travel with Phobos about one half cycle of Mars. We just have to be careful that we don't get captured. In doing this we will reduce our own speed, even so, we still can't allow that to go below 40,000 miles per hour."

"Hope my insurance is up to date," said Geoff, "but how is my wife going to prove I was killed by a collision with a natural satellite in the vicinity of Mars?"

"Hand of God, sorry, old man," responded Richard.

Geoff asked if he had time to look over the jets and give them a quick clean.

"Best not," said Henry, "they've been OK up to now, and from experience I know that more things fail after a spot of maintenance than at any other time, especially cars and jet thrusters."

ॐ ♈ ॐ   ॐ ♈ ॐ   ॐ ♈ ॐ

A large crate was delivered into the office for Julie's attention. It was heavy and soon had the team eyeing it and wondering what it was. Julie came in later after an early appointment at the gynaecologist.

"False alarm," she announced, "I'm not going to be taking a leave of absence due to being pregnant, because I'm not." A tear showed in one eye. "Never mind, we keep on trying."

"That's what I'd heard," said Gary, rudely, "you've been trying it all over the place in your house, on the stairs, in the shower, and the noise, cor blimey. Someone said your poor husband has ordered so much zinc from the chemist that they have a shortage. I don't know how these rumours get out, but quite a few people in our street know you try a lot." Gary smiled wickedly.

A stapler narrowly missed Gary's right ear.

"Just for that, Mr Gary Pinkleton, you can take the lid off that crate, and if you are all nice, and kinder to me, I just might let you have a little something each."

"I could be very nice," said Gary, tempting fate, "just let me know if your husband can't cope."

"Gary," screamed Julie, "ENOUGH!"

He went quiet and opened the crate.

"Oh rocks," declared Gary, "super."

Walking over to the crate, she took out several rocks and handed them to the people in her team. "These," she said, "came from that meteorite that crashed in Turkey. This was for our little museum, although there is still plenty to share out between us. I'd better take one up to the boss so he can admire it on his new glass desk. That will keep him usefully occupied for hours."

"Don't forget to take some home for hubby, so he can get his rocks off on the settee for a change," said Gary, going out of the room and slamming the door behind him.

"What the heck is wrong with Gary today? I've never seen him like this," said Julie.

Mike answered, "It was because his overtime for last month was not paid, for all the extra work he did monitoring our comet. He was really looking forward to the extra for something special he had planned with his girlfriend."

"That wasn't my fault," protested Julie. "I'd better go and talk to him."

"Before you leave," said Mike, "a quick update on Phobos."

"Oh, yes please," replied Julie.

"The moon has reached a height of nearly 75,000 miles above Mars, which by my calculations is just below the point where gravity won't pull it down again for the speed it is going," said Mike. "Another couple of days should see it break free. The comet, oddly enough, should liaise with it at that same point and time."

"Amazing, absolutely bloody amazing. You just couldn't make this up if you tried. Almost looks like they are playing tag, or pass the baton," said Julie.

The format for dangerous manoeuvres was now well established, with Henry reading out the requirements while Richard or William managed the jets. Geoff had made sure the telescopes were all pointing where any action was likely to be, although they were slightly early. Their expected arrival at the designated spot was just 30 seconds ahead of Phobos, so they had had to burn a lot of gas to reduce their speed so that they could get into the best position to make contact. This time the contact was hard and violent, with 'Comet' almost pushed out of the way. The bump was very loud but the grinding sound produced by the moon rubbing against the side of the comet, as it tried to continue its upward motion, was almost enough to burst ear drums. Forward jets were applied with maximum thrust to push against Phobos. It would be a terrible disaster now if 'Comet' started to cave into the pressure and break up, however, they had no choice, they had to take the risk. Fortunately the moon was at its apogee and began to swing around in its orbit of its own determinism. Now they used a combination of jets to change the way that Phobos moved, initially forward, subsequently pushing strongly towards the ground.

By the time they had reached a position halfway around Mars the moon had begun to lose its forward momentum and was dipping seriously in towards the planet. They gave a huge final blast of the reverse jets to push Phobos dramatically towards the planet's surface. The moon tried to recover its height, but by now its death was inevitable, it gave up the fight and went down, screaming through the thin atmosphere to splatter itself on the Martian floor below.

On 'Comet', they worked rapidly to adjust their speed and trajectory to come up out of Mars's gravity, and head for Earth at a reasonable speed. Oddly enough they were on almost exactly the same course that they had been on previously, although their speed had dropped quite low, just under 48,000 miles per hour forward motion.

Geoff watched the moon as it fell towards the red planet. It seemed to take an age with no visible signs that it was disturbing anything, and they were almost out of visible range when finally it smashed into the central plateau of Mars. Geoff could almost hear the thud of the impact as it hit, vibrating all around it, sending up a plume of red dust high into the sky as if reaching out for 'Comet', before spreading through Mars's thin atmosphere to cool the planet a little by blocking the warming rays of the sun. The dust cleared enough to show an enormous crater within the western volcanic region of the red planet, with the debris from one ex-moon filling much of it.

ॐ ♈ ॐ   ॐ ♈ ॐ   ॐ ♈ ॐ

Julie had gotten in to the office early despite a very late night call with NASA on the subject of Phobos, and now as her team joined her she was able to start the day with the news of the tragic event. "Gather round, I've got a sore throat and can't shout. I had a late session with NASA last night and I've just been confirming the situation from our perspective."

"Oh dear, what's our comet been up to now?" growled Mike.

"Plenty by the sounds of it," said Gary. "We left it expecting it to rendezvous with Phobos."

"Correct," agreed Julie, "and then, apparently, the two did meet up, and they slipped behind Mars together."

"No, no, that cannot happen," exclaimed Mike. "They should have either collided or kept on going along their own paths."

"Well, you know our comet," said Julie, "it does what it wants to do. Anyway, that was all the news we had on that until I came in today, because our moon was blocking any sight of anything coming around Mars."

"What super timing we suffer from," suggested Gary, blushing a little. "Sorry, that was not a reference to your husband."

"OK," smiled Julie, having made peace with Gary by getting him his special overtime payment through.

"Now here comes the good bit," interjected Mike, "I can just feel it."

"You're not wrong, Mike," said Julie. "So, when we did get to view Mars again, there was no sign of Phobos and our comet was some distance away from Mars, still heading in our direction. Gary I'd like you to plot that course please and check the speed it is going, it seems much slower."

"Was that it?" asked Mike, disappointed.

"Not quite," said Julie. "As Mars turned round on its axis I was able to spot a very large new crater, and a lot of red dust! Right in the Tharsis region. All I can say is that it's a good job it landed where it did and not on us, or it would have really caused a real catastrophe."

"So it would seem the comet restrained this moon as well, altered its course, and then sent it to its death for misbehaving," muttered Mike.

"Yes, looks that way," said Julie. "Please do a lot more analysis on this as we need to be exact in any data we publish. See if we can get anything on the effect of the earthquake across the central region of Mars. In the meantime I will talk to ESA, and NASA when they come online, and let them have the great news, it looks like our comet has done it again."

"I wonder what it will do for a finale," said Gary.

"It will have to be something pretty spectacular," said Julie, "after all the tricks it has been responsible for, so far, I'm expecting a very special end to this adventure."

"Bit of news for you to think about," said Mike, "while you, Julie were nattering with NASA I was doing some real work. To be honest, I was curious that nothing had changed within the asteroid belt. Everything seemed to be as it was before the comet passed through. However, I did find something."

"Don't say it," said Gary, "the comet has lined up a bunch of asteroids to spell out a rude word."

"Not quite, and you're being silly now," said Mike, "let's be professional here."

"You're beginning to sound like Julie," said Gary, "have you been promoted or something? Oh, never mind; spit it out."

"Fat chance," said Mike, glancing at Julie. "Anyway, we are all pretty familiar with that asteroid Bennu's, elliptical orbit that will come close to Earth at some time in the near future."

"Yes," said Julie, "didn't NASA recently get the rocket back with a sample of scrapings from the surface of Bennu?"

"Correct," said Mike, "you will notice they have been very quiet on the subject. No announcements, no major discoveries. I get the feeling the project may have been an expensive failure. Naturally, of course, that is something they would keep to themselves. That is all history, and Bennu has been checked over many times since that rocket took the samples."

"Is this going somewhere?" asked Julie.

"Patience," said Mike, "I was just getting to it. Looking at Bennu now, that is, well after the NASA rocket left and just after the comet went through the asteroid belt, what do you think you will find? OK I will tell you. Bennu now has a small but very noticeable hole dug into its surface. You can just about see the scrape marks of a shovel. Something has taken a big bite out of Bennu and it was nothing to do with the OSIRES project."

"How very interesting," Julie smiled at Mike in a conspiratorial manner.

ॐ ♈ ॐ   ॐ ♈ ॐ   ॐ ♈ ॐ

With Mars behind them they all breathed a big sigh of relief that the worst was over, hopefully. They only had to navigate a course to home and park somewhere without falling into Earth's atmosphere and burning up. "All of which should be a piece of cake after everything we've done," suggested Richard.

"We do need to start looking at options though," said Henry. "For example, let's see if we can get some help from Luna, our moon. What will its position be, and can we use it to slow us down?"

Geoff added, "We will need something to slow us down because the fuel is almost gone. That business with Phobos used up more than half of the tank, so whatever we do, we will need to be economical with what energy we have left."

"Good point, Geoff, and thanks for that data," said Henry. "We will indeed have to be economical."

"It's good we have reduced our speed already with the help of Mars," said Richard, "we have to be going much slower than this, and of course this all means our arrival date will be different, as you suggested, Henry, the moon could help or hinder us. We need to work out where it will be when we need it."

"Yes, plenty of things to keep us busy. Richard, will you get onto base and explain all of this and if they could put up a big net to catch us we would be really happy?"

"A very large safety net or a very big cushion," suggested Geoff.

"In the meantime," said Henry, "it's time we had a little celebration. A while back I found a cheese cake in the freezer but decided that we needed a special occasion to cut it up. This seems like that time. I took it out of deep freeze over a week ago, and it is now in a perfect state for consumption. If someone can make the drinks we can all have coffee and cake. How's about that?"

"Perfeck," said Geoff, hyping a well-known character from an old TV show, and indeed, perfect it was!

ॐ ♈ ॐ   ॐ ♈ ॐ   ॐ ♈ ॐ

"Just had a backhand compliment from NASA," Julie informed her team. "They wanted to know how come we knew about the new Mars crater first. I told them we keep our eyes open to all possibilities, which was followed by a long silence as they couldn't think of what to say. Maybe they thought we had a man inside the comet, oh oh."

"Nice," said Gary.

"Later today," continued Julie, "I have another conference call to talk about the comet, so please update all of your details and let me have them by three PM."

"The comet has certainly slowed down," said Mike, "it is now likely to hit us in June, rather than in March."

"Thanks, Mike, if you can get certainty on that date and exact speed of travel that would be great."

ॐ♈ॐ   ॐ♈ॐ   ॐ♈ॐ

They finished off most of the cake in a slow Sunday afternoon kind of way, ignoring the fact that they were still heading for oblivion with limited capabilities to do anything about it. Going back to Earth was a lot quicker than when they went out, Henry had said several times.

"Looking back at everything," said Henry in a reflective mood, "I can't believe that it is over 2 years since Donald and the apes left for Earth. So much has happened since."

"Yes," said Richard, "if I can recall all the details I will certainly put a novel around all of this."

"It would have to go under science fiction though," said Geoff, "nobody would believe any of this actually happened."

"Indeed, you'll have a job getting a novel like that published, much too far-fetched. It's probably time we let Cambridge know how we are doing, would you do the honours again, please, Richard?"

"Hello, Cambridge, this is 'Comet', Richard speaking. Here is our current status. We are all in good spirits despite our impending doom. We have eaten the delicious cheese cake we had been saving for a special occasion so our stomachs are quite happy. Hope you noticed what happened to Phobos as William wants to know if that was worth an extra bonus? We are now very low on fuel, so looking to you for any bright ideas to slow us down and get 'Comet' parked in a non-decaying orbit, somewhere safe. 'Comet' signing off."

Twenty minutes later they got a reply on the radio. The controller in Cambridge was just so excited and kept telling them what a fantastic role they had played in keeping Earth safe, and so on. He congratulated them all on having gotten through everything they had had to endure. That alone made them feel so much better and at last appreciated. "We are working on options for you to park 'Comet' somewhere safe, however, they are limited. Most likely scenario is above the Earth; we will confirm that estimate and get back to you within 8 hours. Now, a question, I need to know if Geoff is there? I will pause for 2 minutes while you get him."

Geoff was there in the comm's room listening to everything said, and now wondering what was to come. "Maybe to tell me they'd got a special insurance that covered death by misadventure in space!"

"Hello, Geoff," continued the voice, "this is a specially recorded message just for you."

Geoff listened more intently.

"Geoffrey," exclaimed a very shrill voice. "Of all the useless pieces of meat! How on Earth did you get yourself into this pickle?" Geoff was of course unable to reply, but his eyes got very moist. The shrill voice relaxed a little. "I hope you are finding something to chuckle about out there, and don't be too long, I haven't had a good cuddle in ages." The link was closed.

Geoff couldn't handle that, couldn't even look at anyone. His eyes were somewhat blurred as he pushed his way out of the room, back to his small bedroom to have a gentle sob into his pillow.

The next message came in from Cambridge as they completed their dinner. "Still working on a parking orbit option but we need more accurate data. Please send all current statistics of travel, distance and velocity, and repeat hourly, on the laser link." Richard did as requested.

They were now able to pick up general radio transmissions from Earth. Geoff scanned them to see if there was anything being said about their 'Comet'. He was alarmed when BBC world service announced the Russians had a fleet of rockets with nuclear warheads ready to destroy the comet now heading for Earth. The Americans had had a fire at their launch pad and would not be ready to launch any rockets for some weeks. Geoff knew what he had to do.

"Hello, Ingor, come in, RO-ING, this is M6-GEF. Are you receiving me?" Although closer to Earth, there was always going to be a good delay for any response, that is if the other end were there and listening in, ready. Geoff waited impatiently, while Henry passed on the message to Cambridge via the laser link that the Russians intended to shoot them down.

Finally, a while later, some noise, a crackle, followed by, "Hello, Geoff, this is RO-ING. Nice to hear you after so long. Did you take a trip to the moon, ha ha?"

"Nice to hear you too, old friend, however, I am in trouble, and it was much further than the moon."

"Oh," said Ingor after the usual delay, "is your wife upset with you because you didn't answer the doorbell again, oh oh?"

"Much worse than that, Ingor. You know that comet your military want to shoot down, well, you'd better be sitting down as this is top secret and highly political, besides which it might shock you! Anyway," carried on Geoff, "I and three scientists are inside that comet and we don't want the Russians to shoot us down. We have slowed the comet down, and hope to miss the Earth. Please broadcast this message to your military."

One delay later. "Geoff, you having a joke on me, no? It is not possible for you to be inside a comet."

"Ingor, no joke. Very serious. I swear it is the truth. You can get it verified by seeing that the comet has slowed down. Please, old friend, our lives are in your hands."

Yet another delay. "I will see what I can do," said Ingor very seriously, "I'm sorry if I don't get message through in time."

"Do your best, my friend. If you see a great fireball in the sky, you will know I won't be able to talk with you again. Good luck." Geoff realised that had come out all wrong.

"Yes, goodbye and luck, my friend. I will sign off now, and try to take message to television station, maybe they can help. Cheers," replied Ingor some time later.

While waiting for Cambridge to come back, the three scientists had been working on their own ideas, scribbling many different formulae on the board, rubbing out parts until they had something tangible. In fact three tangible options.

"Number one," Richard reiterated for Geoff's benefit, "is to allow the moon to pull us in. It will be directly in front of us and will hide us from Earth. We would use whatever fuel we have left to keep dropping into lower orbits until the fuel is all gone and we crash onto the moon. Best estimates suggest a drop-glide of 20,000 feet, if we aim for the Sea of Tranquillity to crash land in the dust, it might just be enough to cushion the impact."

"Is that really the best we can do?" asked Geoff. "I had heard that moon dust was fine and so hard that it could cut like glass. Even 'Comet' could be ripped open if it has too much moon dust to contend with."

Surprised at Geoff questioning their science, Henry had to admit that so far this was the best option, "Unless you can think of a better way?"

"I'll work on it," frowned Geoff, unaware that he'd crossed some line.

"Option two," said Richard, "is to use the fuel to fire at certain altitudes above Earth to stabilise an orbit. This is very risky especially if we run out of fuel at the wrong time or turn off the jets too early." Geoff hadn't found anything to say, so Richard continued. "The final option is to steer a course just past Earth, slam on the jets to break our speed, and drift around while we wait for a rescue."

"Number three sounds least risky," said Geoff, "surely though, the fuel situation is the unknown factor. We could end up with no braking power and keep driving hard towards the sun."

"Agreed, Geoff," said Henry, "you have hit the proverbial nail right on the head. We've already told Cambridge what we came up with and are waiting for them to improve on at least one option."

The men all went their separate ways, as much as they were able within the constraints of a small hollowed out rock, to contemplate their possible lack of future.

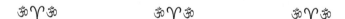

Everybody and his dog were watching the sky for the approaching comet that would impact heavily on the survival of mankind, depending on where it came down. Most people had binoculars, many had telescopes. Hundreds of people had congregated in Hyde Park, in London, to stand together as their potential annihilation approached, even those with naked eyes witnessed something very odd, but amazing, something special to tell their friends about. Looking up they were waiting for the comet to come into view from behind the moon, and it seemed like a very long wait.

Thelma had been collected by car earlier and escorted into the control room at Cambridge, where she was greeted by a fat controller, who made sure she was comfortable and supplied her with hot drinks. She expected to see Dave there, until she was told he was on another mission, so she sat close to the one screen that seemed to show the progress of the comet and watched. She was feeling a bit lonely, a lot anxious, but was determined to put on a brave face as she sipped her green tea and asked the man sitting at the consoles, "What are all these screens for, there seems to be a lot?"

The man explained briefly that in a normal space flight they would be monitoring remotely all of the serious functions that went on inside a spaceship, however, with 'Comet' they had no direct feedback, and the consoles were being used to track speed and direction as well as to simulate any changes suggested for these. His main console was picking up data from a satellite that was tracking 'Comet', a bit like a GPS for the space above our skies. "That will be the best one for you to keep your eye on," he said.

"I take it that is the moon, but where is 'Comet'?" queried Thelma.

"You will see a large green dot when it comes from behind the moon," she was told, so she sat there, hands in lap, clasped together, praying for Geoff.

ॐ ♈ ॐ   ॐ ♈ ॐ   ॐ ♈ ॐ

The broadsheet media had already written the headlines and much of the story for the following morning, depending on whether it was Armageddon, or rescued from Armageddon. The story for the first one included descriptions of a very large crater somewhere in the southern hemisphere, followed by earthquakes and tsunamis, and accompanied by utter panic and the destruction of a great many cities. The second one described how a Russian rocket had reduced the threatening killer rock to lots of small pieces, ensuring a brilliant fireworks display. They went into some detail of what was known of the Russian missiles as well as where they would be launched from. Both stories were purely speculative, as they had to wait for specifics to get reported so that a lot of blanks could be filled in, either way they knew those headlines would sell a lot of papers.

Most people, including newspaper editors, were putting their faith in Russia, seriously expecting an almighty great explosion to light up the sky and reduce that nasty comet to pebbles. They didn't know anything about anybody being inside the comet, or what it had achieved for the scientific community; they just wanted it blown up for posing such a potential threat to the world.

ॐ♈ॐ   ॐ♈ॐ   ॐ♈ॐ

Before 'Comet' lost temporary radio contact with Earth, from having the moon in the way, Cambridge came back with a host of suggestions on extending the life of the fuel, saying that the best of all three survival options was to attempt an Earth orbit. So, the three scientists, with Geoff watching, made ready to put plan-2 into operation.

Following the surface of the moon around, 'Comet' and crew came into the empty space between planet and satellite, applying some braking, adjusting the angle of approach to Earth, and rechecking their instruments to confirm they were on the correct course. It was all looking very smooth until William noticed the creamy white exhaust from a rocket climbing out of Earth's atmosphere and heading in their direction.

They watched it for some minutes, mesmerised, and all the time it was getting closer. The rocket with its warhead primed was coming directly towards them at an increasing, and alarming, speed. It would seem that they would have no say in how they died, the Russians had decided for them.

We have to do something, thought Geoff, but he was feeling soporific and as apathetic as the others, just staring ahead, unable to think, or even to evaluate fully what was happening. His mind went blank, with the image of the rocket burned into his retina, his own impulses trying to fight back, with thoughts turning to Thelma, and for a second he didn't even know the rocket existed, he was so lost to his feelings of despair.

Something in the way that the rocket grew so large disturbed him enough to wake him from the trance he had almost been in, and he decided he would do something, even if it was the last thing he ever did in this lifetime, he just couldn't sit still, do nothing, and simply wait to get smashed up and burnt to death. He glanced briefly at the other three who were still locked in position, frozen, mesmerised.

Pushing William aside, Geoff lunged at the controls for the starboard jets, hitting them hard with all the energy he could find, and held them down for dear life. Nothing happened for several micro seconds. Everything was now in slow motion, while the rocket crept forward foot by foot until he could almost read the Russian words imprinted on the fuselage. Without notice, time returned to normal as he was jerked to one side forcing him to release his grip on the controls. His action had sent 'Comet' spinning wildly to one side, with the motion so violent that even with internal gravity they were all thrown around like rag dolls.

This seemed to shake the scientists from their trance and they started to analyse the situation verbally. Still disorientated, they were left clinging to whatever they could hold on to. From the floor Geoff saw the huge rocket pass by, literally not more than 20 feet away. He felt and heard its loud roar; it had missed them, but only just.

ॐ ♈ ॐ   ॐ ♈ ॐ   ॐ ♈ ॐ

It was 1am on Saturday June 10. As the comet finally came around from behind the moon, sunlight reflecting against its grey surface, making it visible to the many people watching from the world below, looking so small, it was hard to see it as a major threat to mankind.

When the Russian rocket came into view everyone in Hyde Park in London just cheered and cheered. That changed to a group feeling of despair as the rocket just passed the comet by. Those with telescopes swore blind that the comet had moved out of the way. This was met with derision and wild scepticism, as most preferred to blame the miss on the inability of the Russians to produce technology that worked as planned.

ॐ ♈ ॐ   ॐ ♈ ॐ   ॐ ♈ ॐ

Now calm and alert, Richard and Henry agreed that they had to stabilise the spinning motion of 'Comet'.

"We will need to slow the spin a little at a time," said Henry, "if you can control the starboard jets, gently, I will work with the port ones to make sure we do not over compensate the recovery."

They worked at it for a good 10 minutes; first 'Comet' drove to one side then the other until between them they achieved something like a balanced motion. Their direction of travel was now directly towards the moon.

Henry turned to Geoff, "Thanks for reacting there. We were just stupefied. I just couldn't move or think. A bloody good job your reactions were on the ball, or we would all be in little bits by now."

Geoff smiled back in acknowledgement, still breathing heavily.

ॐ ♈ ॐ   ॐ ♈ ॐ   ॐ ♈ ॐ

As time passed, those with telescopes informed those around them that the comet was heading for the moon. It had changed direction, and incredibly, it had slowed down. Again the sceptics talked down this latest report, believing instead that the movement of the rocket had turned the comet around, and at any moment the Russians would send up another rocket, and actually hit the rock this time. They waited and waited. No rocket.

ॐ ♈ ॐ   ॐ ♈ ॐ   ॐ ♈ ॐ

Comet gradually stopped going around, directionally it was about 30 miles from the moon which meant it would still be very painful if they crashed onto it. Speed was much reduced, Richard estimated it at 100 MPH, but the fuel was almost completely gone. All of that spinning had actually done a great job in reducing forward motion. Now why hadn't they thought of that move?

"What would happen," Geoff wanted to know, "if the 'Comet' became gravity free? Would it still be attracted to the moon?"

"Yes, I'm afraid so," said Henry, "changing the gravity waves of the 'Comet' would not stop the moon's gravity pulling us in with a bump."

"Wait a minute though," said Richard, "what if we could nullify or lessen the force of the moon's gravity on the 'Comet' by making it lighter?"

"How?" said Henry rather confused.

"By using the force dissipater. We already use it to modify the force of gravity within 'Comet'. If we could direct it towards the part of the 'Comet' that was heading downwards it should at least slow down the effect of the moon's gravity on us."

Henry was looking at the approaching moon, eyes wide open. "Good thinking, Richard." Shouting for all to hear, "Hold on to something we are going to lose gravity very soon."

Henry didn't wait for compliance; he manipulated the dissipater, pointing its effects towards the front of 'Comet'.

Geoff and Richard grabbed for a chair and strapped in just as they started to feel themselves feel very light. William was in the research lab, and they all hoped he had heard Henry.

The 'Comet' slowed, although it was still moving too quickly. Richard suggested a short burst from the forward jets should help. The last dregs of fuel were already in the pipelines, which fired the jets for that few precious seconds, after this the jets worked no more. Henry meanwhile had boosted power to the dissipater. After these two things took effect, they seemed to be moving very slowly towards the moon. Gradually the moon came to meet them and the bump was very gentle indeed.

The dissipater was turned off and gravity returned, although the 'Comet' had come to rest at a slight angle, which was not a major concern, in fact, it didn't matter at all now that they had actually landed somewhere. They all stopped still, then sat down heavily, with William joining them, still in one piece and not too bruised from what had just happened.

"We are actually parked on the moon," said William after looking through the window, "superb, guys. Now that was a great achievement on its own!"

After slapping each other on the back several times, the four men in the 'Comet' realised that although several disasters had been averted, they had no way to get off the moon. That, however, wasn't a huge problem. They had plenty of supplies and would just wait for a rescue. Cambridge wouldn't let them perish on the moon, surely? They would find a way to get them home.

~ CHAPTER 13 ~

~ WATCHING AND WAITING ~

To the people in central London it seemed like the comet had vanished or somehow merged with the moon's brightness, as though it no longer existed. Some voices wanted to know if it had gone around the moon, but those with telescopes were insistent now that the comet had actually landed on the moon's surface, without creating a new crater and still in one piece. This time even the sceptics were quiet, as the news sank in that they were not facing the end of the world, at least not this night. Some who had had a strange death wish, or an acceptance of fate, felt cheated and disappointed, for, after so many predictions of doom had failed to materialise, they felt for sure this comet would bring their demise, if not considerable destruction. Abruptly, as the mood of the crowd changed up to hope for the future, the gloom left them, and they started to feel happy just to be alive.

The crowd stayed for several more hours, mostly in silence, not quite believing what hadn't happened, yet most certainly, not understanding what had happened. A few, that had recently taken up religion fell to their knees and thanked their God, although nobody in the crowd noticed a craft come into land very close to the comet.

ॐ ♈ ॐ   ॐ ♈ ॐ   ॐ ♈ ॐ

In the Cambridge Space Control Centre, Thelma had watched the 'Comet' move across the moon towards Earth, and had been mortified as the white dots of the missile went straight towards it. She sat extremely still, frightened to move, gasping loudly as the white dot missile went by, holding her hands so tightly together, just wishing and hoping. She had seen the green dot wobble a bit and change course for the moon. Finally the green dot disappeared completely as it seemed to melt into the moon. Everyone in the control room was standing up cheering or shaking hands with someone else, although she didn't know what was going on. The fat controller came over, kissed her on the cheek, and said, "You can stop worrying now, your man and the rest of them are safe, they've landed on the moon. Now we just have to wait for Dave to pick them up."

She was overwhelmed, couldn't speak, and just stared at the console, tears pouring down her face, worn out with worry, happy, yet still apprehensive.

ॐ ♈ ॐ   ॐ ♈ ॐ   ॐ ♈ ॐ

Exhausted with the wild adrenalin reactions they had had to endure, the four men continued to sit heavily in their seats in the comm's area, looking out across a barren landscape with Earth just rising in front of them. The North Pole was just visible and Europe was easily picked out with very little in the way of cloud to hide the major land masses. They could pick out Britain quite easily, almost dead ahead, and yes, there was Manchester, even, with rain clouds all around it. The blue and white planetary image made their hearts beat faster as they thanked their own personal guardian angel for getting them here all safe and in one piece.

Geoff turned the telescope onto his home town in southern England, muttered that the grass and trees could do with a good trim, and turning to Henry said, "If there is any more left of that cheese cake, now would be a great time to finish it off."

So while they sat looking out on their home planet, they shared the last slice of cake, and they laughed heartily as Geoff complained about the car parking chaos around his home, caused by mothers picking up their offspring from school in their enormous four by fours. After some time Geoff moved away from the telescope console to allow the others to view their own family homes.

"I've only got one more question," declared Geoff.

"Only one?" queried Richard, "this really has to be the last one you know, because this trip is all but over."

"There is only one question in my mind at present," said Geoff, "I am sure I will have some others before we get rescued. Are you ready for what is close to being my last question in 'Comet'?"

"Oh, alright," said Richard with a smile.

"For some time now," began Geoff, "I have been wondering why."

"Why what?" asked Henry.

Geoff responded, "Why in the name of science did you go to all the bother of dragging a huge rock to the edge of our solar system, do a mind swap with gorillas so they could chisel out an interior, just to fit your equipment inside it, when you could have stayed down in the rocket and achieved just as much but with less bother, and you would have already been home by now?"

"Well, for a start, Geoff, we'd have been totally messed up without you there to fix the mainframe, so we actually needed the mind transfer apparatus to get you there," replied Richard.

"Seriously though, Geoff," said Henry, "it was all done in the name of scientific experimentation. It was about finding ways to limit the time man would need to spend in space without wasting their lives away. It was about doing things we'd never tried before, and these were great bonuses to the huge volume of data and images we captured of the solar system which alone made it all worthwhile."

"So this was all one great experiment to see what was feasible?" said Geoff.

"Oh yes," agreed Henry, "and thanks to your help it was a resounding success!"

They all smiled, wallowing in the moment.

Two things happened almost at once. A very loud tune, that sounded distinctly alien, started to play from the main corridor, announcing that someone was at their front door, causing wide-eyed surprise within 'Comet'. This was followed by a radio message that came through from Cambridge telling them that they should open the external airlock hatch as some people were waiting to take them home.

They switched the outer door control to open, to allow access, and went to greet their rescuer. The man came in and he sealed the outer hatch before entering through the internal hatch, removing his helmet as he walked. When the man took off his helmet fully and dropped it gently to the floor, Geoff immediately recognized the face, having been on the inside of it for so many years.

They shook hands warmly, as well as one could with hands still inside a spacesuit. It was another magical moment for Geoff. "Hope it wasn't too old and painful for you?" he managed.

"Not so bad," replied Dave, "I've been working the muscles a bit, and that was quite a strain, body wasn't used to it."

"Too much time spent sitting down," admitted Geoff.

"I couldn't get used to the darned hearing aid though, and had our people examine the ears inside very closely. They found some internal damage to a tiny bone which they fixed, and the hearing is somewhat better," Dave smiled.

"Bloody hell, that sounds like a bonus, you really must have worked hard to get fit enough to come up here, and just let me say that we are so bloody glad to see you!"

"Likewise," said Dave, smiling broadly.

Henry was looking at the two speakers with some amazement. "Errm, excuse me interrupting," he said with a big smile on his face, anticipating what might be happening, "do you two happen to know each other by any vague chance?"

"Hello, Henry," said Dave in Geoff's body, "it's me, Dave!"

"Bloody hell," the three scientists chorused. "Hello, Dave, how the hell have you been while we've been having the time of our lives?"

"I've had my problems," said Dave, "I'm just happy that you are all back in one piece and I can get my body returned, so that maybe I can carry on with my life."

"Yes," agreed Geoff, "that will be quite a relief, even though yours is better than mine!"

"I know exactly what you mean, Geoff," said Dave, "you do get kind of used to being inside your own body." Addressing them all, he said, "If you can all get suits on I will go and put everything on standby and turn off unnecessary power usage, then we can all get back to Earth. They have big plans for this little baby, although, for now it can take a well- earned rest."

Nobody could raise the interest to inquire what 'Comet' might be used for next; they just put all of their energy into getting out of the beast that had been their home for far too long. They donned their spacesuits and got out of 'Comet' pretty quickly. Geoff grabbed his collection of notes and pictures, stuffing them inside an internal pocket, before looking around for a small pouch. He wanted one more souvenir. The suiting up didn't take too long for they were all extremely excited and eager to get out of 'Comet'. The usual checks had to be completed though to make sure each suit was airtight and there was enough oxygen. After Geoff had completed his first spacewalk his suit had been thoroughly checked over for any damage, fortunately none was found, and the safety assessment showed it was in good order, with more than enough oxygen left to get across to the shuttle. That done they were ready to leave, after turning around and giving the inside of 'Comet' one last look.

The external hatch opened to a wide airless barren terrain, which at the same time felt so inviting. About 40 feet away they could see their rescue vehicle, a small shuttle that gleamed slightly from reflected Earth light.

They walk-bounced across the small divide laughing, in good spirits, happy that this incredible adventure would soon be over. Geoff looked up, seeking his home planet. "Ah there it is, Earth. What a very welcome sight it is," he said, giving it a very big wave, standing there for a few seconds before giving another high wave and almost losing his balance. His focus gradually shifted to the space around him, the empty void in front of him, the far distant mountains of the moon, the ridges and the dusty plain to one side. He turned around, feeling like a king again surveying his kingdom of Earth, the moon and a multicoloured universe of bright stars. As if to own this moment in history, this brief interlude when he could wish for nothing, he just stood there rejoicing in the moment.

Still exhilarated, he used the heels of his boots to gouge out his name in the dust. Scraping out a large 'G', he then started on an 'E', before the others joined in to make his name immortal, creating deep letters; 'OFF'. They stood back to see their handiwork. It was impressive, and might even be viewable from Earth with a decent telescope.

After this, they walk-bounced slowly across to the shuttle, happy that things had turned out so well in the end, with Geoff thinking to himself that he was "over the moon", then laughing at the concept. He was feeling happy and light, and it wasn't just the lessened moon gravity that made him feel so intoxicated by it all, while feeling so relieved. He was more than content that things were coming to a conclusion. That he had been able to be a part of this most incredible story and had been able to contribute just a small amount of himself was beyond awesome, it was utterly staggering to someone who before this had all started, imagined his life to be almost over. He knew he would never be bored ever again, not with the rich tapestry of memories and experiences he had gotten from this *trip of a lifetime*.

"This really tops it all for me," said Geoff, scuffing the dust with his heavy boots, and collecting some moon dust into the small pouch. "I've had the most amazing adventure of my life, saw and done things I could never imagine, and all after I'd been retired. But this, this really takes the biscuit; this is just so amazing, so utterly bloody amazing. I, me, Geoffrey A Robinson, I'm only walking on the bloody moon!"

ॐ ♈ ॐ   ॐ ♈ ॐ   ॐ ♈ ॐ

Julie was using her home telescope to watch for the comet. She personally had plotted its course, watched it for weeks, and saw it wobble making predictions difficult. Now it was close to home and by her calculations would demolish a lot of Antarctica. The devastation could possibly hit South America and the Falklands, or possibly South Africa. There was no point in alerting anyone as they just couldn't get out of the way in time. Besides, there were plenty of people worldwide doing the predictions and spreading the gloomy news.

Mark was with her, listening to her matter-of-fact comments as things developed.

Now like millions she was watching things play out. She saw the comet avoid the rocket, and that made her blink, "What the hell was that?"

"What?" asked Mark, sensing the confusion in her voice.

"The rocket missed the comet by a very short distance, I could swear..."

"Swear away."

"I could swear that the comet actually moved out of the rocket's path. Now that's impossible! Why didn't that rock shatter into small pieces?"

Amazingly, the comet visibly slowed its approach to the moon, landing in what looked like a controlled manner, with no impact, not even any moon dust disturbed.

"The comet has landed on the moon," she said with excitement, emphasising 'landed', "and I mean it didn't crash, it just gently came to rest on the surface. Now that is just too fantastic for words."

Mark didn't often hear that tone of excitement any more, even when Julie was watching the stars; still, he noted that she was still well able to form words.

"Oh my golly..." she managed, almost unable to contain her elation. "A small spaceship has landed close to the comet."

Mark wondered if she was making this all up, but that wasn't her style. "Let me look," he pleaded. He saw the small ship close to the dark shape of the comet, and backed away from the eyepiece in total surprise; now he felt lost for words. There was a feeling of unreality about all of this. A short time ago the world was threatened with an epoch ending disaster and now they were talking about a spaceship on the moon. "So I guess the end of the world is not going to happen today?" he said, sounding almost disappointed. "Do you imagine those are friendly aliens up there that saved us?"

"Let's wait and see," she muttered, "after the events of today we are deeply into the uncharted, and just about anything could happen. This is so fantastic; I have trouble coming to terms with any of it at the moment."

Nothing else happened for a while; eventually a man left the spaceship and walked over to the huge rock. He just seemed to vanish into the shadows.

They kept watching, although it was almost a half hour later before anything else happened. Five figures now seemed to appear out of the shadows and walk towards the ship. Her telescope was better than most and she could really pick out a lot of detail, could almost see the faces of the people there, if they would just turn in her direction, and take their helmets off. "Silly thought," she told herself.

She saw one man turn around and look towards her. Waving as if he could really see her. She waved back, with a huge smile.

"They won't see you wave in here," mumbled Mark, irritated that this was all taking so long after the Earth had been declared safe. The man stood still again and gave her another wave as though he had seen her waving to him.

Julie watched the momentous moon walk, witnessed as they walk-bounced across the moon's surface, and saw the figures stop. Yes, they were making marks in the loose dusty surface, spelling out something for posterity. Julie expected the word to be 'Peace' or 'Love', or some such, and it wasn't until the men resumed their walk to the ship that she was able to see what they had left behind in characters 12 foot high. "GEOFF," she spelt out half to herself, "now what does that mean?"

"It's a man's name," suggested Mark, a little sarcasm creeping into his voice, "short for Geoffrey."

"Oh," she agreed, deciding right then that she was going to meet those men, soon, especially Geoff, for they would surely have a most amazing tale to tell.

The ship took off with Julie following its progress. She was very keen to see where it would go. If it went away from Earth it would surely be alien. If it went towards Earth it would be even more amazing to think that somewhere on our planet the technology was advanced enough to build such a craft.

Mark asked if it was worth him staying any longer, a question that implied a different question of whether his wife would be in need of a little loving, or should he just go to sleep.

"Wait for me," she said sweetly, "this is almost played out." Indeed it was, for the ship went in neither expected direction. It went outwards from the moon, and circled back behind planet Earth. It could have gone into space beyond the shadow of the Earth; it was not reflecting much light so it would be almost invisible anyway. The ship could also of course be heading for its home on an Earthly continent, if that's where its home base was. There were no more clues in the sky. She had a feeling though that she would come to know all about it sooner or later. In the meantime she turned off the recorder, shut her telescope and PC down, took the hand of Mark and led him to their bed.

ॐ ♈ ॐ   ॐ ♈ ॐ   ॐ ♈ ॐ

The first thing that happened after they got back on Earth soil was for Geoff to be reunited with his own body. It was strange to see his own body, with Dave inside, as it was strapped very securely into the special seat. Ultimately it was his turn to get securely positioned in a similar seat opposite. After that everyone left the room. He felt a little buzz, a small jerk and very soon he was being helped out of the chair. He looked into a mirror and recognized himself at once. The narrow jawline, the laughter lines, the deep blue eyes. He was back and immediately felt the stiffness of the old muscles and the general aches he had been used to for so long, it was so good to be himself again though, he felt much more comfortable in his own skin.

As he came out of the special area he found Thelma waiting for him, smiling eyes full of tears that splashed down her face. He picked her up and hugged her so close, for minutes and minutes, as he felt his eyes moisten too. After this short eternity where words were unnecessary, they walked slowly out of the building, still holding each other tight, back to their own lives.

ॐ ♈ ॐ   ॐ ♈ ॐ   ॐ ♈ ॐ

Over the length of project BACKDOOR, an enormous amount of scientific data was recorded and pushed back to Cambridge where it was stored in huge electronic libraries. There was so much of it that it required ten maximum capacity virtual tape libraries to hold it all, with another ten to hold a full backup copy. Geoff was brought in to organise the way the data was stored and to arrange it better. This was attached to a huge new mainframe computer system.

When it was ready they held a ceremony at CSC to celebrate the release of this data to the whole scientific community around the world. Once registered, just about anybody with a real interest in space exploration and knowledge gathering would be able to log on and access the information. This was all raw data, which was something astronomers loved, however another project was underway to index the petabytes of data to make it easier to locate specific items or trends.

On the day of the ceremony to welcome back the astronauts, and officially hand over the data gathered to the British Astronomical Society, to manage and authorise access, anybody that was anybody was in attendance. Julie and her team were there. Her boss insisted on coming as well, however, Julie was in such a good mood that she didn't allow even that to ruin the day.

Other scientific representatives from around the globe also attended, making it a day to remember, not just for the release of the astronomical data, but also for the chance to mingle with peer experts.

A set of three large video screens had been arranged at the front of the hall, with a PC terminal in front that had a big golden ribbon around it. Geoff had the honour of cutting the ribbon. "You cannot believe the pleasure it gives me in symbolically making this data available to the whole world. Let me just say that being a tiny part of this incredible project has changed my life in so many ways, and for that I will be eternally grateful. Let's not forget the scientists that made this possible, truly great people. The praise, however, should go to CSC, who with extreme vision and purpose launched this amazing experiment to find out what was feasible, which in turn, has already revolutionised our understanding of our home in the Milky Way." With that he cut the ribbon as the crowd cheered.

Immediately the screens lit up to show the reason behind the comets and the mini ice age that had cooled the Earth down somewhat. Each screen had an image of Betelgeuse, one in infrared, one showing in radio waves, and the middle one showing the normal optical view. The audience found that all very pleasing. These were the images

that the world had almost lost out on seeing due to dust clogging up their telescopes. It started from the point where the mainframe had started to work again, back inside the rock, allowing the fresh images to be captured. It fast forwarded to show the changing super star increasing in power and size, becoming very bright before sinking back to a brilliant white dwarf. It was a short 15 minutes, with so much packed in that everyone was soon pleading for copies of the films. There was a brief pause after which the screens were showing the recorded view from the telescopes as the rock approached home. The Earth had never looked so appealing, so beautiful with its dressing of greens and blues, not to mention the whites of the cloud. Some minutes were spent in watching the Earth as the rock moved closer. It was an inspiring view. A white streak was seen at the left of the screens, causing some gasps from the people observing this incredibly tricky time, and for the first time, for many, it was clear just how close that missile had come to destroying 'Comet'. About 15 minutes, where 'Comet' had been spinning helplessly, was edited and reduced to 3 minutes, but even that, showing the universe going around at a mad rate, was enough to make most watchers feel dizzy. The picture continued, initially showing the moon approaching at a very fast rate, before unbelievably it slowed down to a crawl, until moon met rock with not even a judder.

Surprisingly, one telescope had been pointing in the direction towards the space shuttle, which was shown landing nearby, on the moon. The audience got to watch that now famous moon walk by the five people, now all Knighted by the king. They saw how Geoff turned around and gave a big wave to Earth, and then scraped his name in the dust.

Julie couldn't help herself, she caught Geoff's eye and gave him that return wave he hadn't been able to see before. As the film was clearly coming to the end, Julie edged her way closer to where Geoff and the other four new celebrities were standing, so that as it came time for people to start to mingle she'd have a good shot at getting Geoff alone.

"You know," she said to Geoff, some minutes later, "I watched you walk on the moon from home on my own personal telescope. It was amazing to say the least. When you turned around and waved I gave you a little wave back, not sure anybody else did, my husband thought I was mad."

Geoff laughed, "That was nice. I had the feeling I was just waving to the planet, even better that you were able to reciprocate. I really was feeling exuberant at that point. You cannot imagine how it feels to walk on the moon after years spent watching it and wondering how it could be."

"I have a vague idea," said Julie, "I've been watching the stars for a very long time. I know that feeling, that urge to be out there."

"Were you aware that it was us in the comet?" asked Geoff.

"Not at all," replied Julie. "I just knew that there was some intelligence associated with everything that had been going on. It was just not feasible, not possible for a moon to come and push you along, without damage, and suddenly fly away. Which happened twice!"

"You should come and meet Henry," said Geoff, "that is if you can get close. He and the three scientists were the brains behind that."

They chatted some more, until Geoff spotted Thelma talking with Dave, smiling and laughing, and felt a pang of jealousy. He slid up behind them and put a hand around Thelma's waist. She didn't turn in a guilty fashion, merely held his hand tight to her body.

There were big plans for the 'Comet' which were discussed in a small conference for selected experts. It would be fully refreshed in terms of equipment, and decorations, with other rooms planned for special purposes including free-fall copulation and other games.

The intention was to get it out to the asteroid belt with a new crew that could be refreshed every other month, and from initial inquiries there was no shortage of volunteers. Its main purpose would be to study the formations of rocks within the belt, analyse their behaviour and generally get to understand everything about them. The radio that Geoff had hooked up was to be replaced with a brand new one, with appropriate signal boosters that would be tested fully to confirm they worked.

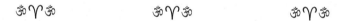

Clewiston Government buildings in Florida were now designated as a US Government disaster relocation area, and work continued to make it an alternative seat of federal administration in the event that a national disaster should occur. The president decreed and congress agreed that every winter for 2 months that Clewiston would be where the country was run from.

The Russians decided to carry on with their moon expedition, asking the British for their support and expertise. A joint project was to be organised to exploit the possibilities of extended living on the moon.

George and Clara never did get a comet or even a small spaceship land on their house, however, as the months blossomed into a really hot summer and a few short months after the 'Comet' had landed on the moon, they did get a nice sized lottery win and were able to buy the home of their dreams. It was a superb bungalow with a cellar and enough rooms and cupboard space for all of Clara's clutter. Several rooms were lined with bookshelves to take the myriad of books that Clara had collected this lifetime and which she couldn't let go of. As for George, he was happy to have some space for himself, free of clutter, and a kitchen that was big enough for him to partition off a section that was always clean and tidy. Best of all though, as George and Clara both agreed, there were no takeaways close at hand, no schools, and that meant their attractive gardens could be kept litter free!

ॐ ♈ ॐ   ॐ ♈ ॐ   ॐ ♈ ॐ

Geoff's daughter, freshly returned from a 15 month trip around the world, came to visit Thelma and Geoff. She was full of interesting comments about different places visited, and all while this thing with the comets was happening. Fortunately the comets had not disrupted their trip. She was clearly thrilled and couldn't stop talking or showing some of the pictures they'd taken. Geoff and Thelma listened and questioned, eventually Sophie ran out of things to say about the trip and conversation switched to more mundane things.

Over dinner Sophie asked, "And what have you been doing with yourself, Dad all this time? Auntie Jean said she hadn't seen or heard from you in ages. She thought you were ill."

"Oh you know," said Geoff, "a bit of this and a bit of that. Did some work with CSC on their mainframe, fixed their radio for them."

"Super," said Sophie, a little condescendingly, "glad you are keeping busy in retirement. Come on, Mum I will help you with the dishes."

Thelma had banned Geoff from washing the dishes after what happened the last time. "What a result," Geoff told himself again, taking his 2 year old grandson into his shed where he'd installed a telescope. While mother and daughter did the dishes, grandson Jimmy was given a shortened version of the big trip.

"Look up there, Jimmy, see that great big moon? Perhaps one day you will go up there, but do you know what you will find?"

Little Jimmy shook his head in wonder.

"Granddad was up on the moon, and I left my name in the dust for you to find."

Jimmy smiled. He liked games where you had to find things, and the moon looked like an interesting place to play.

"Oh yes," said a reproachful female voice, "just what stories are you telling my son?"

Before any reply could come out, Thelma entered and showed Sophie the new telescope. "It's superb, you can really see every detail of the moon, and if I point it towards the market I can see if they've sold out of my organic eggs."

"Oh very useful," sniggered Sophie, but stood aside as Thelma looked into the telescope eyepiece.

"Take a look," said Thelma, "you won't get a better shot of the moon."

"Oh OK," agreed Sophie. "I can see a lot of mountains. Oh and below that there is something big and black. Could that be the famous comet we hear about?" She didn't wait for a reply but focused on a small area close to the black shape. "How do you increase the magnification? It looks like some words or letters in the dust."

Geoffrey increased the magnification.

"G E O," mumbled Sophie stepping back and looking towards her father, before making a dive back to the eyepiece for confirmation of what she thought she saw.

"It's your name, Dad!"

"I know," said Dad, "I wrote it!"

She stared at her dad, incredulous. "You mean, you really have been on the moon, and that was you in that huge rock?"

"That was me," said Geoff, feeling emotion welling up within him. "Me, the most useless piece of meat on planet Earth, who has trouble hearing a doorbell. I walked on the moon. Yes, I did. I spent months cramped up inside that huge rock. Helped where I could and survived to tell the tale." He moved to one side to produce the pouch that he had filled on the moon. "I brought this little trophy home from the moon, real moon dust. Careful how you touch it, it can rip your skin off."

Sophie gingerly touched the trophy and found it sharp but inviting.

"Here," said Geoff, "are some of the places we passed on our journey home," mimicking something Sophie had said earlier when showing pictures of her journey. "This one is Mars; you can just see the big crater that the moon Phobos made."

The original images that Geoff had made were black and white prints, and not always very clear, but he had persuaded some technicians to give him full colour image prints of all the bodies they had passed by, and Geoff knew them all off by heart. "This was Kerberos, the moon that originally came from Pluto and gave us a push back to Earth as far as Saturn, oh and this one is the most amazing moon, with its own atmosphere circling Jupiter, Ganymede it's called. It is bigger than both our moon and the planet Mercury."

"You must be very proud of all of this then," said Sophie, coming to terms with the facts.

"I am," said Geoff, "I've got enough memories to bore the pants off anyone prepared to listen, for a very long time!"

"What's that black and white print?" asked Sophie.

"Ah," said Geoff, "that is me standing on the back of the 'Comet' on my first ever spacewalk. I was feeling like a king. It was such a great feeling to be there in open space with the universe around me, I could barely take it all in, but it was a wonderful feeling, if brief."

"You really look like you were enjoying the moment," said Sophie.

"I was," said Geoff, "till I made a proper idiot of myself by getting tangled in the cables, and I fell all over the place. The other two guys had to rescue me!"

Thelma looked at her man, her flow of admiration exceeding anything she had ever felt for him before, and she had loved him deeply for many years.

"This is that Russian rocket that nearly blew us up," said Geoff moving on to something less personally embarrassing. "We were all somewhat mesmerised watching it come directly towards us, just paralysed."

"That must have been frightening," said Sophie, beginning to understand some of the dangers her dad had been in. "There are so many aspects to the trip in that carved out rock, I'm surprised you aren't jumping up and down still at the excitement of it all and just having survived it."

"I did that while I was on the moon," he confessed. "I was so jubilant that it was all coming to an end, happily. That I would get to see you all again, and get to talk with my grandson."

Sophie, his daughter, eyes wide, was re-evaluating everything she had ever known about her father. "I can't wait to tell Sam," she said, "while we have been having a gorgeous time travelling around the world, doing marvellous things, meeting great people and generally seeing the best this world has to offer, my dad, MY DAD has been saving the world, *and* walking on the moon. Dad, you are incredible."

"I still can't believe it myself. I scuffed the surface of the moon, I left my footprints behind, my name is in the dust, and I lived to tell the tale over and over again." They all laughed. "But even if I do say so, and I'm not normally one to praise myself, I was absolutely bloody marvellous! I really, really, did walk on the moon."

"That truly would have been a gigantic leap for anybody, but not for my dad," laughed Sophie, giving him a kiss, and the biggest hug of his life.

~ CHAPTER 14 ~

~ AFTERMATH ~

The full crew of 'Comet' took a long well-earned rest, although they met
frequently, either at CSC or socially. Their lives had certainly changed since
they returned to Earth and each had a new vitality about them which
encouraged them to take on more interests. There was always something to
talk, or reminisce about.

Henry had moved into a nice large house on the outskirts of Cambridge, in
Barton Road. It had been an expensive purchase, although that hadn't been a
problem thanks to the generous wages and bonus CSC had provided.

Geoff and Thelma moved into a smart town house on the outskirts of Royal
Tunbridge Wells, in one of the more exclusive areas. CSC had been most
generous in rewarding him for the inconvenience of being snatched from his
own home to become a part of the 'Comet' team. After settling in, Thelma had
insisted on finding a small job locally at a nearby paper shop.

As for William and Richard, with their stash they were able to afford very
nice apartments close to the university they were working at. Money hadn't
been a problem to any of them as CSC had made them relatively well off. They
all still had a strong work ethic and they all found it hard to sit around when
there were so many thoughts active in their minds.

Henry had taken on the chair of space engineering at his old university,
keeping him relatively busy. Geoff had started to write a novel based on his
experiences in space, not entirely factual as he liked to introduce humour and a
little odd craziness at times, but it was one more on the list of hobbies he had
taken up. Richard had taken up ballroom dancing and was kept busy with that,
when not being a scientist. His doctors were completely puzzled at how his

back and neck had healed completely. They put it down to the lessened gravity and cosmic waves. William became well known as a visiting professor at different universities, lecturing on different aspects of working in space, and demonstrating how gravity waves can be made to work for the individual. Ever since Dave found himself back at Cambridge, in Geoff's body, he had been working closely with the technical teams to improve space equipment. He was particularly involved with improvements to 'Comet', and had worked out a whole series of enhancements. With help from others, he prioritised what needed to be done, from internal decoration to luminous paint outside, so that it might be seen from Earth, while working away in some rock clustered part of the solar system.

It was a good 15 months after they returned that Geoff started to have the most vivid dreams. Sometimes it was about aliens dressed all in black, other dreams had him floating above a wild jungle looking down at dinosaurs. Gradually these dreams became more solid, more real, until he became convinced they were an actual part of his memory. He called up Henry for some help in explaining what was happening to him, only to find that Henry too had been having the same dreams. Henry contacted William and Richard who both related graphic dreams they'd been experiencing, then decided they needed to get together to see how closely their dreams matched, so he invited the three men to his house for the weekend.

Over afternoon tea and cakes, each described the content of the dreams they'd been having, until they all looked up at each other with a knowing look. Henry spoke first, "So Kirk is not a figment of my imagination."

"And we really were abducted by aliens," added Geoff. "Those funny words that keep coming to my mind are not just my inventiveness at work then, they are real Sirisian words?"

William added, "I was really shot by aliens and fell in love with one, no wonder I haven't fancied any local girls lately."

"This is all too fantastic," said Henry. "Who on Earth would believe us?"

"Nobody," concluded Richard, "that doesn't mean we can't use what we learned while on the alien worlds to the benefit of mankind, even if we have to do it under the carpet as Kirk might have said."

They all had a great desire to put their adventure into words, to bring it to life, to write it all down, but they also agreed that for now it was best to keep it all between themselves, even though they were ecstatic to have the knowledge back that had been pushed to the back of their minds by Kirk, to protect them, and they fully understood why.

For a start, it was now so long after the trip had ended that everyone would think them crazy if they suddenly started to talk about the time they spent on another planet, even though it explained so well why 'Comet' was so many weeks behind the last batch of comets in journeying back home. Additionally, with aliens on the planet from this Seventh Star system, any talk of them getting data from the Sirisians could get them killed.

"Oh, by the way," said Henry, "CSC finally got around to rescuing 'Comet' and began preparing her for the next trip. I was sent a pile of stuff they found on board, our notes and a load of clothes and so forth that we acquired on Sirisia. Oddly enough nobody thought it strange that we would have brand new clothes that couldn't possibly have come from Earth."

"When did you get that?" asked William.

"About 4 months ago," replied Henry, "I was busy, tied up with university projects and just threw it all in the spare room, only now did I realise what it all was, but we will need to keep it all safe."

Looking through the clothes and other items from Sirisia, they each pulled out their own things. Geoff was pleased to find his little medal and immediately put it around his neck, unwilling under any circumstances to put it away, it meant so much to him, being symbolic of everything associated with their adventure.

The scientists were already engaged in their own research projects, so making use of the information from Kirk, they started to add in little experiments that had been done on the effects of CO^2 into their discussion papers, not specifically talking about climate change, merely laying the foundation for other scientists to pick up on some real data and run with it.

Some months later when Geoff returned from his golf lessons, Thelma had a message for him, "Very odd, he didn't say who he was, sounded a bit foreign, just repeated that you were needed at Henry's house tonight, and can you do your best to be there."

"Strange," agreed Geoff, "can't imagine what could be so important." He tried to call Henry on the phone, but got no response. "Hope nothing has happened to Henry," he said to Thelma, "I'd best be off. I'll just grab my weekend bag." His wife made him a sandwich to eat on the way as he'd likely miss dinner by the time he arrived.

Once in the car that he had named Comet-2, he was soon on the M20, and then the M25 going north. Geoff switched to hands-free driving and allowed the car to take him through the Dartford tunnel and a good way up the M11 towards Cambridge before taking back control. In the meantime he'd had a brief siesta, eaten his sandwich and given Henry another call.

"Yes," said Henry, "I received a similar call, and I didn't recognize the caller, although it might have been Dave just thinking about it. It's the sort of thing he used to do in our time as students at university, calling people together for an impromptu party."

"Hmm OK, but it sounded a little more important than a party," said Geoff, "I guess we will find out shortly. I will be with you in about one hour."

When Geoff did arrive he found William and Richard had already joined Henry, and the talk was about which takeaway options they should order. "Evening all," said Geoff, "I'll have a vegee pizza with extra garlic please. So who was the mystery caller that got us all together?"

"Evening, Geoff," said Henry, "well, it was none of us, and so far no sign of Dave. His phone was on divert with a message to say he was unavailable until the middle of next week. I do recall he was on a special project related to 'Comet', so that might be what he is doing."

Sitting in the lounge they were suddenly aware of figures blocking the sunlight coming through the glass surrounding the front door.

"This could be our mystery man now," said Henry, who being a popular tutor was always getting students call around, "or it might just be someone coming for a cup of tea." Henry opened the door to a young couple.

"Hello," said the man, "sorry to barge in, as we usually do, we were arguing all day about what you meant when you said that light was no inhibitor of speed."

"Hello, Stephen and Wendy, no problem, you are always welcome," replied Henry. "These are my three friends, William, Richard, and Geoff, who helped keep me sane while we were in the 'Comet'."

"Oh amazing," said Wendy, "I always wanted to meet you all, this has made my day, never mind that silly question. Can I interview you all, one at a time, sometime, for the college newspaper?"

"Yes of course," they all agreed, now being used to dealing with the media.

"I was just about to make a cup of tea, you can have a quick chat with them while I'm away, and they can talk about me and tell you about my failings."

"That won't take long," said Geoff, "I can't think of any."

They chatted about the four being in 'Comet' until Henry came back with a great big teapot and tea mugs. The two new visitors asked other questions including how they relaxed while on the 'Comet'.

"Not so easy," said Richard, "Geoff was our main cheerleader and one idea he came up with was to paint the dreary grey walls. You recall we had our own little garden, which we tended; well Geoff used the colouring from the fruits and vegetables to create some coloured oily water to change how the walls looked. Some of it was an awful pale yellow colour, although he made some nice purple. In any case, it helped to brighten up the walls."

"That must have been fun," said Stephen, "and gave you something to distract you from normal duties?"

"It did," agreed William, "and some of the painting was very good. I especially liked the Union Jacks that Geoff painted, you could still see, and sometimes smell, streaks of the various fruits and vegetables that went into the paint, even so, it all helped our mood."

"Don't remind me," said Geoff, "one wall was a mass of raspberry pips!"

"Ah," said Henry, "more visitors. Good job I made a large pot."

He opened the front door and nearly fell backwards in surprise, and then he grabbed the hand of the man in front of him, shaking it warmly, and almost dragging him into the lounge. "Look here, guys who we have come visit us?" he said, while putting his finger to his lips so that the man wouldn't say anything incriminating.

William, feeling hopeful went to see who else might be there, and he was almost knocked over in a frenzied rush, as a young female literally took a running jump to land in his arms. "I can't believe it," said William, smiling and looking happier than he had done in quite some time.

They all sat down and Henry did the introductions. "These are two of my students, Stephen and Wendy, and my latest guests, from err, Oxford, are Kirk and Pudding."

The conversation dried up a little as they all looked at each other in surprise. "I really didn't expect to see you both again, err so soon," managed Henry. "Was it you by any chance that left those telephone messages?"

Kirk admitted guilt, and Henry gave one of his loud laughs that displayed some of his nervousness.

Kirk said, "I had a bit of a job finding you all because the addresses you gave me were wrong, however, some kind people did pass on your new locations, after that I just had to find your telephone numbers."

"You did well, it's not an easy task to find where people move to," said Geoff. "Henry has just made some tea. I take it you are staying for a while?"

"Oh yes, we are," said Kirk, "and I'd love a cuppa, milk and two sugars please."

By this time the two students felt like they were intruding and made their excuse to leave, but not before Wendy had arranged dates and times to get her interviews.

Turning towards Geoff, Kirk asked Geoff how it felt to be back in his own body after being in the borrowed one for so long.

"Fantastic," replied Geoff, "even if it creaks and pains me frequently, I have to say it's much more comfortable. I'm not one to encourage body swapping!"

Pudding hadn't relaxed her hold on William; they were snuggled together in one comfortable easy chair, with a certain amount of kissing going on, and little to show for the two Earth years they had been apart.

Now with just the six of them in the house Kirk said, "So sorry to suddenly appear like this. I have some news that you really need to hear about."

"No problem at all, it's so wonderful to see you again. We were just deciding what to order to eat, let's give the takeaways a call with our requests, after that we can start to discuss everything, although if we wait for the food, and talk while we eat, it will make the words easier to digest," smiled Henry.

As they waited for the food to be delivered, Henry said, "It's only in the last few months that our memories of our time with you came back to us. Before that we didn't recall anything about Sirisia, our abduction, or even the Toothie dance. That was quite a trick to make us forget so much."

"Yes, again, sorry for that as well," said Kirk. "It was a protective mechanism, and I think you can understand why?"

"We do get it," agreed Richard, "we never had the opportunity to inadvertently blabber anything we shouldn't have said."

They sat around the large dining table to eat, the decorative lace tablecloth soon becoming stained with drips of different sauces, which nobody noticed as they all tucked into the food selection spread across the table.

Pudding had prised herself away from William and now sat between him and Richard.

"Do you like spicy sauces?" Henry asked Pudding in Sirisian.

"If it's mild," said Pudding in English with an Oxford voice, "but I prefer to taste the natural flavour of each food."

"Impressive," said Richard, "you have made great progress with English."

William smiled towards Pudding in appreciation of her learning English so quickly, while Henry nodded admiringly in her direction.

"My colleague here has been through the basic English language course," said Kirk, in between filling his mouth with a large samosa. "William, I was hoping you would complete that part of her education so that she is totally proficient and understands some of the quirks of living here."

"That depends," said William, looking afresh at Pudding, "how long you will be staying."

"I, myself," responded Kirk, "have only a few days before I must go. Pudding has been assigned as permanent liaison officer between you four men and Sirisian high command, and will be here for some time, that is if you can find somewhere for her to stay?"

"Oh, that won't be a problem," said William smiling quite happily, now positively glowing at the prospect of having his beautiful lady friend stay with him.

"What is this Sirisian high command?" asked Henry. "Sounds very important. Clearly things have been happening while we have been taking it easy."

"Glad to hear you've had a good rest," smiled Kirk. "Yes, Earth has become more high profile on Sirisia. Now for the two major items of news that have changed inter-species politics and brought us two all the way out here." He finished off the lamb tikka and wiped his mouth.

Henry insisted on getting another bottle of Riesling from the kitchen, while Kirk got his thoughts together. "OK," said Henry, "I'm guessing this is something that affects Sirisia, please do go on."

"The second part, yes," said Kirk, "however I will start with the more dangerous item."

Henry filled the glasses, while they all moved their chairs back a little to a more relaxed position.

Kirk continued, "That situation I told you about involving treachery from the Seventh Star system has moved on. As you probably noticed, the effects of their previous propaganda campaign have become less potent as regards the climate. People are more sceptical about the claims of disaster."

"Yes, agreed, even the BBC has not been pushing the subject down our throats quite so much," said Richard.

"The Seventh Star system planners have also noticed this and have been working on other ways to bypass the sensible people on Earth, and impose their own authority."

"I suppose politics forbids you to act directly?" asked Richard.

"I'm afraid so," said Kirk, "at least we have you. You are our little gem in all of this."

"We will do what we can," said Henry, "as unofficial representatives of Earth, but it won't be easy, please tell us what we can do."

"For a start," continued Kirk, "you can get me a crate of that Riesling to take home, it is sensational."

"Done," said Henry.

"Seriously though," said Kirk, going on with his message. "The Seventh Star system, let's just call them Sevens from now on, to make it easier to spit out what I need to say, are sending a lot more people to Earth. They are committing resources and will be spending a lot of your money to bribe those in power. There will be several things going on. One, they will continue to push climate change as an imminent disaster looming. Two, they will keep wars and conflicts going, and three, they will keep pushing the political mood to accept a single world government with absolute power. It would never be a part of your democratic system, with accountability going right out the window, so you would never be able to get rid of the unelected elite."

"So," said Geoff, "a lot more of the same old stuff going on, only a lot more intensive."

"Yes," agreed Kirk, "it is going to get nasty. I will be with you for two more nights if you can find me a bed, please Henry, and I plan to go over all of that stuff in some more detail."

"A bed is not a problem if you don't mind sharing a room with Geoff or Richard, I'm assuming William will be able to make space for Pudding in his room," said Henry.

They each had come with very small bags and Henry had them deposited in the appropriate rooms.

Kirk started to speak again. "If you can imagine all the star systems locally, in a three dimensional array, you will see, certainly in my imagination, that the Sevens's system is to the bottom right, while Sirisia is to the bottom left. Now all the main star systems we deal with are generally to the left of Sirisia, when you view my image. Sevens are usually excluded from much of what we do, although they do come to many conferences. We regard them as pariahs, which some other systems do not. I'm just saying all of this so you can get the idea that there are many other things going and our influence is limited as we still have to work within the political framework we all agreed to. That doesn't stop us having spies or making attempts to undermine bad governments, or to change things, although, even as a major player we have to stop ourselves from doing too many things at the same time."

"So, just like Earth," said Richard, "you have to deal with other societies within certain protocols, and you keep fighting to make things better."

"Indeed, except that some of these space societies can be very vicious, not to mention single minded," said Kirk. "One of these little troublesome things that brought me here revolves around trade, science and knowledge sharing."

"Well, OK, you've painted a very depressing picture to put us off ever joining these space societies, at least until we have guns as big as theirs," said Henry.

"Even so, you also have to put up with deceit and mistrust," said Kirk, pausing to get his thoughts together. "I have been asked by my government to seek your assistance in a little matter concerning ownership of one specific substance."

"Did I hear that right," laughed Henry, "you want four old codgers from a backwater planet that can barely navigate its own backyard to *help* a much superior star system with some matter?"

"That's about it," agreed Kirk smiling. "Let me spell it out."

"Let's go back to the comfy chairs in the lounge; I really do need to be sitting down in comfort to hear this," said Henry.

Kirk spelt it out. "There is a dispute over ownership for the process to make a valuable substance called aggra. It is between us and the Kirisian Star system. Kirisians are a sister system to us. When they broke away many legal agreements were made, some discussing ownerships of patents and so on. You will understand when I say that we currently issue licences for other systems to make aggra which makes it very valuable to us. Now the Kirisians have taken the issue to consolidation, saying that the separation treaties we signed gave them the right to ownership of certain licences, aggra included.

"Hmm, OK I get the picture," said Henry, "how on Earth can we help?"

"Consolidation requires that we bring in a third party to investigate these claims on our behalf. Kirisians will be doing the same, each third party will summarise what they found while investigating the treaties. That summary has to be pretty clear as the decision will be made against the most potent one."

"Are you suggesting, as I think you are," said Richard, "that these third parties need to understand the implications of the scientific information written into the agreements, so it's not just about the legal aspect of it all, it's about sorting out what chemicals and manufacturing processes were included, and for that you need scientists?"

"Very well put," agreed Kirk, "yes, although it's even more complicated, the third party will have to know our science back to front. This would mean highly intensive tutoring before the analysis even begins."

"That sounds like quite a lot of work," said Henry. "Could take us some time to complete. I'm not sure we could all be away for an extended period."

"Once the process kicks off we will have only 4 months to complete it all. There are some formalities to go through before we get to that point," said Kirk. "In return it would establish a power source of scientific knowledge on Earth in the form of you guys, and you could use that to bring Earth up to a good scientific standard. Besides, we really do not want other space societies getting their hands on our scientific databases."

"Shall we sleep on that," said Henry, "it's well past midnight, and I don't know about anybody else, I feel the need to digest what you've been saying, Kirk?"

"Sensible," agreed Kirk, "we two have already had a busy day, let's get some rest and I will fill in the details over the next day or so."

Over the long weekend they went through with Kirk what their assignment would mean for them, and they tacitly agreed to help out.

Aside from the aggra situation, they worked on what they needed to do to improve the political aspects of Earth in relation to climate change. Firstly, they had to challenge all aspects of false science that was blaming mankind for the fact that the climate was changing, they also had to get across how undemocratic a one world government would be by making that concept news. All the guys were asked to write articles against one world government and use their celebrity status to get it discussed on TV and in the media. The idea being that by laying a foundation against the concept they would make it harder for the Sevens to make headway.

Geoff wondered what he was doing in this party of scientists, "I see you've included me," he said, "in all of this, which is nice of you. It seems though that I'm going to feel like a spare thingy at a wedding, with nothing real to do."

"I didn't include you just because you're a nice guy," answered Kirk, "you will need to be working at least as hard as the others. Your job will not be scientific. You'll be there to keep these guys working smart. You'll be the one that paints the greyness brighter. You will be there to break the logjam when they get stuck. I understand how you helped motivate these guys during the trip home. From all the reports I've read, and I must tell you in secret that I do have access to most confidential items, they have been full of praise for the way you helped in all sorts of ways. You can do it again and help them get the result we need."

"Oh OK," smiled Geoff, feeling a little happier.

"Additionally," said Kirk, "just before you left Sirzero you mentioned something about security of data. I followed that up with my seniors, and they all agreed it was something we should build into our computer system, so they want your input on that."

"Wonderful," said Geoff, now feeling 10 foot tall, "magnificent even, I'd like that!"

Kirk presented them all with an outline of what they needed to do to prepare for their trip to Sirisia, a large binder each. "Get everything in motion and arrange to be absent for at least 4 months," he said. "I will be back at the start of November. In the meantime, read those packs and if you need clarification Pudding will help or request further assistance. There are many pages of scientific terms and definitions. You need to be fully conversant with them all."

"Four months away?" asked Geoff. "My Thelma will hit the roof. I can't possibly think up an excuse to be away for that long."

"Hmm, interesting point," said Kirk, "have you Richard or Henry a wife or female friend that would object to you going away?" They both shook their heads. "In that case, Geoff, bring Thelma along."

Geoff's mouth opened to say something, only the words were missing.

"Yes," said Kirk, "bring her along. Tell her you are going on that trip of a lifetime, once on the ship it will be easier to explain, bit by bit, where you are going and why."

"I can do that," smiled Geoff, "I'll start it off as a mystery tour that will stop her asking too many questions."

"Er, excuse me," said Henry, "looks like I have another caller at the front door." They heard him opening the door, saying very loudly, "Dave, hello, this is a nice surprise. I thought you were busy working on 'Comet'. I gave you a call and your voice message said you'd be away until next week."

"Hello, Henry," said Dave. "Well that was the plan, but there were some very odd things about 'Comet' I had to come and speak to you directly about."

Bringing Dave into the lounge, Henry said, "We are all here so you can ask anything you like. These are my guests, our good friends Kirk and Pudding."

Dave shook hands with the guests, wondering what an odd name Pudding was, but looking at her more closely decided that it was somehow perfect for such a sweet looking example of womanhood, although her eyes looked a lot oriental.

"We should go somewhere private really, Henry, because what I have to say shouldn't become public knowledge," said Dave.

"Dave," said Henry, "come and sit down a moment. There is something I need to tell you first. A secret we were not able to tell you about, and it involves these two good people here."

Dave sat down frowning, not sure what to expect. Henry continued, "Did you ever wonder why 'Comet' was about 4 months behind the last batch of comets that were swept out of the Oort Cloud?"

"Well, yes," said Dave, "but this is another matter."

"It is all connected with the questions you have," said Henry, "and trust me; we didn't deliberately keep things from you."

Dave was frowning harder, having difficulty in coming to terms with Henry's statements.

Kirk stepped in at this point, saying, "Henry if we are going to spill the beans to Dave, perhaps he should first know that it was at my command that you were not able to explain all of this earlier. You see, Dave, I had their minds, or at least certain memories within their minds concealed. Only in the last few weeks have their minds been restored with the knowledge of what went on in that four month period."

Dave was looking even more perplexed and miserable, not comprehending any of this.

"There is no easy way to let you down lightly on this," said Richard. "This man here is an alien and we spent the 4 months travelling or on his planet."

Nobody said anything for a while, Dave started to say something but his mind went blank.

"Those questions you have about the red boxes and the new controls on the external hatch of 'Comet' can all be answered, but are very much a part of that adventure we had over those few months. I'll go make a cup of tea and we will tell you the whole story," said Henry.

Dave managed a reluctant, "OK," although he just sat staring at the carpet.

Over tea and biscuits, they related how they had been abducted, right up to the point where they were back in 'Comet' feeling very drowsy.

"So, you've only just had the veils lifted on what happened? It must have come as a shock to you all as well to recall all of that?" said Dave after many mugs of tea.

"It was a huge shock," agreed Henry, "especially when Kirk and Pudding turned up."

Eventually Dave ran out of questions and could see that his earlier concerns about changes to the 'Comet' were answered more fully than he would have liked. He stayed the whole weekend becoming fully engaged in the new projects, and was very keen to see a real spaceship, despite being heavily occupied in refitting 'Comet'.

"That's settled, for now, I'll see you all in November," said Kirk on the final Monday bank holiday of the year, well after breakfast had been digested. "Oh, by the way, William, please don't forget that Pudding is here to do a job as well, apart from being liaison she must have first class English before we depart."

"She will be more English than my granny by the time we are through," smiled William.

"Good," said Kirk. "Just one other thing to mention. Geoff you were talking on the trip back from the Toothies's home world about the operatives from the Sevens's system, and how we could handle them. I found out a little more about the brainwashing they do on their operatives, and it seems that there are some keywords that can turn off the control mechanism. Details are in your packs, the pronunciation is not easy, so be sure you practice that very well with Pudding."

With that, he was done talking, shook hands all round, was tempted to do the goodbye dance, but thought better of it for now. He picked up the crate of Riesling that the supermarket courier had delivered, before walking out of the front door.

"He never told us how he got here without being intercepted by our air force," said Geoff.

"Oh, we have to keep some secrets," said a smiling coquettish voice.

Immediately the six heads came together to start planning their next moves. Henry had already decided how to introduce some politics into his science presentations. They split up the different aspects of climate change bad science they wanted to attack and started making some notes on their upcoming scientific papers.

While they were busy writing, talking and trying to plan ahead, the doorbell went yet again.

"Well hello, it's Julie isn't it?" asked Henry.

"Yes, Julie Banks from the British Astronomical Society, we have met several times. I was in the area and decided to take up your invite to visit any time."

"Well, do come in, Julie, all of my space related friends are here, and we've just been discussing our next projects," said Henry. After introductions they sat around the lounge, each with a fresh mug of green tea.

Julie told them she was in the middle of a scientific paper on their trip back through the solar system, and would really like to collaborate with one of the famous four.

"From what perspective are you attacking this?" asked Richard.

"Well," said Julie, "I started off by approaching it from 'isn't nature weird and wonderful?' until I realised it is also predictable, you just have to know the parameters."

"So, you want to explore otherwise unknown influences on our environment, expand our current thinking on the subject and put the science there that drives the various effects we experienced?" asked Richard.

"Wow," said Julie, smiling, "spot on, you are very incisive."

"Strangely," said Henry, "we were just discussing a similar idea. We all plan to research different aspects of it for papers we will publish shortly."

"Looks like I dropped in at just the right moment," said a very happy Julie, showing them a summary of her analysis so far.

"I live pretty close to your office, Julie," said Richard. "Henry and the others have their hands pretty full, so why don't you and I work through this and issue a joint paper?"

"Perfect," smiled Julie.

Henry was so convincing when introducing the notion that an unelected world government was scientifically unworkable, that his students took to it readily. It is said that everything can be reduced to a mathematical formula, and that's just what he did, he created a series of expressions, guiding his students to a point where it all too clearly didn't add up. As budding scientists they could not rationalise the incoherence of a system that was not supported from the ground up, which perfectly illustrated why a one world government that was imposed, not accountable or even elected, would not work mathematically. A small group of students decided to start their own fledgling political movement on the basis of this set of formulae, and they soon spread the word within the college, until most students saw it for the truth and joined in to canvass their own members of parliament on the subject.

News of the small political movement also became a newsworthy item, with Henry being invited to the TV studio to explain how his formula produced the result it did. "It's fairly straightforward," he started. "This was originally an exercise for my students to use maths to understand our political environment. We kick off with a basic mathematical definition of a world body that is unelected and effectively unaccountable, and then by extrapolating the way it works, in a set of sub-formulae, it finally comes to the point where it doesn't add up to a formula for real democracy. For the unelected side we get a minus, while the opposite or democratic side gives us a plus value, meaning complete incompatibility. A one world government imposed on nations just would not work out well for the people of this planet, per these results." He went briefly through the formulae, boring most people who had not a clue about such things, but delighting and enlightening those few that understood enough mathematics to see what he was getting at. The TV station received lots of comments about the program, while those in Westminster took careful note of the mood of the people that this demonstration had produced.

Richard and Julie got their research paper published, while Henry and Dave did a paper on adverse effects from carbon starvation. William started some research on how to purify our skies, while introducing Pudding to every aspect of life in Britain, and they had a great time doing that.

The famous five had acquired a large following, especially on social media, also many ordinary people that were hungry for more of their refreshing approach to life and science.

Geoff was also extremely busy during that period leading up to November. He wrote another book, this time a factual account about his journey through the solar system, using the notes and images he'd collected along the way. It was called 'The laymen's guide to the solar system'. Additionally, he spent some time with the mainframe systems analyst at CSC that knew most of what there was to know about the mainframe architecture. He was quite happy to explain to Geoff, in simple terms, just how the mainframe computer worked to keep data secure by the way it was designed, purely at a physical level. At a software level, Geoff read up on how to implement a securely protected system. If he was going to sell the idea to the Sirisians he told himself he'd best have as much information as possible on how things worked here.

Wherever he went, Geoff looked out for any individuals that matched the descriptions Kirk had provided for the operatives from the Seventh Star system, and when he saw a likely candidate he would utter the magic phrase that he'd memorised, "krooack beyflaf." Although he could never tell if it had turned off any impulses in anyone, he kept looking and trying.

All too soon November came along.

END OF BOOK ONE

Lightning Source UK Ltd.
Milton Keynes UK
UKOW04f0607310118
317091UK00001B/20/P